FORBIDDEN FREEDOM

ALSO BY JASMIN MILLER

Kings Of The Water Series

Secret Plunge - An Accidental Pregnancy Sports Romance

Fresh Meet - A Single Dad Sports Romance

Second Dive - A Second Chance Sports Romance

Fake Start - A Fake Relationship Sports Romance

The Husband Checklist - A Brother's Best Friend Romance

Mitchell Brothers Series

Baking With A Rockstar - A Single Parent Romance

Tempted By My Roommate - A Friends to Lovers Romance

Mitchell Brothers Box Set

The Best Kind Series

The Best Kind Of Mistake - A Workplace Romantic Comedy

The Best Kind Of Surprise - A Surprise Pregnancy Romantic Comedy

Published: Jasmin Miller 2022
jasmin@jasminmiller.com
www.jasminmiller.com
Editing: Rebecca, Fairest Reviews Editing Services;
Emmy Ellis, Studioenp
Proofreading: Karen Hrdlicka, Barren Acres Editing
Cover Photography: Xram Ragde
Model: Lucas
Cover Art: Najla Qamber, Qamber Designs & Media

FORBIDDEN FREEDOM

JASMIN MILLER

BLURB AND CONTENT WARNINGS

Gemma Fiore can't decide what's worse: sharing a forbidden kiss with a stranger on her wedding day, or her husband being murdered before the marriage has even been consummated.

Matteo Santarossa never planned to steal a kiss from a married woman . . . it just happened. He hadn't planned to kidnap her either, but when gunshots are fired, decisions get made fast. And Gemma Fiore? She's the kind of woman he's ready to make risky decisions for.

The heat between Gemma and Matteo is nothing either of them can seem to control. It doesn't help matters that they're hiding away at his cabin, which only has one bed, while he nurses her back to health.

However, when Gemma learns her kidnapper, the same man starring in her darkest forbidden fantasies, is planning to marry her cousin, she knows it can't last.

The question is, does she go back to her father, knowing he'll promise her to yet another business associate? Or can she stay with Matteo against her family's wishes and break the sacred promise she made to her dead mother?

Forbidden Freedom is a standalone forbidden mafia romance with a HEA and no cliffhanger. It features mature themes and content that may not be suitable for all audiences. Reader discretion is advised.

Content warnings: sexually explicit scenes, murder, physical assault, kidnapping.

To all women who thought they couldn't get out of a difficult situation, but then they did anyway.
You're amazing!

CHAPTER 1

GEMMA

"**S**on of a bitch." I push through the hotel room door and slam it shut behind me. At least I try to, but the automatic stopper catches it, closing it with an unsatisfying click.

Stupid door.

I'm not even sure who I'm angrier with, my papà, for actually marrying me off, or my new husband, who had his cock sucked by someone who wasn't me less than an hour after we said our vows.

Going into this arranged marriage with one of my dad's business partners, I knew it wasn't going to be some fairy-tale love story, but I was at the very least hoping for decency and respect between Luigi and me. That I would be treated like a person and not just as property or an accessory.

I guess I was wrong.

My chest feels too tight, the material of my wedding gown threatening to crush my rib cage and steal my breath.

My fingers blindly grasp for the top pearl button at the

back of my neck, attempting to undo it, which isn't an easy feat. I manage to unbutton two of them before I huff out in frustration. This isn't going to work. None of this is. What I wouldn't give to scream, or better yet, to punch a hole in the wall. But I don't do things like that, or rather, the precious and obedient daughter of Lorenzo Fiore doesn't.

Instead, I ball my hands into fists and try to alleviate some of this festering aggravation. My jaw is clenched so hard, I'm worried I might actually break a tooth if I can't get out of this damn wedding dress in the next moment. I guess I could call my cousin, Ally, or someone who works for Papà to help, but I don't want to see anyone right now.

Thank goodness I decided to change into a more casual outfit after we welcomed our guests at the wedding reception. This way, I should have a good half an hour before someone searches for me, maybe even forty-five minutes, if I'm lucky. Either way, I'm beyond grateful for this break. No way in hell would I have been able to keep a smile on my face after catching my husband cheating on me. I can only pretend to be the devoted new wife for so long.

My gaze lands on the desk, and a spark of hope blooms in my chest. I walk over and rummage through the drawers, excited to find what I was looking for . . . a pair of scissors. With an actual smile on my face, I snatch them and get to work. Careful not to cut myself, I start at the neckline and slowly make my way down the front of my body.

The pressure eases off my chest, and I sigh in relief when it allows me to fill my lungs with much-needed oxygen. The dress loosens around my hips, and I stop cutting and simply step out of it. My slip follows, both forming a large pile of chiffon, lace, and silk on the carpet.

Ah, freedom. At least for a short time.

I slip out of my shoes and walk to the floor-to-ceiling windows. The desk lamp near the suite door is the only light source, and I welcome the dimness as I walk up to the glass. From the forty-second floor, Manhattan seems miniscule from the bird's-eye view, yet also vast and enormous with all its skyscrapers.

A movement to my left snaps my gaze away from the city skyline and to the armchair situated in the corner.

It's plush . . . but, more importantly, it's occupied.

The person in it is swallowed up by the surrounding darkness. Once my eyes have adjusted to the low lighting, I'm able to make out a large man. Who is he? And how the hell did he get up here past security? Do they know him?

I swallow, trying to fight against the weight that's pressing on my chest and robbing me of breath. Again.

"I have to say, you're not anything like I expected. Luigi Rizzo usually likes his women quiet and obedient. Somehow, you don't strike me as either." His voice is dark and deep, like a cool touch on my overheated skin.

"Who are you?" I inhale deeply, my chest expanding with the fresh oxygen.

The rise and fall of my breasts is a painful reminder that I'm standing here in nothing but my bustier, thong, and garter belt. My hands itch to cover myself in front of this stranger, but I refuse to give him the satisfaction of my embarrassment.

If I've learned one thing from my papà, it's that Fiores don't show their fear. Or their emotions for that matter. I might have been kept home the last few years like a damn prisoner, but I've watched my male cousins receive their lessons from Papà or my uncle. Even when they thought I

3

wasn't paying any attention to them. My papà, and now my new husband, expect me to be a compliant princess, which I usually am around men, but I'm not a damn robot.

The stranger unfolds his legs and pushes off the chair. He's tall, close to one of my cousin's six-foot-five height, and instinctively, I take a step back.

"I'm a friend of the Martino family. They wanted me to talk to Luigi." His steps toward me are slow and casual, clearly demonstrating who's in charge here.

And the Martino family? My brain scrambles to remember any information about them.

To my knowledge, my family doesn't have any beef with them, but Luigi does, which means now that I carry his name, I do too.

Fuck.

He makes his way closer to me, and even though I'm itching to wipe my damp palms on something, I refuse to show him an ounce of my discomfort. That's what these guys usually get off on. They expect a woman to quiver in their shoes or to run away.

My eyes have finally fully adjusted to the dark, and with the stranger angled toward the light, I'm able to get a better glimpse of him when he's only a few inches in front of me.

Holy shit. He's a breathtaking masterpiece in a gray suit.

Dark hair, brooding eyes, a sharp jawline peppered with stubble.

His gaze travels down my face and over my body until it stops at my chest. He lifts a hand, one of his fingers reaching out to brush the skin between my breasts. I can't breathe. I can't move. His touch holds me hostage as my whole body reacts to it, a low and pleasant hum radiating through my blood.

What the hell is going on?

The contact is brief, not lasting for more than a second or two, but it feels like he just imprinted himself on my skin.

He lifts his thumb to his mouth. "Mmmm. Delicious, just like I knew you'd taste."

It's then I notice the slight burn on my skin where he touched me, and the speck of blood that's now smeared over several inches of my skin. Somehow, I must have unknowingly cut myself with the scissors. And . . . and this guy just tasted my blood.

Swinging my eyes back to his, I'm trapped in his penetrating gaze once more. Every neuron in my body fires, and it's difficult to form a coherent thought.

The same thumb he just touched to his lips is suddenly in front of my mouth, and he stares at me intently. "Open up, sposa."

My brain latches on to the fact that he just called me 'bride,' a terrible time to be reminded of my marital status and the reality that I'm expected to consummate my marriage tonight. My stomach churns at the idea of Luigi putting his repulsive dick inside me, but I push it back down. I can worry about that later.

Pressure against my lips snaps me out of my thoughts as this stranger presses his thumb in my mouth. My tongue acts on its own, twirling and sucking around it, as if on reflex. Or maybe it's my subconscious enjoying this small instant of defiance, of doing something terribly forbidden, because I know I'll never feel even an ounce of the same attraction for my husband as I do for this stranger.

5

Sometimes, our bodies form a connection that is purely based on instinct, which is the only reasonable explanation I can come up with for my reaction to him. His mere presence has turned my brain into a buzzing mess of static.

The sound that escapes his throat is almost feral, and before I have a chance to react, he pulls his thumb from my mouth and drags it down my chin and neck. When his hand closes around my throat and squeezes softly, a shiver of pure pleasure runs through my entire body.

His eyes are dark, liquid pools of pure lust, and I'm sure mine mirror his.

Agonizing moments later, his grip tightens at the same time he slams his mouth on mine. His lips are rough, his tongue invading my mouth like he owns it. His other hand lands on my hip, his fingers digging into my naked flesh and tugging me against the hard planes of his body.

A moan bubbles up in my throat, and he swallows every last bit of it.

I've never experienced anything like this, my senses completely overloaded.

I brush my hands against the expensive material of his white shirt. It's soft under my fingertips, but the urge to rip it to shreds, so I can feel his hot skin underneath, is almost irresistible. His masculine woodsy scent surrounds me, and his thick length presses into my stomach.

Without thinking, I rise on my toes.

I need more of him.

I need him to touch me.

Everywhere.

I need him to turn my world so far upside down that it can never be righted again.

Just when his fingers brush the top of my panty line, a noise in the hallway snaps us out of this all-encompassing spell.

Taking a step back, I stare at him.

What the hell just happened?

And what was I thinking? Someone could have walked in on us. And if there's one thing Papà has drilled into my cousins and the rest of the Fiore family, over and over, it's to not fuck up. There are no second chances in the Mafia, not even for family.

We stare at each other until one corner of his mouth lifts, and he gives me a little salute.

"Ciao, passerotta. Until we meet again."

With that, he leaves me standing there with my lips still parted, my panties wet, and an ache between my legs I've never felt before.

And he called me little sparrow, an endearing little bird.

The entire scene, every forbidden moment, replays in my head as I put myself back together and try to mentally prepare for my new life. For my new husband. It doesn't matter that all I can think about is the handsome man I just made out with and actually . . . *liked* it. Does that make me as bad as my cheating husband?

Either my dad or Luigi must have gotten impatient for me to come back to the reception because the instant I open the door fifteen minutes later, someone from the security team is already waiting for me.

Without saying a single word, we take the elevator down and head to the reception, which is taking place in the hotel's beautiful ballroom. The wedding planner and staff outdid themselves, turning the room into a fairy tale come to life.

7

Everything from the romantic and elegant table decorations to the delicate light-pink-and-white flower arrangements, the stunning sparkling chandeliers, and expensive personalized menu, is absolute perfection.

The security guard stays by the door, and I stop a few feet into the room, taking it all in before I'm spotted and have to play the bride role. I try to feel an ounce of happiness, of excitement for this day, this huge life event, for my future. No matter how small it is, I desperately long to find it, but I only come up empty.

I bet you'd feel differently if you married the handsome stranger you just encountered in your hotel room.

The thought pops in my mind, forbidden and unwanted, and I fight the heat that threatens to overtake my body once more. I shouldn't be fantasizing about another man on my wedding day, for crying out loud. I married the man, and even if it wasn't my choice, I need to find a way to deal with it, to make the most of it.

I *have* to.

I promised my mamma I'd do it because family is everything, and sometimes, sacrifices must be made.

A hand suddenly wraps around my upper arm and drags me to the side.

"What the hell do you think you're doing?" My dad's angry voice hits my ear. "You know better than to just wander off like you did."

"Sorry, Papà. I went to my room to get changed." I wiggle my arm, trying to put some room between us, but to no avail.

"I don't give a fuck. And I'm sure Luigi doesn't appreciate his sposa suddenly disappearing."

I scoff. "I'm sure he didn't even notice. He appeared rather occupied wh—"

Papà's grip tightens on my arm, and I yelp quietly, trying to pull back, but he's got an iron hold on me.

"Papà, you're hurting me."

"It seems like somebody needs to teach you a lesson if you're acting like a brat."

For a second, he squeezes even tighter, cutting off my circulation almost entirely, but then he quickly frees my arm, steps up beside me, and grins widely at the man approaching.

"Ciao, Luigi."

My husband.

Double my age at forty, a little plump around his middle, and with a slightly receding hairline.

The image of him getting a blow job earlier reenters my mind, and I bite the inside of my cheek to remain quiet, even though I'd like nothing more than to call off the marriage for infidelity, but I can't.

This is my life. It might not be perfect, but it's going to be okay. Right? It has to be.

Luigi steps up to me and kisses my cheek. "Ciao, bella. There you are. My beautiful bride."

I want to turn my head, to move away from him so he can't touch any part of me, but ever the dutiful daughter, I stay frozen in place. Like this isn't really my life to live but someone else's. Except I've played this role for so long now, what if I've already become her without even knowing it.

The overly pungent smell of perfume that surrounds him makes me nauseated to the point I want to throw up, but then he takes a step back and smiles at me, and I return it with the fakest one I can manage.

Family is everything.
La famiglia è tutto.
Two hours later, my husband is dead.

CHAPTER 2
GEMMA

"**I**s our family always this obnoxious?" My cousin, Alessandra—who goes by Ally—leans in, whispering the words to me behind her tall cocktail glass. She ordered a fruity, colorful concoction that came with a pineapple slice at the rim and even a little umbrella.

I don't know why I'm so surprised to see one of our family's establishments serving something like this, but I am. Despite the fact this is an actual bar. At least on the ground level. The illegal gambling club in the basement is a whole different story, which is the reason why we—as in Ally, me, and almost every other female in the extended Fiore family— aren't usually allowed here.

Gotta keep our precious weaker sex home in front of the stove, taking care of the kids while the men handle all the important business. Such a crock of shit.

Talk about old-fashioned.

Although, I'm not sure we miss much by not being invited. There are a lot of my female relatives here tonight, which usually doesn't end well because they're loud and catty.

Sipping from my glass of Prosecco, I shrug. "I was just wondering the same. Maybe it's better to skip these gatherings in the future."

She nods, with a bit too much enthusiasm, her blond hair almost finding its way into her drink. "I know, right? Next time, we'll convince them to let us stay at home."

"We would have a lot more fun by ourselves, that's for sure."

"Mmm-mm." She makes a loud slurping noise with her straw when her glass is almost empty.

I hide my chuckle behind my hand. The last thing I need tonight is to be reprimanded for my inappropriate behavior. I'm a grieving widow, after all.

Ally's phone buzzes in her hand, and she releases a loud breath. "Finally."

She unlocks the screen in record time, her face turning into a grimace. "Damn it, just a spam message. I hate those fuckers. So annoying."

"Whose message are you waiting for?"

Her head snaps up, and her wide eyes stare at me like she forgot I'm right in front of her. "Mmmmm . . . no one. Why?"

I tilt my head to the side and stay quiet for several seconds, letting her sweat a little. "We both know you're a terrible liar, so spill."

She presses her lips together and just keeps staring at me.

"What are you hiding, Ally?"

Her mouth opens, just as our aunt, Maria, walks up to us. Oh no.

Maria gazes at me with an overly sullen expression before

12

pulling me into her soft chest. "Polpetta, I haven't been able to talk to you yet. I still can't believe Luigi is dead. What a tragedy. He was such a good man." She inhales deeply and examines me from top to bottom. "Goodness, you look terrible. Not that I blame you. A widow at only twenty. And on the day of her wedding. Some might think it's a bad omen. Maybe the Morelli family still has some bastardi left who would agree to take you anyway. Wouldn't hurt to ask, I suppose."

Her nose wrinkles when she says *Morelli* like she just smelled something bad. No one likes that family, but I guess Aunt Maria thinks a Morelli bastard is all I deserve at this point.

Do not punch her. Do. Not. Punch. Her.

Despite her rudeness, the fact that she still insists on calling me meatball because I once was a chubby baby girl is reason enough to dislike her. Add to that, I'm pretty sure she was the one on her knees in front of my now-dead husband, and she just catapulted herself to a whole new level of rancor.

Pulling out of her grasp, I run my hands down my black dress, trying to focus on the soft material instead of the rage that's threatening to spill out of me. I don't need any drama tonight.

Papà wasn't happy when I told him I would wear black clothes and nothing else. No hats, and certainly no veil. It's not like anyone thinks I'm a real grieving widow anyway. Not sure who this sham is supposed to fool, but I'm not planning on wearing black for a whole year either, that's for sure. Tradition be damned. I don't put my foot down too often, since it's not worth the consequences, but this time, the little spark that started to ignite on my wedding day made me do it.

Ally coughs, and I'm pretty sure I heard the "Bitch," she tried to disguise.

It breaks through the red haze in my brain and allows me to unlock my jaw without breaking any bones or teeth.

Because I can't let it go completely, I'm unable to help myself and lean closer to my aunt, only stopping when my mouth is a few inches away from her ear. "Better keep those comments in check, Maria. We don't want anything bad to happen now, do we?"

She recoils at my words. "Are you threatening me?"

I give her the sweetest smile I can muster, standing a little taller than before, grateful, once again, I'm only related to this horrendous woman via marriage and not by blood.

With my hand on my chest, I shake my head at her. "Why would you ever think such a thing?"

I can tell by the way her eyes turn into slits that she's not done with me. But then something behind me catches her attention, and she gasps. Her eyes are widening so far that I'm afraid her eyeballs might pop out of their sockets.

"Figlio di puttana." Aunt Maria spits out the curse words before she turns and leaves, our conversation completely forgotten.

Thank fuck.

Ally whistles under her breath and finishes the last of her drink, her gaze trained on the same spot Maria's just was. "Son of a bitch, indeed. Who invited Matteo to the party? I didn't even know he was back. And why is he talking to our dads?"

"Matteo?" I turn around and scan the crowd. Apprehension and unease coil in my stomach at the name, and the second I spot *him* across the room, that feeling only intensifies.

It's really him.

The man from my wedding night.

It's been three weeks since I last saw him in that hotel suite. Three weeks since he kissed me and turned me to putty in his hands.

I've thought about him a lot since that night, replaying the way he touched me and how he made me feel more alive in that moment than I'd ever felt before.

Was it stupid to kiss him? Probably.

But no one has ever regarded me the way he did. Like I was more than just a possession, more than just a means to an end. Like I was a real person with a heart and a soul and not just a body.

When I lie awake in bed at night, I sometimes imagine how things would have played out if the noise outside the hotel room hadn't stopped us. Would we have gone further? Would I have . . . would I have let him . . .

"Earth to Gemma." Ally elbows me.

Two, three, four more times until I take a step to the side and hiss at her, "What?"

"He's staring at you." She giggles. "Holy shit, it's intense."

I blink, then blink again, everything coming back into focus, especially the man who has haunted my dreams ever since the day my husband died.

Ally clears her throat. "Why are you staring back at him like that, Gem?"

Straightening my spine, I tear my gaze away from the group of men across the room before I gain any unwanted attention from my dad or someone else in the family. "What?

I wasn't. I was zoning out, looking at nothing and no one in particular."

She nods, like what I just said made total sense. "Ah mmm, uh-huh, of course. Who's the liar now?"

My skin tingles with discomfort.

I didn't tell anyone about my encounter with *Matteo*. Gosh, why does even his name have to sound sexy?

Stop thinking about him that way.

He might have killed your husband.

Matteo was there to talk to Luigi, so he probably killed him.

Good. I'm glad.

Ah fuck. I'm going to go to hell for that.

That's exactly why I didn't tell anyone.

I'm a nutcase.

Ally's elbow makes contact with my side again. "Oh my gosh, he's coming our way."

My poor heart feels like it's trying to jump out of my chest, but I ignore the impending heart attack. After taking a big gulp of my wine, I press my glass into Ally's hand. "I have to go."

I'm gone before she can protest, or worse, before she can ask more questions. It's both a blessing and a curse knowing someone as well as Ally and I do. Hiding stuff from each other is a real challenge.

My heels click on the gray vinyl floor as I hurry through the throng of people, past the closest restroom, and down the staff-only corridor until I come to a door that says: "Employees Only." It's mostly used as a break room with a table and two chairs cramped in one corner and a small sink in the other one.

I step up to the mirror and flinch at my reflection. My face is flushed, my eyes wide. Too wide, too wild.

Is this what I looked like the night I met him?

The feverish feeling is certainly the same.

Turning on the faucet, I let cold water run over my hands, rubbing it up my wrists and lower arms too.

I close my eyes and focus on my breathing and the sound of the running water. I've done the same thing a million times during meditation, so this should be a walk in the park.

Only, it doesn't work this time. Neither my racing pulse, nor my spinning mind, calm down.

Squeezing my eyes shut so tightly it's almost painful, I try again.

It has to work, or I have to come up with an excuse to go home. Papà wouldn't be happy with me, but that's not anything new.

I open my eyes and turn off the faucet.

Then I glance into the mirror and squeak.

Matteo stares back at me with the same intensity he did before. He doesn't say a single word, just stares at me like he's never truly seen me. His gaze roams over me from top to bottom before it makes its way back to my face, heating up my body even more under his scrutiny.

It's too much. Too intense. My brain is overwhelmed at the way my body reacts to him. Again. The last time I was able to write it off as a reaction to my husband's infidelity, but what's my excuse this time?

I swallow and break eye contact, attempting to focus on what I was doing before he interrupted me, and grab a paper towel from the dispenser to dry my hands.

Once I'm done, I toss it into the trash and turn around. "What are you doing here, Matteo?"

The corner of his mouth ticks up. "You know who I am?"

I shrug.

"Answer me."

When I stay quiet, he stalks toward me. Yes, this man doesn't walk, he stalks. My inner submissive fights the urge to back away from him and obey. Since *I* don't want to do either, I stand my ground and let him close the distance between us.

Just like that, he's invading my space, overpowering my senses once more.

My hormones sigh in relief at his scent, like they're welcoming an old lover instead of a cold-blooded killer. But man, he does smell good. I'm not even sure what it is. Something woodsy with a hint of oranges. Whatever it is, it's addictive.

Two seconds later, he's touching me. It's an innocent touch, only his fingers at my temple, brushing a strand of hair out of my face, but he might as well be running his fingers all over my naked flesh with the way my body ignites into little bursts of flames everywhere.

I wonder if he can see the reaction in my eyes, or if I appear composed on the outside.

His fingers brush down my throat, and I fight the desire to lower my lids, blinking rapidly instead.

Then his hand circles my throat and he squeezes. "When I ask you a question, passerotta, I expect an answer. Understood?"

He tightens his grip, and my gasp gets stuck halfway down, so I nod.

"Good girl."

A shudder runs down my spine at his words, fueling the fire inside me.

What might have been an innocent spell the first time we met feels like more of a curse now. Doing this with him, allowing him to touch me at all, is forbidden, and we both know it. So then why does it feel so good . . . so right?

The pressure lifts off my neck, but Matteo keeps his hand in place. "Let's try this again, shall we? Do you know who I am?"

This time I can swallow, and I have to do so several times before I can talk. "I know your name."

He contemplates that for a moment, his eyes boring into mine. "Did Alessandra just tell you?"

My stomach tightens at the mention of my cousin's name, but I push the strange feeling aside. "Yes."

I don't tell him that I heard whispers at the reception about a Matteo Santarossa being seen at my wedding, or the fact I googled him later that night. I didn't find a lot of information anyway, just a name and photo of him and his father at some social event a while ago, but it allowed me to put a name to his face. I also made sure he wasn't a serial killer or something else crazy, at least not that the public knew about.

He nods at my answer. "She's a couple years older than you, so she probably remembers me from before I left."

"Left?"

"Yes."

I huff out a breath at his refusal to elaborate. "Where did you go?"

His teeth bite into his bottom lip as if my irritation is

19

amusing to him but he's trying not to show it. "Nowhere and everywhere."

My gaze is fixated on his lips, my mind replaying the way he just bit into it.

I shuffle my feet and shake my fist at myself—only in my head, of course.

Figures that the first man I'm attracted to is a cryptic stranger I know almost nothing about.

"Stop looking at me like that, passerotta." The words come out clipped, but even that's not enough to snap me out of my daze.

This inner sex goddess he's awakened is out and ready to play. She makes me want to rub myself all over this mountain of a man, no matter how wrong or dirty that is.

The more I think about it, the better the idea sounds.

Apparently, all common sense has left my brain because I lean in and stare him straight in the eye. "Or what?"

I see the exact instant something snaps inside him. His eyes flare with so much heat they might burn me alive, but I'm here for it.

And I'm ready.

My mouth opens right before his lips crash on mine. He devours me, there's no other way to describe it. He moves my head until it's tilted exactly the way he wants it, and his lips move against mine with so much skill, I moan into his mouth. His tongue tangles with mine in such an erotic way that I know my panties are already damp.

The groan he makes reverberates through my whole body, and I reach out with my hands to steady myself. How I go from wanting to balance myself to my fingers tangled deeply into the hair at the back of his head, is a bit of a mystery.

What I'm finally understanding is how people can be obsessed with kissing. Ally has told me before how much she loves it, but since both kisses I'd had weren't memorable, I thought it might not be my thing.

But one thing's for sure, I will never forget the way Matteo kisses me, not in this life or the next. It's imprinted into my veins and will continue to live there forever.

He pulls back, our heavy breaths filling the air around us. "You taste just as good as I remembered."

What is someone supposed to say to that?

I tighten my hands in his hair, the ache in my core growing to monumental heights.

So I do what any self-respecting woman who's been accosted by the same handsome stranger for a second time would do: I grind against him, frustrated that my dress won't allow me to alleviate this blazing need inside me.

A growl escapes his mouth. "My control is only so strong. I'm trying to be a gentleman and to not fuck you up against the wall right now."

"Please." The plea escapes my mouth before my brain can fully process it. Not that I'm sure what I actually asked for anyway.

For him to fuck me?

I definitely wasn't planning on losing my virginity in a break room at my family's bar. Then again, I never wanted to marry a guy I had no interest in because of stupid family traditions either, but I did it anyway.

Matteo's mouth moves along my jaw and over to my ear, where he sucks on my earlobe. The pressure between my legs increases, thrumming like a live wire. How is it possible that it feels so different when he touches me than when I pleasure myself?

This is so much more powerful. Hotter. All-consuming.

"Please what?" His hot breath fans over the shell of my ear.

I shiver in response. "Do something."

I'm not even sure what exactly I want him to do, but I know I don't want him to stop whatever he's doing anytime soon.

His chuckle is low and throaty, and it's the sexiest sound I've ever heard.

He arches a brow. "Something?"

"Touch me. Just touch me, okay?" There's a beat of silence between us as my desperation takes charge of my mouth. "Please?"

"If I was a better man, I wouldn't even be here with you, but we both know I'm not. Plus, you asked so nicely." And with that, he gives me what I want.

His lips are back on mine, his tongue in my mouth, and his fingers . . . those fingers are finally touching me. Starting at the top of my dress, they descend, stopping to squeeze one breast, then the other, before following his previous path down my body.

They finally get to the bottom of my dress and make their way underneath it, and I whimper. His knuckles brush along the inside of my thighs, and I rely on him to keep me upright. Holy crap, he hasn't even touched my throbbing pussy yet, or anything remotely in the vicinity, and it's already better than anything I've ever experienced.

Not that there was ever anything beyond a kiss, but that's beside the point.

His fingertips reach the seam of my panties and trace it, and I'm practically panting. I'm almost glad he stopped kissing me, considering I need every single ounce of oxygen I can draw into my lungs.

As if he can read my mind, his mouth is back on mine, just as he pushes my underwear aside to plunge one long finger inside me. I gasp into his mouth, and he slowly pumps in and out of me. Once, twice, three times, before adding a second finger.

"Fuck, you're so tight, baby." He withdraws his fingers, spreading my arousal all along my folds and clit before he circles it.

My head falls back, and I groan in pure bliss because he knows exactly what he's doing, and I'm here reaping the benefits of his skillset. Continuing his delicious assault, he switches between rubbing my clit and thrusting his fingers deep inside me to the point where I'm so worked up that I explode.

"Yes, come all over my fingers like a good girl."

The orgasm is so strong that I sink my nails farther into his shoulders to keep upright. If it's too much, he doesn't say a thing.

It takes me a long time to come down from my high, and even longer to withdraw my claws from him.

"So beautiful." He draws me against him, this time kissing me slowly, with a tenderness that tightens my chest. Like I'm precious.

Distracted by his erection pressing into my stomach, I

move back enough to rub my hand over his pants. He's hard and massive, like he's ready to explode.

"Porca puttana. You'll be the death of me."

A huge grin spreads on my face at his cussing. "I take that as a compliment."

I reach for his belt, but he stops me with a hand on mine.

"Not this time. We better get back to the party. People will notice we're gone."

I freeze, stunned he doesn't want me to reciprocate. He doesn't strike me as the kind of guy who cares what other people think of him. He has that fuck-off vibe all around him like an impenetrable shield.

Hmmm.

Suddenly feeling slightly awkward about this whole encounter, I nod and brush my hands over my dress, hoping like hell no one out there will notice anything amiss.

"Look at me." He sounds exasperated, like he's already regretting what we just did.

I mean, for fuck's sake, I just let him finger me to the first orgasm I've ever had with another person. In the break room. At my family's bar.

How did I go from accepting to be married off to appease my family to having this stranger please me in a way that's so forbidden? I'm not sure I'd survive if it came out. And let's not forget that he's also the guy who might have killed my husband. He told me he was there for Luigi, and a short while after he disappeared, my new husband was shot and killed. If I wasn't so relieved about not being married anymore, I'd probably be more freaked out.

When I don't react to his demand, one of his fingers goes under my chin, tilting it up to meet his gaze. His pupils are big, the brown of his irises so smoldering, it resembles a fire blazing behind them. "No one can know about this."

I'm officially a dirty little secret.

Figures.

My back straightens and I pull out of his grasp.

Even though I know I can't tell anyone anyway, his words still sting.

It also makes me want to punch him in his beautiful face, and I'm really not a violent person. That's for the men in the family. So, instead, I clench my fists so hard that my nails dig into my palms.

Since obedience has been drilled into my head for as long as I remember, I nod. "I understand."

He brushes his hand over his stubbled jaw and stares at me. "You do?"

I nod again but avert my gaze. "Yes, of course."

I turn around quickly to check my reflection in the mirror, just so I have something to do that doesn't involve staring at him. My fingers fly over my brown hair, finger-combing it as best as I can before I get started on fixing my makeup.

I completely ignore Matteo, and when I'm done and turn back to him, he's gone.

For the second time.

Both times, he slipped out before any more could happen. If it wasn't for the fact that he makes me feel things I've never felt before and that he made me come so hard I saw stars today, I'd get a complex. Or maybe I already have one.

I stop in the bathroom on the way back to pee then walk back to the bar. Thank goodness the lights are dimmed enough to allow me to hide some of my shame and embarrassment. For the first time, I wish I would have let Papà talk me into wearing one of those stupid veil hats after all.

Ally's eyes widen when I walk up to her. "Where the hell have you been? I was about to send a search party for you."

"Sorry, I needed a break." I don't dare look at her, afraid she'll see straight through my bullshit.

She tries to burn a hole in my head, then huffs because I don't take the bait.

"Yeah, I don't think so, Gem. You can tell me later once this snoozefest is over. Apparently, my dad has some announcement to make, and then we can get out of here." She bumps her hip against mine, her new drink almost sloshing over the rim. "Deal?"

I finally glance at her. "Deal."

Uncle Antonio—who goes by Toni—whistles loudly, and all conversation ceases. Both he and my dad are big guys, but Uncle Toni has gained some weight around his middle over the years. He stands near the stage with my dad and clasps his hands together.

"After our recent tragedy with Gemma"—all eyes turn to me, thanks so much for that—"we wanted to give her the appropriate time to grieve her loss, but at the same time, we were also ready to welcome a new member to our family."

A sour taste forms in my mouth at his words, and I don't like where this is going at all. Especially considering Matteo just joined the two of them.

This better not be what I think it is.

Ally leans close to me. "I swear, if they sell you off again, I'm going to have a word with both of them."

Although her words are whispered, they're sharp as a whip.

26

I nod, focusing back on the three men, just as Matteo gazes at me and winks.

Beautiful bastardo.

Uncle Toni smiles and claps his hand on Matteo's shoulder. "Help me congratulate Matteo on his engagement to my beautiful daughter, Alessandra. Welcome to the family, son."

What the fuck?

CHAPTER 3
GEMMA

I've never wanted to kill anyone in my life, always thought the violence that seems to flow through each family member's veins might have skipped me. Looks like I was wrong and I just never had the right target in sight.

My fingers are twitching from the sheer effort it takes not to grab someone's gun as Matteo saunters over to Ally and me. Swaggers, even. That fucking asshole. Forget the gun. I want to gouge his eyes out with a fork and make him eat them.

My rage is a living, breathing thing, and I must be a witch or something else supernatural because the fact that I can pull myself together enough to survive the next minute is nothing short of otherworldly.

Matteo reaches us with Uncle Toni and my dad, and the three men are smiling like they're children having a blast at the fair. Ridiculous. The man of the hour embraces a still stunned Ally with a side hug, placing his hand firmly on her lower back, and that's all I can stomach.

He's touching her.

He's crushing her against his body like he wasn't just devouring me less than half an hour ago.

Right here in front of me.

"Scusa." I turn and walk to the bar. I need something stronger than wine. Pronto.

The bartender is cleaning glasses when I slide onto a stool. I raise two fingers. "Sambuca, please."

He gives me a curious once-over but does as I ask. I watch him while he fills the two shot glasses with the clear liquid and adds three toasted coffee beans each. He's getting his lighter from the counter, but I stop him before he sets the liquid on fire.

Normally I love watching the blue flames dance across the top, but today, I'm not patient enough for that.

I place one of the smooth glasses against my lips and tip it back. The liquid burns down my throat, the anise flavor strong on my tongue, turning slightly spicy when I chew the coffee beans. A tiny shudder runs through my body as the alcohol sets in, and I reach for the second glass.

"No coffee with it?" Matteo's voice comes from behind me.

I stiffen at his words. It's a normal question, and a valid one too since I sometimes prefer drinking my Sambuca in coffee rather than straight up, but anything that comes out of this man's mouth would drive me up the wall right now. So I ignore him.

Instead of sitting next to me, like a normal, polite person who's not supposed to know me intimately would, he squeezes between me and the barstool. His suit jacket brushes my naked forearm, eliciting goosebumps all over my skin.

Apparently, this man has never heard of a personal bubble before.

Trying my best to ignore him, I lift the shot glass and down it too, sending a tight-lipped grimace his way and crunching loudly on my coffee beans.

He lifts his eyebrows. "Ah, don't be like that."

A noise vibrates in my throat, and I'm slightly horrified that it sounds like a growl. Considering I'm about to rip his head off, it's more than fitting, though.

It appears that he likes his stupid face on his shoulders because he doesn't comment on the close resemblance to my feline spirit animal.

After a quick chat with the bartender, he grabs the tumbler of amber liquid he's handed and takes a sip. "Just out of curiosity, is there something wrong with your cousin that you don't want me to marry her?"

Wow.

The nerve of this man.

I snap my head around to look at him. No, I'm incapable of simply looking at him. I glare at him with such an intensity, he should wither under it.

Aware of the bartender and possibly other ears close by, I keep my voice low. "What the hell is wrong with you?"

He presses his lips together. "Why do you think something's wrong with me?"

One, don't kill him. Two, don't kill him. Three, don't kill him.

Nope, I don't think three breaths will do for this man.

Not sure anything will.

I clench and unclench my hands in my lap. "I can't

believe you have the fucking nerve to talk to me about marrying my cousin considering what we just did together."

Maybe I should find an empty room somewhere and do some push-ups or something to release some of this energy. Someone will notice soon that I'm not my cool, well-behaved self.

Remember how that empty room worked out last time?

Ah crap, never mind.

No more empty rooms for me.

Matteo lifts his glass to his mouth again, and my traitorous eyes follow every single movement, like they're addicted to him and don't want to miss even the most miniscule motion he makes.

Like the way his lips mold around the rim of the glass, or how his Adam's apple bobs every time he swallows the drink. And let's not forget the way he licks his lips next to catch the errant drop that's escaped.

What would it feel like if I licked up his throat to catch it? Would he feel warm under my tongue?

What the hell?

One orgasm, and this man holds my body and brain hostage.

This is just . . . no. Not on my watch.

He sets his glass down and turns around to face the room, like he doesn't have a care in the world. Well, he most definitely doesn't look like he's getting stabbed with a hundred imaginary knives like he is in my head. Which is a real shame, even more so when he says, "So does that mean there's no second round then?"

He did not just say that, did he?

I *must* have imagined that.

After a minute, he says, "I thought you'd be up for more."

The audacity of this guy. I just want to punch that sexy mouth of his.

"Fuck you, Matteo."

"That's what I was hoping for."

I jump off my stool and get as close to him as I can without raising any suspicion. Well, not any more than our conversation might already have raised anyway. "There's a special kind of hell for people like you, and I hope you're going to rot in it."

"You wouldn't be the first one."

"I hope you get hit by a truck."

"Been there, done that."

My jaw is so tight, I'm seriously afraid I might break a tooth or two.

"Gemma."

I freeze at the voice, turning in the direction of where it came from and attempting to hide the sigh. "Frederico, hey."

My cousin—who's like a third cousin twice removed or something obnoxious like that—walks toward us, stopping in front of me. He takes my face in his hands and kisses me twice on the cheek. First left, then right. "Ciao, bellissima."

I draw back as soon as I think it won't be considered rude. Whereas I don't even consider him "real" family, we used to be close when we were kids. Then he grew up and started working for my dad, and nothing good can come from that. He's also been a little too supportive in my dad's endeavors to keep me on a short leash, so I try to stay clear of him as much as possible, even though it's not an easy task since he's usually always at our house to see my dad.

He stays close to me, which doesn't help my annoyed

state in any way whatsoever, so I lean back as far as I can without toppling over, the two shots definitely not helping my balance any.

He tilts his head and regards me. "How are you? I haven't really seen you since . . . you know."

"The wedding?"

He nods and leans even closer so he can whisper, "I'm used to seeing you every week. I called and texted several times, but you never got back to me."

My Matteo-induced irritation makes me want to snap at Frederico as well, and it takes all my effort to keep my voice normal. I succeed, mostly. "Yes, sorry about that. I've been a bit . . . uh, distraught after everything that happened."

He rests his hand on my arm and squeezes lightly. "We should get together soon. You know, I'm always here for you. I can help you with whatever you need."

I tug on my dress, overcome by the urge to make sure I still look impeccable in case he's reporting back to my dad. "Mmmm, yes. Sure. I'll let you know."

"You do that. I can check in with your papà too, to make sure you're okay." Then, without warning, he grabs me by both arms and yanks me against his chest, wrapping his arms tightly around me.

It feels like a switch was flipped inside me, and I'm pushed into a corner with no way out. My stomach quivers at the feeling, and I'm thrown back to five years ago to the moment when I was trapped in a similar fashion and unable to get away. It was another set of arms, a skinnier body than Frederico's, but my brain doesn't seem to understand that little fact.

When I shiver all over, his hands are suddenly ripped off

me, replaced by an arm that's pressing me against a warm body. My brain registers the woodsy smell with a hint of oranges, and I almost collapse against Matteo, wrapping my hands around his waist like he's my lifeline.

"Santarossa." Frederico practically spits out Matteo's last name like it's the most disgusting thing that's ever passed his lips.

Matteo's muscles tense underneath my fingers. "Fuck off, Gallo."

Frederico's nostrils flare and he glares at Matteo. "What's your problem? If I remember correctly, you're holding the wrong Fiore in your arms."

"It's none of your fucking business what I'm doing or who I'm holding. And you'd do well to remember that." The words come out of Matteo's mouth with what sounds like forced restraint, like the low rumbling of thunder before the earth-shattering boom.

I don't know if they already have a beef with each other, but right now, I don't even care. All I know is that I have the sudden urge to be anywhere but here. My feet feel steady again, or at least steadier, my little mini-freakout almost forgotten.

Gathering my strength, I push off of Matteo's hard body, mentally saying goodbye to his abs and tight back muscles. Although he's a major asshole, I'm still sexually frustrated enough to appreciate his male beauty and what I'm guessing is the body of an Adonis hidden under his suit.

But before I can take a step from the guys who make me feel strangely claustrophobic with their standoff, several things happen all at once. A loud bang pierces the air around us, just as an invisible force hits my chest. It reverberates through my entire body, the sensation jarring and unlike anything I've ever experienced before. My ears ring immediately, and I'm so disoriented from the sensory overload and the surprise of what I'm guessing was an explosion that I stagger several steps until someone grabs me.

Two seconds later, Matteo's face comes into view. He regards me with wide eyes, his mouth moving, but I can't hear much past the ringing in my ears and the occasional *pop*. It feels like I'm underwater and everything is muted but a few faint sounds.

People around me scramble in all directions, and I see more than one guy with their guns raised. Light filters in from one of the open emergency exit doors where people try to escape the chaos and the line of fire.

I still have no clue what's going on or what just happened, but my survival instincts kick in, and I try to get around the bar and closer to the exit. Matteo is still beside me, and since the *pop, pop, pop* sound is louder than before, I'm guessing he's either the one shooting, or whoever else is, is a lot closer than a few minutes ago.

My brain feels jumbled, and I don't want to waste any time by peeking around.

I'm almost at the end of the bar when a firm hand pushes me to the floor and around the corner. Matteo appears next to me, his hand still on my shoulder. He seems completely unfazed, like this is just another day at work, which might actually be the case for him.

My stomach turns into knots at that thought because, let's face it, I've let this man do things to me no one else has ever done, all while I know nothing about him. I'm not sure what that says about me, especially now that he's supposedly engaged to my cousin.

A man walks around the corner, his gun aimed straight at us. Matteo is the first to pull the trigger, and the other man slumps to the floor, the fresh wound in his chest oozing blood onto it. I stare at the man, my brain incapable of fully processing what just happened.

Matteo taps my arm to get my attention, and I focus on him. His lips are moving, but I fail to make out any of his words. I huff in frustration and shake my head while pointing at my ears.

His head bobs up and down in understanding. Then he points to the exit and gestures for me to stay low. At least I think that's what he means.

I swallow, and he makes a shoo motion at me.

All right. Here goes nothing.

I get on my hands and knees, figuring that might be the safest option for me, and crawl. Yup. It feels just as fantastic as it sounds, which is not at all. Especially taking into account that I need to move around the dead guy on the floor.

Matteo's right behind me, urging me on with the occasional tap to my leg. I'm almost at the door, so I get up to run the last few feet.

Turns out that was the wrong thing to do, since something hits my side almost immediately. It feels like someone threw something at me, but I can't be sure since I don't stop to check. For a moment, I stumble, but Matteo's strong hands are right there, keeping me upright once more, and we finally make it out into the night.

I gulp in fresh air, my lungs burning, and I stumble across the asphalt, going wherever Matteo leads me. With my hand firmly in his, we make our way to a black car. He tugs his keys out of his pants, unlocks it, and helps me into the passenger seat. The smell of leather and oranges takes away some of the horrible smell that's assaulted my nose for the last ten or so minutes, and I welcome the change.

The car ride that follows is a bit of a blur. I don't think it takes very long, but I can't be sure. We drive into an underground garage, where several bulky men dressed in black from head to toe are waiting for us. Matteo hops out of the car and comes around to open my door, but instead of offering a hand, he just stares at me.

His face is a stone-cold mask, and I have no clue what's going on behind his eyes. But he doesn't look at all happy.

I unbuckle and turn to him. My poor heart is pounding behind my rib cage, and I feel dizzy and weak. It's not as bad as it was when all hell broke loose at the bar, but I'm pretty sure I'm in shock. A bead of sweat runs down the nape of my neck, and the ringing in my ears is still ridiculously loud and annoying, even though I think I'm starting to hear a little better now that we're away from all the noise.

Matteo's chest rises and falls, and he finally unfreezes. He offers me his hand, and I take it, wincing as a searing pain shoots through my side the second he pulls me up. His brows furrow as he examines me, one hand holding me upright, while the other moves over my body.

When his hand comes off my body, it's covered in red. He shouts something to the men at the same time the pain on my side turns to an excruciating level. Dark spots jump out of nowhere and blur my vision, followed by a wave of dizziness.

Then everything turns black.

I WAKE up to low murmurs around me and my side throbbing like nobody's business. The sensation of my body being torn in half is gone now, but it doesn't necessarily feel much better.

I open my eyes to see a man next to me I've never seen before. He touches my side and pokes me with something, adding to the existing agony. I flinch and try to move away from him.

He grimaces. "Hey there, you're back. Sorry about the poke. I thought you'd appreciate the local anesthetic before I get started on your wound."

I close my eyes for a moment at the realization I can hear him. It still sounds like I'm underwater—with the ringing still there as well—but it's so much better than before that I'll take it.

My gaze settles on the man once more. His focus is on the side of my body he just poked. He's handsome with more boyish looks than Matteo's rugged ones, but with dark hair just like Matteo's. He appears to be around the same age as Matteo, maybe in his early thirties?

He probably feels my stare on him and glances at me with his dark-blue eyes. "It'll only take a few minutes until it's all numb and we're good to go."

I nod and clear my throat. "What—" I sound like a dying frog, so I try again. "What happened?"

"Teo, get her some water, will you?" He brings his gaze back to me. "All I know is that a bullet grazed your side, and that's why I'm here. As for what happened to get you into this state, I have no clue. You'll have to ask the big bad wolf about that."

"The big bad wolf? Ugh."

He chuckles at my reply.

A bullet grazed my side.

I got freaking shot.

My brain feels fuzzy, and I'm having a hard time putting all the puzzle pieces together of what went down at the club. It was all so fast.

On the other hand, my brain doesn't have any issues remembering everything that happened with Matteo, no matter how much I try to pretend like the whole thing was only a figment of my imagination. Which is disconcerting, and I might need to see someone about that.

I'd also really like to forget everything that took place afterward with the engagement announcement of Matteo and . . . "Ally."

"We're trying to find her." Matteo's voice comes from somewhere close by, and I try to lift my head, but the other guy shakes his head at me and pushes me back down on the bed. At least I think it's a bed.

"You need to lie down and stay down, please. I promise, as soon as I'm done with you, we'll prop you up so you can drink, okay?"

A sigh slips past my lips, but I nod. What a mess.

I really should have stayed home tonight. I should have stood up to my father, like I've dreamt of doing so many times before. For so many reasons.

Matteo's words register in my scrambled brain, just as he walks up on my other side.

I turn my head so I can look at him, my heart skipping a beat. "Ally's missing?"

"Yes."

A single word. Only he would think that's enough information for me.

"Elaborate, please." I try to keep the frustration out of my voice, but I'm not sure I succeed. Everything sounds wrong to my ears right now.

"We think the Russians took her."

It's dead silent for a heartbeat while I stare up at him. I must have heard him wrong. He couldn't have possibly said the Russians took my cousin, right? "Excuse me . . . who took her?"

"The Russians."

He regards me like I'm a little slow, which in my defense, I am at the moment, but that still doesn't mean he needs to be rude.

"The Russians took Ally?"

He rubs his brow as if he's trying to fight off a headache. "Yes, Gemma. The Russians took Ally. Do you need it in writing?"

The glare I give him is supposed to kick him hard in the balls, but of course, nothing happens. "Why?"

He takes off his suit jacket and places it on a chair by the window. "That's what everyone's trying to figure out."

I'm temporarily distracted by him rolling up his shirtsleeves, exposing two strong forearms that are thickly veined and lined with several tattoos. He crosses his arms over his chest as if he knows exactly what I was doing.

Focus, Gemma.

The local anesthesia must have started working since the

pain in my side has subsided, and with that, my brain function is slowly coming back as well.

The other man clears his throat. "I'm going to clean the wound now, okay? It might take a while, considering how much fabric is lodged in there. I'm going to give you some antibiotics later too, just in case. We don't want you to get an infection."

I turn his way. "Thank you."

He gets to work, and I focus back on Matteo, who's watching us like a hawk.

I ignore his scrutiny. "So that was the Russians at the bar?"

His fists open and close several times before he answers, "Yes. They blew up one of the walls on the side to gain access."

I scrunch up my nose. I can't believe they blew up part of the bar. "Did they take anyone other than Ally?"

"From what I know, she's the only one."

None of this makes sense, and this conversation hurts my head, a dull throbbing near my temples getting more intense by the second.

Matteo's phone rings, giving me a small reprieve.

After checking the screen, he swipes it and brings it up to his ear. "Lorenzo."

The reprieve is short-lived when I hear the name. Is he talking to my dad?

His gaze finds mine, holding me hostage under his scrutiny. "Yes, she's with me."

Sounds like it's my dad. But why would he call Matteo?

"She's being taken care of."

He pauses and listens to the reply.

41

"Keep me updated on Alessandra. I want to know every detail. If they want something from us, I'd imagine they'd contact Toni first. Even though the Russians aren't known for their patience, so you better find her fast. I want my fiancée back and that Russian bastard to pay for what he did."

Another pause.

"No, Gemma stays with me until I have my fiancée back."

Then he hangs up.

CHAPTER 4
GEMMA

Matteo's words sink in. "Did you just say I'm staying with you?"

I jolt upright, briefly forgetting about my injury.

Thankfully, the doctor restrains me with a firm hand, and I don't get far.

"Gemma, lie still. Teo, if you talk to her, go closer to her so she stops moving around so much. Otherwise, I'll do more damage here than good."

Matteo pinches his lips together but does as asked. He grabs the chair with his suit jacket on and pulls it to the other side of me, opposite the doctor.

Leaning back with one of his ankles resting on his knee, he looks like the cocky bastard he turned out to be.

"Yes." He stares me straight in the eye and finally answers my question. His expression is similar to my dad, giving no room for discussion. It makes the hair stand up on the back of my neck.

I'm also convinced this man doesn't understand how to have a proper conversation with all of his one-word answers.

My blood boils under my skin, and the urge to strangle him is almost blinding. "I'm not staying with you. No way."

"You are."

"I'm not going from one prison to the next. I'm sick of it." I tip up my chin, no matter how pointless it is in my current position.

He tilts his head in the same direction mine is and leans forward. "What are you talking about? You don't live in a prison. You're the revered Mafia princess."

"Who people think I am and who I really am are two very different things." I narrow my eyes at him. "You of all people should know that, Mr. Engaged-to-be-Married-to-Someone-Else."

He doesn't appear impressed with my remark, but I don't care.

It needed to be said.

And I meant it too. Maybe something finally snapped loose in my brain when I got shot, but I'm so tired of people's bullshit and their promises and behaviors not matching up. If you promise me ice cream, give me the damn ice cream.

Before either one of us can say another word, a mechanical noise sounds from somewhere outside the door, followed by several beeps, and then heels clicking on the floor.

"Honey, I'm home."

The female voice is loud and cheery, and the woman seems to be walking in our direction.

I swear to God, if he has another fiancée or whatever else, I'm going to strangle him right here, right now.

The doctor peers up. "Is that who I think it is?"

Matteo's chest deflates with his next exhale. "Yup."

"I thought you changed the security keycode?"

He sends a look to the ceiling before rubbing his hand over his face. "I did."

The doctor chuckles at that. "Sounds about right. There's a reason her nickname is Lunatic."

I have no clue who they're talking about, but I'm not sure she sounds like someone I want to meet. Since no one cares about what I want though, there's no way out of this.

Matteo pushes out of his chair just as a woman walks through the door. She's sporting a huge smile and seems like she might be in her mid-to-late twenties. Her hair is a beautiful honey brown, and her red dress is both sexy and sophisticated. Unlike me, this woman has a gorgeous hourglass figure.

Would I ever be able to look like that if my dad hadn't put me on such a strict diet when I was a teenager?

She spots Matteo right away and instantly throws herself at him, engulfing him in a tight hug. "Matty."

Matty?

He groans into her hair but returns the hug.

The doctor grins and shakes his head.

The woman's gaze skims over me before it lands on the man sitting next to me. "Please tell me my eyes aren't deceiving me. Ash Rylant in the flesh?"

"Hey, Luna."

Luna Lunatic. How precious.

She walks over to Ash and brushes her fingertips along his shoulders until she stands next to my head and bends down. "And Gemma Fiore." Her gaze flickers over to my wound before focusing back on me. "I heard about the shooting. Are you okay?"

My brain feels like it's ready to explode, my life suddenly full of puzzle pieces I'm trying to connect and information I need to catch up on.

Such a loaded question. *Are you okay?*

Honestly, I have no freaking idea.

Three weeks ago, I was forced to marry a man, someone I barely knew or liked, who cheated on me before the reception was even over, and ended up dead a couple of hours later. Oh, and that was after I made out with a total stranger, just because he lit a fire in me no one else ever has. All with a single look. Then I repeated that same mistake today and came all over his fingers, right before his engagement to my cousin, and best friend, was announced. The same one who got kidnapped only minutes later when the Russians attacked my family's bar and I got shot in the process. And now I'm being held prisoner by my cousin's fiancé.

I don't think I'd call that okay.

But the only thing that escapes my mouth is a snort while I blink at her. "Not really."

She purses her lips. "I didn't think so. The wound doesn't seem too bad, so I think you'll be okay, at least physically. Right, Doc?"

The tips of Ash's ears slowly turn pink, but he keeps his eyes focused on my wound.

"Luna, get away from Ash. He needs to focus," Matteo barks at her.

She shrugs but steps away. "Fine."

"Did Dad send you?"

Wait a second. Is she his sister?

She shakes her head and walks over to the chair Matteo had been occupying and plops into it, crossing her legs. "Nope. I heard what happened and wanted to make sure you guys are okay."

Matteo leans against the wall and crosses his muscled arms over his chest. "You know, that's why they invented phones."

"Thanks so much for the tip, smart-ass. You know I'd rather see you in the flesh."

"Which you did. So you can leave now."

Seems like I'm not the only one he's rude to.

A real sunshine, that one.

She pouts at him. "But I just got here. Let me talk to Gemma for a little bit. She must be bored out of her mind with you two old snooze-balls here."

Ash gasps. "What? I'm younger than Teo."

Luna shrugs. "Not by much. You just turned thirty, and he's thirty-two."

Matteo grinds his jaw. "You two are insane. Ash, call me when you're done."

Ash nods, focusing back on his work.

Luna leans closer, her eyes as wide as saucers. "Is it true my brother got engaged tonight?"

"What the fuck?" Ash stops once more.

I'm starting to wonder if Matteo was right, and these two really are insane.

Maybe also kind of fun, though.

Luna couldn't be any more opposite to her brother. There's this spark in her eyes that screams of adventurous days and wild nights, a spark I once had, too, before my life changed forever.

Would I be more like Luna now if things hadn't changed? This confident woman who appears so full of life?

Apparently, my body has turned into the proverbial water cooler because Luna and Ash catch each other up on what transpired tonight at the bar. I'm not sure where Luna got all the information from, but it's as if she was there.

She scrunches up her nose. "I still can't believe he got engaged." Her gaze bores into Ash. "You really didn't know about it?"

The doctor shakes his head. "Not a single clue."

Luna tilts her head to the side. "We must be missing something. He's been acting all sorts of weird since our cousin died, but marrying some random woman he doesn't know is so not Matteo."

"I can still hear you," the devil himself calls from behind the slightly ajar door.

"Grumpy butt," Luna mumbles then sighs. "I wish Mom was here. She was always the only one who could talk sense into him or my dad."

At that, Ash pauses, his expression soft. "She was good at that."

Luna nods, and with that, their conversation comes to a halt, and Ash concentrates on my wound again.

My brain is spinning from all this information, and I'm still not sure if I should be laughing or crying about this whole situation.

If someone told me a few hours ago how today would pan out, I'd have howled in their face. Everything that happened sounds insane; it *feels* insane.

I yawn behind my hand when Ash finally pulls back, the needle and string still in his hand.

48

"All done?" I glance at him, hoping the answer is yes.

"Almost."

Thank goodness.

As entertaining as it was to listen to these two gossip about Matteo, I could really use some sleep.

Ash nods at Luna. "Get your brother, will you?"

The siblings walk in less than a minute later, Matteo appearing annoyed to no end.

How incredibly satisfying.

Ash regards his friend. "I don't need to tell you how important it is to make sure her wound doesn't get infected. Wash it out twice a day with water and put some antibiotic ointment on it before applying a new bandage. No shower for the first twenty-four hours. And we'll check the stitches next week. If there's any sign of infection, call me immediately. I'm going to leave you with antibiotics as a precaution, as well as pain medication. Any questions?"

The last bit was directed at me, and my wide eyes must say it all because he chuckles.

"No worries, Gemma. You'll be okay. You're lucky the bullet only grazed your waist. And Matteo has lots of experience with wounds, so you'll be in good hands with him."

I'm not sure if it's possible to be in good hands with that man, but I say, "Thank you," anyway.

So far, Matteo has brought nothing but chaos into my life.

And pleasure.

But I'm going to smother that hussy right this second.

No more anything with Matteo.

Luna gasps, and I'm not sure if her eyes or her smile are bigger. "Gemma's staying here?"

"Yes," Matteo grumbles at the same time I say, "No."

No way am I staying here with *him*.

Matteo ignores me, his gaze on his sister. "She's staying with me until this whole situation is resolved. Her father agrees she's safest here for now."

Oh my God, he's such a liar. That is so not what happened.

"Maybe you should get her out of the city and take her upstate." She scans the white-and-gray bedroom. "No one wants to stay in this boring place anyway. Plus, Gemma can get a nice break and get better far away from this mess."

Matteo closes his eyes and exhales slowly.

Mmmm. Maybe that's not the worst idea after all. I'm sure I can figure out a way to avoid Matteo most of the time.

I think I like Luna.

Not just because of how vibrant and full of life she is, but also because she seems to annoy the shit out of her brother. It's not her fault she's related to him, so I can't hold that against her.

I yawn for what feels like the five hundredth time in the last five minutes, and Ash stands. "Time for Gemma to get some sleep. Teo, come here and help me to slowly prop her up so she can have some water first."

Instead of coming over, Matteo goes to the nightstand and grabs something black from it. He pushes on it, and the mattress slowly lifts.

Ash's eyebrows rise. "And you didn't think to tell me that earlier?"

One of Matteo's shoulders shrugs. "It's new. I forgot about it."

"Of course you did. It sure will come in handy when

someone's injured." Ash takes the water cup from the night-stand on the other side of the bed and brings it to my mouth.

Matteo watches the interaction, but I'm too happy for the water to fill my dry mouth and run down my throat to care about him right now. And too tired. So very tired.

Getting shot apparently zaps the energy right out of you.

The water is gone too fast, but I'm not sure I could keep my eyes open for longer anyway. I have no clue what time it is, but it must be the middle of the night by now.

THE NEXT TIME I wake up, the room is bathed in sunlight.

Did I sleep through the whole night?

I rub my hand over one eyelid and groan the second I touch hard eyelashes. Of course, I didn't wash off my makeup last night. With everything going on, that didn't even occur to me.

"Are you in pain?"

My heart leaps at Matteo's deep voice.

Stupid man.

But that was a good question. I definitely don't feel fantastic, that's for sure, but I don't hurt as much as I expected I would.

"I'm fine," I croak, my voice raspy with sleep. I shift around to see where he's at and immediately regret it as pain shoots up the entire right side of my torso.

Nope, it definitely hurts like hell. I hiss through my teeth. Shit. That's bad.

"That's what I thought." He gets out of the chair and comes over to me.

"What . . . what are you doing in here?"

"Making sure you don't die on my watch."

"How reassuring."

"You're welcome."

Is he this infuriating on purpose?

He steps up to the bed and reaches for the sheet.

With an overwhelming sensation of dread running through my veins, I grab it before he can and hold on to it with all my might. "What are you doing?"

He gives me an exasperated look but stops his advance. "I want to check your wound."

"Oh."

"Also, I might need to give you a sponge bath."

My chest and face instantly grow hot as I stare at him to see if he's serious. "No way."

"So you'd rather stink?"

I try to sniff myself inconspicuously, but I don't think I succeed, since the corner of his mouth twitches. I flick my gaze at the ceiling. "Is it that bad?"

He shrugs. "Could be worse, I suppose."

"Ugh." I throw my arm over my eyes. This is so embarrassing.

"You can wait until tonight when we're at the cabin and take a shower there."

My forehead pinches together, and I move my arm just enough to peek at him. "The upstate cabin Luna mentioned?"

"Yes."

I roll my lips together. "You're seriously taking me out of the city?"

"Yes."

"Do you often kidnap people?"

The corner of his mouth twitches again. "If necessary."

Damn him. "And my dad agreed to this?"

My question wipes all expression off his face.

"I don't need his permission. Plus, he wants this family union so he's smart enough to stand down."

I stare at him, unsure of what to say. This man is nothing like anyone I've ever met before. Not that I've had a lot of contact with people outside our family or security team. And even they usually keep their distance.

I set my jaw, not wanting him to bulldoze me into doing his bidding. "What if I don't want to go with you?"

He takes a step closer, and I wonder if he's had it with me since patience doesn't seem to be his strong suit. "Then I'd say tough shit. This isn't a wellness trip or a vacation. You're coming with me. Deal with it."

I swallow the lump in my throat and don't say anything in response because, really, what's there to say? I can't overpower him, even if I wasn't injured, and he doesn't strike me as the kind of guy you can convince otherwise once he's made up his mind.

Well, he can take me to his cabin, but I don't have to like it.

Once I'm better, I'm going to make his life a living hell, that's for sure. At least, I'll try. There are lots of ways to carry out revenge, and I'll find the right one for this infuriating stranger.

He holds out one of his hands but doesn't advance any farther. "Can I check out your wound now?"

I press my lips together until I barely feel them anymore but nod. "Fine."

I don't like this, but I'm also not stupid. Even though I'm usually not around my dad during his business dealings, I've seen my fair share of wounds over the years when injured men came back to our house.

Finger by finger, I loosen the death grip I have on the sheet and slide it aside enough to give Matteo the access he needs and not a single inch more.

He gives me a silent *Really?* look, while I mentally shoot him a *Is that a problem?* one back. Maybe he'll rethink this whole trip to the cabin, or go by himself and leave me here.

After dragging the chair right next to the bed, he sits and stares at the huge hole Ash cut into my dress yesterday. He apologized but said it was necessary to access the wound without aggravating it more. Matteo brushes his fingers along the frayed fabric. Goosebumps erupt on my skin, and I flinch at the sensation of the skin tightening around my wound.

"Sorry." He tries to touch me as little as possible and peels the bandage off with a tenderness that surprises me.

We both stay silent while he inspects my wound and cleans it with the water he put on the nightstand. Once it's dried, he puts on the antibiotic ointment and applies a fresh bandage. I flinch and groan several times, but he never stops.

When he's done, he picks up his things and stands. "You need to eat something so you can take your medicine. What do you want?"

I close my eyes for a second. "Whatever you have is fine. Just coffee works too."

He inclines his head and turns to leave.

"Matteo?"

He peers at me over his shoulder. "What?"

I lick my dry lips. "Do you have clothes for me to wear?" I

inhale deeply before pushing out the next words. "I also need to go to the bathroom. Could you . . . could you help me get there, please?"

"Sure. Will you be okay for another few minutes?"

"Yeah."

"I'll be back." Just like that, he's out the door.

I continue to stare at the spot he just disappeared from. He's different today, almost clinical in the way he talks to me. He didn't even argue with me. On the contrary, he was almost . . . nice.

My brain has a hard time putting this version of him together with the man who only yesterday looked at me with fire in his eyes and made me orgasm without asking for anything in return. How's this the same man?

But maybe that's a good thing?

He's an engaged man now, after all, and I have no claim on him whatsoever. Maybe that's the reason for his change.

For a very short, very fleeting instant yesterday, there were possibilities for us, of what could be if the stars somehow aligned correctly. Now, there's nothing.

If there was ever a future for us, it was over before it could even begin.

Just as promised, he comes back with some clothes under one arm and a tray in his hands. He sets it down on the nightstand, and a quick glance at it has my mouth watering. There's water and juice, a banana, and a plate with two pieces of toast with what appears to be butter and jam. My stomach rumbles at the sight. Simple, regular food like this hasn't been on my meal plan for years.

"Here." He hands me the bundle of fabric, then turns around to give me some privacy. But not until after he grabs the remote for the bed and tilts it up, making it easier for me to sit up.

It all goes painfully slow, and when I'm finally out, I stare at his back in disbelief. He doesn't even try to get a glimpse of me in my underwear. That should make me happy, right?

I take off my dress, thankful it was one that was wrapped in the front, and focus on the clothes in front of me. A soft white T-shirt and some sweatpants.

It's a white shirt. *White.*

My chest rises while I stare at it. "You don't have a black shirt?"

He sighs, and when he speaks, the bite is back in his voice. "I think we both know there's no need for you to wear black."

My heart misses a beat at the way he says those words with so much conviction. "But—"

"Are you telling me you mourn the man you were ordered to marry?"

"No." The word is out of my mouth before I can stop it.

I should feel bad about saying it out loud, or about feeling nothing at all, but Matteo is right. I don't mourn Luigi, I never have. Not in the way a wife should have mourned her husband. Not considering this handsome stranger occupied my thoughts, even before my husband was killed.

"You don't have to pretend with me, passerotta."

I press my lips together. Am I that easy to read? Did I just waste years of my life pretending to be someone I'm not for nothing? I'm pretty sure my dad and everyone else in the family buys it, everyone except Ally . . . and now Matteo.

He rolls his shoulders back. "Stop overthinking this and

put the damn shirt on. It'll make it easier for me to spot if you're bleeding."

An image of my dad's disapproving expression pops into my head for even considering wearing white, but I push it aside and cling to Matteo's last comment. It *will* make it easier to keep an eye on my injury. No one can argue with that, right?

With renewed determination, I shove my arms through the sleeves, immediately regretting it because the movement tugs at my wound. "Damn it."

Matteo is at my side in an instant, helping me get my arms into the sleeves and sliding the soft fabric over my head and down my body. The shirt is way too big for me, easily falling to my hips when he helps me stand with a hand behind my back.

With his head right next to mine, my breath hitches with him lingering there. His breath whispers over my ear, and his woodsy orange scent invigorates my sense of smell. The combination of it has my heart fluttering.

He clears his throat and draws back. "Let's put the pants on after your trip to the bathroom."

"Okay."

"Put your arm around my middle and hold on as much as you can."

I do as he says and wrap my left arm around his lower back. Since I can't reach all the way around, I clutch a fistful of his shirt and hang on for dear life.

We carefully make our way to the en suite, and I flinch with every step we take. You never realize how much you use certain body parts until you injure them.

Matteo reaches inside the room to switch on the light.

The bathroom is mostly white with gray undertones, very similar to the bedroom.

"Is your favorite color gray?"

He frowns at me. "No, why?"

I bite my lower lip. "Just wondering."

He ignores my randomness and walks me right up to the toilet. "Do you need help here?"

I grimace at the thought and glance at my feet. How mortifying. "I think I've got it, thanks."

"I'll be right outside the door." He lets go of me slowly and walks away, clicking the door shut behind him.

Once I'm done peeing, I carefully move to the sink to take a look in the mirror and immediately regret it.

Now I know why he wanted to help me bathe.

How on earth did they all keep a straight face around me?

My dark hair, which was in beautiful waves yesterday, resembles a complete rat's nest today, and my eyeliner and mascara are smeared all around my light-brown eyes. My face, neck, and arms have streaks of dirt and blood all over them, and I easily resemble an extra on a cheap B-horror movie set.

"Matteo, do you have any washcloths in here?" I brace myself on the edge of the counter, not trusting the slight dizziness in my brain and body.

He opens the door and bends down to one of the cabinets under the sink, brushing my leg in the process. I suppress the shiver, remembering how terrible that last body ripple was for my injury earlier.

Matteo stands back up with a gray washcloth in his hand, leaning around me to turn on the water. Once the washcloth is wet, he wrings it out and wipes my face. I don't even attempt to protest, focusing on staying upright by clinging to the counter instead.

Once I appear at least a little more human, he gets the sweatpants from the bed, holding them out in front of me to step into. I have to steady myself on his shoulders before I topple over, making things more awkward by the second.

I attempt to look everywhere else but at him. "Thank you."

He grunts in response, before gripping one of my arms to help me back into the bedroom. When we reach the bed, he studies the food intently.

"Do you want to eat while you stand? It might be easier."

I hate the thought of standing any longer with my dizziness, but the alternative isn't very appealing either. "Yeah. Bending, or any kind of movement, seems to yank at my wound."

While keeping a firm grip on my elbow, he leans down to pick up the orange juice and turns my way. "Open."

"What?"

"Open your mouth."

I break eye contact and lick my dry lips.

"You let me finger-fuck you but get all shy when I want to feed you?"

Damn it, he's got a point.

And I'm really thirsty and hungry too.

"Open. Your. Mouth."

Without looking at him, I comply and cup my mouth around the rim of the glass the instant the cold firmness touches my lips.

"Good girl."

Warmth rushes through my body at his words, showing

once more how completely out of whack my body is for reacting this way.

I drink most of the juice before he places it back on the tray.

He gets a piece of toast next, and this time, I open my mouth before he can say anything.

Or so I thought.

I'm completely aware of just how close he's standing to me while he says, "Open wider."

I do as he says and bite off a piece of the jam toast, enjoying the sweet flavor in my mouth.

"Now swallow."

Two words spoken in a low rumble, and my gaze flicks up to his immediately, almost like a reflex. My heart beats to a wild rhythm when I see the fire in his eyes.

Despite the state I'm in, heat rushes through my body, all the way to my core.

It's the first time he's dropped the clinical gaze and has regarded me the same way he did while he devoured me.

Holy shit.

This man is dangerous to my health, and I'm not sure if I like it or not.

He's engaged.

To your cousin.

That little nagging voice in the back of my mind is enough to snap me out of my lust-filled haze.

And I'm glad.

All in all, this man and I are nothing. He will join my family on someone else's arm, share someone else's bed, and I'll have to watch it all happen from the sidelines.

He feeds me the rest of the food in silence, and when I'm done, he grabs the pills.

Instead of letting him put them in my mouth, I draw back a few inches and take them out of his hand.

"I can do that."

He shoots me a stormy look but doesn't prevent me from swallowing the medicine with the water he holds out to me.

Twenty minutes later, we're in his car—a large SUV this time—and I'm propped up with pillows and blankets so my body is jostled as little as possible. Once we're out on the interstate, the gentle rocking movement puts me to sleep.

Sometime later, Matteo's voice pulls me out of my sleep. He must be on the phone, so I keep my eyes closed, planning on drifting off to sleep again.

Despite the fact he's almost whispering, his words have too much bite in them for my brain to ignore. "Nikolai Vasiliev is hiding Vladimir, and someone has to pay for what happened. The tracker I put on Alessandra should make it easy to find him, yet we still have no clue where Nikolai is keeping her."

My heart is beating so hard, I'm sure Matteo can hear it.

Find *him*. Not her.

Not them, just *him*.

What the hell is going on?

CHAPTER 5
GEMMA

Pretending any kind of normalcy with Matteo once I overheard the snippet of his phone conversation earlier is impossible. Once he dropped that bomb, I couldn't go back to sleep and just stared out the window for the rest of the drive. I'm not sure if Matteo knows I accidentally eavesdropped or not, but he hasn't said anything. The whole thing doesn't make any sense; maybe I imagined it, I was in that half-awake, half-asleep stage, after all.

We drive up to his cabin, and I'm surprised I actually like it. It's modern, all dark wood and glass, and not at all like the shabby small one-room shack I pictured. Somehow, it still manages to look cozy.

I point out the windshield. "Isn't this too big to be called a cabin?"

Matteo shrugs. "When my grandpa bought the property, it only had a little cabin on it. The name stuck, even after he built this many decades later."

This piece of information is so normal that I stare at Matteo for a moment as he pulls into the garage and turns the engine off. He even smiled a tiny bit when he mentioned his grandpa. This man is such a conundrum; he makes my head spin.

I desperately want to get away from him for some time to think, but I'm packed in tightly with all the pillows and blankets, and I'm not stupid enough to cause myself more pain than necessary.

So I stay where I'm at until he comes around to my side and helps me out of my cushioned spot. I follow him to the door that leads us through a mudroom and straight into the kitchen. It's an open floor plan, and I'm immediately fascinated by the modern interior mixed with the exposed wooden beams and the enormous fireplace on the other side of the living room that's encased in an all-stone accent wall.

Beautiful and mesmerizing.

"Come on, I'll show you your room." Matteo walks past me and waits by the stairs with a black duffel in his hand.

I want to ask what's going on with my cousin, but I know he won't answer me. Just like my dad never does. I used to ask a lot of questions, but he shut me down fairly quickly, telling me little girls shouldn't be asking questions about the business, or much else really.

I shake my head at Matteo and his offered hand and grip the rail instead. Eventually, I make it upstairs without keeling over and follow him into the bedroom off the hallway. I stop and stare in awe at the huge bay window complete with a reading nook. How perfect. Too bad I don't have any books with me. After a quick glance around, I don't see any here either.

Matteo sets the duffel on the bed. "My sister packed some stuff for you. Let me know if you need anything else. I had food delivered this morning, so I'm going to make us something to eat."

"Okay."

"Anything specific you want?"

I shake my head. "Whatever you want is good."

He's quiet, bringing my gaze to his. His eyes are narrowed at me like he's annoyed. I think back over our conversation but I can't think of anything I said that would make him react this way. Maybe it's just his regular grumpy-butt attitude like Luna mentioned.

After a long exhale, he says, "Do you want to eat up here or downstairs?"

"Mmm, whatever is easier for you." Just the thought of walking back downstairs has me wincing, but I'll manage if I have to.

He stares at me, like he's trying to read my mind, before he turns around and leaves, closing the door behind him.

I release a pent-up breath.

Then, curiosity gets the better of me, and I go to the duffel and open it.

Inside, more outfits—similar to my T-shirt and sweatpants one—greet me, and I'm oddly grateful for them. It's not what I'd normally wear, but it'll be a lot easier and more comfortable while my body heals. Underneath the clothes are toiletry bags with everything I could possibly need as well as a bunch of underwear. I don't even look at it, it's so weird to have someone else pack that for you. I reach around the bottom of the bag to see if there's anything else, just as my fingers touch something hard. Paper. Is that a book? I grab it and pull it out, and low and behold, it *is* a book.

How on earth did Luna know how much of a bookworm I

am? I turn it around to study the back cover, and my stomach flutters when I see it's a paranormal romance. Exactly the kind of escape from reality I need.

The window seat is sadly not an option right now, but the recliner in the corner might be. I walk over to it and slowly make my way into the seat, thankful the chair has a remote that allows me to recline into a comfortable position.

Matteo comes to my room sometime later, and I haven't moved an inch.

He walks in, and I make the mistake of smiling up at him, still lost in the book world and characters.

Once he's placed the tray he's carrying on the small table next to the recliner and examines me in the chair with the book on my lap. "You like to read?"

"I do."

"Was it in the bag?"

I nod.

He shakes his head. "That woman."

"What woman?"

"Luna. She's incapable of staying out of anyone's business."

I lift the book. "If it means I get things like this, I'm glad she's in mine."

Maybe he's a book snob, who knows? He wouldn't be the first one, especially when it comes to anything romance. If they only knew what they miss out on.

He drags the corner of his lower lip into his mouth as he regards me. "That's what you say now. Ash wasn't wrong yesterday; she's nicknamed Lunatic for a reason."

I purse my lips and close the book. "Maybe I need some crazy in my life."

"Why?"

I shrug my left shoulder. "Reasons."

He doesn't seem satisfied with my answer, but I don't care. I'm actually not sure if I have an answer, at least a good one. Or one that would make sense to anyone else.

My brain has been spinning more than usual since my wedding, suddenly wondering how different my life could have been if I hadn't fallen into my submissive role so easily. Maybe I could have had a more regular life by now, had my own apartment and gone to college, had actual friends and maybe even a boyfriend?

But after my mom died, I almost welcomed handing over that control. The grief was so intense, it felt like I couldn't take on another thing, even if it was making decisions for myself. Eventually, I got used to it, and my father took advantage of that.

Matteo gets the chair from the other side of the table and sits. "I hope you like Mexican food."

I glance at the tray and what looks like a chicken fajita bowl with quinoa, and my mouth waters instantly. "Sure."

I'm also incredibly grateful I don't have to walk downstairs.

Matteo lifts the plate and picks up the spoon. It's then I notice that the meat and vegetables are all cut in small pieces rather than strips.

"Come on, passerotta. Open that pretty mouth for me."

Matteo calling me little sparrow again stuns me, and I open my mouth without thinking about his command and the fact that I don't need him telling me what to do.

I chew and swallow. "I can probably feed myself."

It hurts to raise my arm since everything tugs at my stomach wound, but I'm sure I'd manage somehow. Matteo feeding me is just so weird, and it also creates this strange flutter sensation in my stomach, which is probably even worse.

He sighs. "Or you could let me feed you so that you can get back on your feet as soon as you can."

Damn him and his stupid logic.

So I open my mouth.

But only this once.

He doesn't say a single word during the whole meal, but he's watching me like a hawk. The glint in his eyes goes from annoyed, to neutral, to hot, and I don't miss a second of it because I watch him right back, even though I know I shouldn't. He's not good for me in any way, but my body didn't get the memo. It's impossible to forget the way he made me feel alive, the way he turned my whole life upside down in a single moment. Whatever he unleashed inside me, it's slowly growing, and it's craving more. I'm completely screwed.

When the bowl is empty, and I've downed the water too, he places everything on the tray and picks up the napkin. But instead of using it, he only holds it and brings his thumb up to my mouth. The rough pad wipes over one corner of my mouth before he pushes it between my lips.

My breathing and heartbeat accelerate, but I'm frozen in place. I couldn't move back, even if I wanted to. And I really should.

In a sick twist of fate, I should also be grateful I'm injured and unable to do anything naughty with him. All things considered, I have no claim on this man and should be running as far away from him as possible, I also still want him.

My conscience douses my thoughts like a bucket of cold water, reminding me that I don't take what's not mine, and I definitely don't want to be the other woman either.

Now I just need to find my self-control since that bitch took off without asking me first.

I pull my head back, and he gets the hint, taking his hand away.

He places both hands on the armrests and taps away with his fingers. "How are you feeling?"

There's tension in his voice, but I ignore it.

One of us needs to be the bad guy, and ironically enough, it seems like it's me.

"Same, I guess. As long as I don't move much, I'm okay."

"What's your pain level?"

"Bearable."

"So you don't want any pain meds?"

"No."

As if he smelled something more behind my answer, he narrows his eyes at me. "Why?"

I wrinkle my nose. "I just don't like medicine very much."

"Why?"

This time, he leans forward, almost breaching my personal bubble, the way he likes to do so as frequently as possible. It's slightly more intimidating though, especially paired with an intense look like right now.

I don't give him more than a shrug. He's not the kind of person I want to share my past with and the reality that my dad pumped me full of antidepressants after my mom died.

At first, I thought he did it to help me, but I quickly realized it was for his own benefit because they made me loopy. Information Matteo could possibly use against me somehow later on?

A stifling minute of silence passes, and he releases a frustrated breath. Relief floods me when he backs off, and I watch him as he puts the chair back in its place and picks up the tray.

"Did Luna get everything you need, or is something missing?"

My gaze flickers to the bag on the bed. "Mmmm, I think I'm good, but I'll check again to make sure. I got distracted by the book."

"Just let me know what you need, and I'll get it."

"Okay."

He spins around and walks toward the door.

"Matteo?"

He turns a fraction, enough for me to see his profile.

"Thank you for lunch."

He nods and closes the door behind him.

Nothing's easy with him.

I stare longingly at the book, but eventually, I get out of the chair, cursing the whole time.

Every single movement hurts, and it feels like the whole ordeal takes me about five minutes. At this point, just breathing is difficult, but a much-needed bathroom break is in order. Thankfully, I manage it by myself.

Standing seems to aggravate the wound the least, so on my way back to bed, I open the dresser drawers, as well as the closet door, ready to grab whatever Luna packed and put it away as fast as possible so I can go to sleep.

I swear, I've never been this tired before. And it keeps hitting me so suddenly too.

Once all the T-shirts and sweatpants are put away, I take the toiletry bags and put them on the bathroom counter. I can unpack those later, when I actually need them.

There are a few pairs of jeans and a couple of sweaters that will be perfect for the approaching fall temperatures. The underwear goes straight into a drawer.

The books at the bottom bring a huge grin to my face. It's the rest of the paranormal series I started and totally fell in love with. How nice of Luna to pack all of this for me. She's officially turned into my lifesaver, and I need to find a way to say thanks to her. Maybe I can ask Matteo if I can call her.

I pick up the small stack of books and put them on top of the dresser. I double-check the bag to make sure I didn't forget anything, then throw it in the bottom of the closet.

The bed calls my name, and I half-crawl, half-slide into it until I lie flat on my back, panting a little. Normally, I hate sleeping on my back, but it seems to be the least painful position to be in at the moment.

It's early evening the next time I wake up, and my wound is throbbing like a bitch. Looks like it might be time for another round of pain meds.

My gaze lands on the dresser that's to one side and has my stack of books on it. Wait a second, there's something black between the books. Is that a box? I must have been more tired than I realized to have missed it earlier.

Slowly—and I mean a-snail-could-give-me-a run-for-my-money slowly—I make my way out of bed and shuffle to the dresser. After taking the first two books off the pile, I stare at what is, indeed, a black box. It has a Post-it note stuck to the top that says, *Open me.*

I snort. Not conspicuous at all.

Curiosity gets the better of me, and I lift the lid, gasping when I see what's inside.

A phone.

A freaking phone.

I grab it with shaky fingers, reading the note that was left underneath.

Gemma, I'm sure you'll be bored out of your mind with my lame brother there in no time. I know your phone got lost in all the chaos yesterday, but I wanted you to have one. I had to take certain safety precautions and lock some accounts and contacts. I hope you understand. But my number is open, so call or text me, and I can tell you all of Matty's secrets so you can poke the big angry bear in my absence. ;)

PS. Check your voice message. I was able to retrieve that from your cloud. Luna xoxo

My heart is racing, and I rush to turn it on. While I wait for the phone to start up, I eye the bed. I hate that sitting hurts more than standing, but I guess it'll take a few days, if not longer, for that to change. The phone makes a melodic sound while it finishes loading, and I immediately push the voicemail button.

Tears form the second Ally's voice fills my ear. I barely hear what she says the first time through, and I replay it immediately.

"Hey, Gem. I'm going to keep this quick, but I just wanted to let you know I'm okay. And I mean it. Please delete this message as soon as you're done listening to it and don't tell anyone what I'm about to tell you. I promise I'll explain more later, but for now, you have to believe me that Nikolai won't harm me. We've been . . . he and I . . . uh . . . I know him, okay, and I trust him. He's in trouble for what he did at the bar, but he'd never hurt a single hair on my head. Ever."

There's some noise in the background, and Ally exhales loudly. "I've got to go, but I'll try to call or text soon. Take good care of yourself, and let me know you're okay too, please. It was so chaotic when they took me away that I couldn't see where you were. I'll try and check my messages as soon as I can, and I promise I'll be home soon. Love you, Gem. Keep on shining."

Then the voice message is over. I listen to it approximately ten more times, maybe twenty, and I come to one conclusion.

Ally doesn't sound scared. Not one bit. Quite the opposite actually. And the way she stumbled her way through explaining that she knows him, like they're more than acquaintances.

What did you do, Ally?

My mind races, searching for answers.

I keep dissecting every sentence, every word Ally says until there's a knock on the door. I start and throw the phone into the box before closing it and dumping one of the books on top.

Pain shoots through my middle, and I clench my jaw to keep from crying out.

Way too much movement.

Shit.

Matteo pokes his head in and frowns when he sees me standing there like a deer caught in headlights. "You okay?"

"Yeah." I barely get the word through my teeth.

The door opens all the way, and he walks inside with a water bottle and my two pill bottles in one hand, a plate with a couple of sandwiches in the other. "I thought you might need some meds and food by now."

I nod, fighting the heat that's forming behind my eyes. Man, that really fucking hurt. Damn it.

He opens the pill bottle and shakes the tablets out on my outstretched hand. "You don't have to act a certain way for me. If you're in pain, you're in pain. End of story, got it?"

I nod and accept the water bottle from him, taking several big gulps with the medicine.

He studies me. "Better?"

"Yeah, thank you."

He tilts his chin in acknowledgement, then peeks at his watch, and I'm momentarily fascinated by the fact he actually wears one. Not many people do anymore, to the point it strikes me as almost sophisticated now.

"The twenty-four hours are almost up. Do you want to take a shower after you're done eating?"

"Gosh, yes." The words come out as a half-moan, and heat creeps up my neck immediately.

"I'll be back soon then."

His words don't register until the door closes behind him.

Wait, what?

I shake my head. It doesn't matter. I have more pressing

things to do, like checking out my phone and contacting both Ally and Luna.

I also need to find a safe spot to hide it. Matteo didn't say I couldn't have one, but I don't want to chance it either. Otherwise, Luna could have just given it to me instead of smuggling it into my bag. Definitely not worth the risk.

Grabbing one of the sandwiches Matteo left, I take a big bite and open my contacts to dial Ally. Even though I didn't expect her to answer, my heart still sinks a little when her voicemail pops on.

The beep sounds, and I clear my throat awkwardly. "Hey, Ally, it's me, Gemma. I only just got access to a phone and listened to your voice message. I hope you're still doing okay, but shit, what the hell is going on with you and Nikolai? It sounds like you've got a lot of explaining to do. I'm, mmh, I'm doing okay here. I don't know if you heard, but I got shot at the bar. It was thankfully just a graze on my side, but it's still a pain. Matteo got me out of there, and he and my dad decided I should . . . uh . . . I should stay with Matteo for now. He took me out of the city this morning, so I have to deal with his grumpy ass for the foreseeable future. Get back to me if you can, please. Love you."

I end the call and blow out my cheeks. My mind is dizzy from all the questions swirling around in it. Should I have told Ally where Matteo took me? At first, I was planning on telling her, but what if someone else listens to the message? What if the Russians come after us to harm either or both of us because of it? As much as I'd like to not be held hostage here, I also don't want anyone to get hurt. And considering what happened yesterday, it's better to be safe than sorry. The last thing I need is to be under fire again. No, thank you.

Even the grumpy ass is a better option than that.

Especially since he's actually not too bad.

Nope, not going there.

I pause to listen for any sounds coming from outside the door. I don't need to hurt myself again. I'm not a masochist.

When everything seems quiet, I pull up Luna's contact. She's the only other contact beside Ally and Matteo, but I decide to text her rather than call. I'm not sure I'm comfortable enough to do that yet. Not only did she provide me with clothes and books, but also with a phone and therefore, a way to contact my cousin and her, so I'm incredibly grateful. And the fact that she got Ally's voice message for me was extra sweet of her.

ME

> Hey, Luna, it's Gemma. Thank you so much for the phone. I cannot thank you enough.

There, that's good enough for a first text.

I'm just about to put the phone away, as three little dots appear at the bottom of the screen. I continue eating while I wait.

LUNA

> Hey, girl. You're so welcome. I'm glad you found it. How are you feeling?

ME

> I'm okay. I'm going to feel a lot better once I finally take a shower.

LUNA

> Yeeeees. I'd be miserable in your shoes. Do you like the books I got for you?

ME

Oh yes, sorry. Totally forgot to say thanks for those too, well, for everything really.

LUNA

No worries. I paid for all of it with my brother's credit card, but don't tell him.

ME

You paid with your brother's credit card without telling him?

LUNA

You bet I did. It's so much more fun this way.

I chuckle, despite myself.

ME

He won't get mad?

LUNA

Oh, he'll totally blow his roof off, especially when he sees that I didn't just buy stuff for you. But it's okay, I'm keeping him on his toes this way. Really, he should thank me for exposing these security risks to him.

Oh my gosh, she really is crazy—in the best possible way.

A noise from somewhere startles me, and I type another quick message.

ME

I think I heard your brother, so I better go. Thanks again for everything.

LUNA

My pleasure. Text again soon, and keep me
updated on your reading. That series is
sooooo hot! But hands off River, he's my
book boyfriend.

With a silly smile on my lips, I go the cliché route for now
and hide the phone in my underwear drawer.

After inhaling the last bite of my sandwich, I drink the
rest of the water and stand by the window for a few minutes.
Large trees line the property, slightly swaying in the evening
breeze. It's so different from the busy city skyline, incredibly
soothing.

*And your dad isn't around to tell you what you can and
can't do.*

The thought circles around in my head, getting louder
and louder, bringing a sort of lightness with it that nestles in
my chest.

Maybe coming here wasn't such a bad idea.

Not wanting to overthink it anymore, I head to the bathroom to pee, then inspect the toiletry bags Luna packed for
me. When I'm done unpacking, I stare at the bottles, containers, and jars on the counter. Every single item is exactly what
I have at home. All of my favorite products. How's that possible? She could have contacted my dad, but I doubt he would
have taken the time to go through my bathroom products.
Not even the staff would have done that.

This is exactly how Matteo finds me, staring at the wide
array of items with pursed lips and a blank stare.

"Why do you look like you've seen a ghost?"

I meet his gaze in the mirror. "Uh, I just unpacked the
bags and . . . and everything's the same as I have back home."

He tilts his head to the side, like he doesn't understand the problem. "And you don't like it anymore?"

I blink at him and raise my eyebrows. "Matteo, your sister bought me the same exact items as I have back home at my house. Did she pay my dad a visit or is she secretly a witch or something?"

"No visit and no witch."

I let that sink in for a moment, but nope, that information doesn't help . . . not at all. "How exactly does she know all of my favorites then?"

"By hacking your data," he says this with a straight face and so nonchalantly that it takes my brain a few seconds to process.

She hacked my data? What the hell?

Then Matteo starts to take off his clothes.

CHAPTER 6
MATTEO

Gemma watches me while I take off my shirt first, followed by my pants and socks, leaving me in only my boxer briefs, which I keep on. For now, at least. They do nothing to hide my hard dick, but I don't give a fuck.

No matter how hard I try not to want this woman, my body has other ideas, even if it makes things complicated.

Having her all to myself without any distractions isn't helping either. But she's injured and needs to heal. If I fucked her now, I'd only cause her pain. And I'm not that much of an asshole.

She finally manages to snap her gaze away from my body, but not until after getting a good eyeful at my naked skin, her gaze slowing down at my tattoos. "What . . . what are you doing?"

"Helping you shower."

She shakes her head. "I can do that myself."

"I'll stay here then to make sure you won't slip and crack your head open."

Her chest rises in quick succession, and she glances around the room, probably hoping someone magically appears and saves her from this situation. "Well, then you can wait outside the door like you did last time."

"You mean the time where you were holding on to it so hard that you almost broke off the counter?"

Her eyes narrow to slits, and I suppress a chuckle. This woman's attitude keeps surprising me. I wasn't lying to her when I said she's not anything like I thought she'd be, or rather, like her dad made her out to be. Like she's his little doll he can do with as he pleases.

If things were different, I'd put a bullet in his head for imprisoning her like this. Does he really think he tamed her? Can't he see that all he's ever been able to do is mask who she is? Her personality? From the second I met her in that hotel room, I saw the eyes of a caged animal: the uncertainty and the fire. The girl who was yearning for a different life than the one that was molded for her. I wanted to corrupt her because I knew it would be just as fun for her too.

And maybe I will. But first she needs to get better.

"Come on, passerotta. I won't touch you, not until you beg me for it." My dick gives a little twitch as the flames in her eyes ignite.

"Fine." She manages to push her sweatpants off by herself but quickly gets stuck when she tries to take off her shirt.

Without a word, I close the distance between us and help her. She flinches a few times, but the pain doesn't seem to be too bad, her medication doing its job.

After tossing her clothes on top of mine, I walk to the large glass shower and turn it on.

Facing her again, I watch her slide a fifth bottle to the front of the counter with one hand.

I nod in their direction. "Do you want all of these in the shower?"

Her gaze stays locked on her hand. "Yes, please."

Ah, there's my submissive little bird.

I place all bottles on the built-in corner shelf of the shower before closing the door and walking to the cabinet. I get one of the waterproof bandages and sit on the chair against the wall. "Come here."

I try hard not to stare at her underwear-clad body while she walks over, but I only have so much self-control and lose the battle when she stands a few feet away from me in a pair of matching black panties and bra. I want to release a growl at the possibility of her father forcing her to wear black underwear too, but I swallow it down. Though at this point, my frown might be permanent.

"I will not shower naked with you." Gemma raises her chin like she's done several times in my presence.

"I expected as much."

"Good."

"Great."

"Ugh."

It's so easy to get her riled up, almost too easy.

Holding her by the back of her thighs, I gently drag her closer, her skin soft under my fingers.

Her breath hitches, but she doesn't say anything. She places her left hand on my shoulder, I'm guessing to steady herself, but my dick might as well think she did it to say hi to him.

Fucker.

As slowly as I can, I take the regular bandage off—glad to see the skin around the wound doesn't appear too angry—before exchanging it with the waterproof one. Gemma moves away when I press around the outside of it, making sure it's sealed everywhere. Other than that, she handles it well.

Once I'm done, she walks to the shower, leaving me sitting here to stare at her perfect round ass that has called to me more than once already. It's so plump, I want to bite it. And one day, I will.

I discard the old bandage and wrapper and step into the shower after her. It's a large space with two rainfall shower-heads and matching handheld ones. She already made herself at home under one, with her face tilted back and the water running down her face and body.

Fuck.

I rub one hand over my face and step up behind her. "We have to make this quick. The faster we get you out of here, the better."

"Okay."

She tells me in which order she likes to do things. Shampoo first, then conditioner, deep conditioner, bodywash, facewash.

She peeks at me over her shoulder. "But let's skip the deep conditioner since that needs to stay on for several minutes."

I nod and reach for the shampoo bottle, staring at the label. You've got to be fucking kidding me. It says, *Like a Virgin*. All I can do is shake my head and squeeze a decent amount of it into my hand, telling my hungry cock for the millionth time today that he's not going to get anything but my hand.

"Lean your head back."

She does as I ask, and I spread the coconut shampoo over her hair then massage it into her scalp. Her eyelids flutter closed as she relaxes into my touch, and I wish we could be here under different circumstances.

Circumstances that don't involve her getting caught in the middle of my revenge plan. Damn it. She got shot because of me.

Aware of the time this has already taken, I hurry to rinse out the shampoo and repeat the process with the conditioner. She's still turned with her back toward me when I pick up the loofah and squirt some bodywash on it. I avoid the label, not wanting to see another ridiculous name like *Please Fuck Me Now* or something equally ridiculous and forbidden.

Although I'd love nothing more than to touch her in all the right places, I refrain from doing so. This might be one of the hardest things I've ever done. I wash each arm and her neck, only brushing the loofah over the exposed skin on her chest before I move on to her stomach. Then I bend down to wash each leg, trying to ignore that my face is right in front of her pussy.

Images from the club and how wet she was pop into my mind, and I indulge in the knowledge that her wetness was all for me. She was as desperate for me as I was for her.

But all of that changed the second her uncle announced my engagement to her cousin. That was a little inconvenient.

It still is, since she hides her attraction to me as much as possible, which could be said speaks for her character. While that might be the case, it just pisses me off. I haven't gotten laid since I got back to the city with my team, and it's been too long. Actually, I hadn't been with anyone for a while before then either. Somehow, being away for two years and constantly on the move made the whole cliché of having a different woman in every city get pretty boring after a while.

It's just my luck that the first woman who gets my dick excited in so long is the beautiful girl standing in front of me now, and I had to meet her on her wedding day of all days.

I move the loofah higher up her inner thigh, and her left hand grasps my shoulder, her grip so tight her fingernails threaten to break my skin.

Yes, baby, leave your marks on me.

Due to her underwear, I skip her pussy completely and go straight to the other thigh, and Gemma lets out a frustrated huff. I press my teeth into my lower lip, trying to distract myself from this walking temptation.

My gaze flicks to her stomach and the scar she has, and I have to remind myself to be gentle with her despite the edgy, twitchy feeling that's coursing through me at the sight. It awakens every single carnal urge inside me, even the ones I've worked hard to push into the darkest corners of my mind. My muscles and veins strain against my skin, and I know I need to let out some of this energy later, before it eats me alive.

"Do you know who did this to you?"

She realizes I'm talking about her scar and immediately tries to cover it with her hands, which makes sense for someone like her, who was taught to look as flawless as possible. It's not the worst scar I've seen, but it's not pretty either. It's more like a half-assed butcher job that bears a close resemblance to a boomerang right above her belly button. That is if the boomerang had fang-like edges and was about seven inches long.

She shakes her head, still trying to get her hands fully

over it.

It takes me several times to swallow the rage down enough to ask, "Does your dad know who did it?"

She stops holding her hands over the scar, and instead, tries to get away from me. But I keep my hands on the backs of her thighs. Firm and unyielding, without hurting her.

Her left hand slaps on her outer thigh when she drops it. "What's it to you?"

The bite in her voice surprises me. Especially since she tried to pull away.

My gaze finds hers as I get up, and the pure rage in her eyes seems to connect with mine, allowing me to breathe normally again.

What's it to me, she asked?

What's it to her after all this time? How is it possible that an incident that happened years ago can still get her this worked up?

I doubt she'd be honest with me though. That's not the way things are between us.

But I do want to know about her dad's involvement in all of this, so I repeat my question. "Does he know who did it?"

There's a visible tightness to her jaw and neck that's impressive for someone who's supposed to be calm and obedient. Is she only like this with me, or did no one else ever notice her fiery spirit?

This woman has been challenging me from the moment we met, not acting anything like the woman I heard about marrying an old family foe, the one she was molded into by her father.

I want to figure her out, strip off every one of her layers to see what's hiding deep on the inside.

At last, she flicks her gaze at the ceiling like she's had enough of our staring match, and says, "I don't know if he knows, okay? He's never mentioned anything to me, but it's not like he's usually forthcoming with any information. The police and my family wrote the incident off as a home invasion gone wrong, that the person breaking in probably wanted to get their hands on my dad's business files or something, and that I was lucky I got away at all."

What she's not saying is that her mother wasn't so lucky. After Ash saw the scar, I did some digging and read about the break-in. It said that the then fifteen-year-old girl was safe but that her mother died at the scene of the crime and the killer was never found.

Thoughts of losing my own mother when I was a teenager slice through my chest. While it was cancer that took her away from us, and not murder like in Gemma's case, our situations couldn't have been more different regarding what happened once we lost our moms. Whereas I had a dad who took good care of us, Gemma was left with nothing but an asshole of a father, who treated and still treats her like she's nothing more than a commodity.

"I'll find out if the person responsible paid for what they did. If they did not, it seems like there's a debt that still needs to be paid."

"Why?" She tilts her head to the side and studies me, as if she can read the answer on my face.

"Because I believe in karma and fate. You shouldn't dish out what you aren't willing to receive in return. Some people need to learn that lesson the hard way." With that, I lean past her and get the handheld showerhead to rinse off her hair and body. "We need to get you out of here and dried off."

"Okay."

I don't know if my words made sense to her, or if she even cares, but I meant every single one of them.

Whoever did this to her, whoever scarred her this irrevocably, has to pay.

He won't get away easily either. Most of the time, I prefer clean and quick kills, since they make my life a lot easier. But there are special motherfuckers who deserve to die a slow and painful death. Gemma's attacker belongs to that group.

Somehow, we'll find him, even if it takes me a while like with Nikolai and Vladimir. No one can hide from me forever, no matter how hard they try. Everyone slips up eventually.

I turn off the water and get one of the towels from outside the door. After squeezing it around Gemma's hair several times, I brush it over her skin. It's a bit of a battle, considering she's still wearing her wet underwear.

I point at her bra and panties. "Let me help you take those off."

It's nothing special, just some simple, smooth fabric, but it doesn't take away from how sinful it looks on her.

She shakes her head. "I'll do it."

"Stop being so damn stubborn. You're just going to hurt yourself even more."

The glare she sends me is so hostile, I'm surprised I'm not going up in flames. Then she snatches the towel from my hand and turns her back to me in a silent invitation.

Not wanting her to change her mind, I unclasp the bra and pull the straps down her arms without making too much contact. As much as I want to make her squirm, I know it hurts her if she gets goosebumps or shivers.

Before I can grab her underwear, she steps out of my reach with the towel clutched to her chest.

"I got it from here, thanks." She's avoiding my gaze, which is fine by me.

I drop my wet boxer briefs and reach for the other towel to dry myself off, then fasten it around my waist.

Ignoring her attitude, I snatch the ointment and new bandage and go to her to take care of her wound. Any longer, and she might decide to bite off my head.

Then I collect both of our clothes from the floor, so I can throw them in the laundry room downstairs.

I stop in the doorway. "Are you sure you don't need help?"

"Yes, I'm good." She peeks at me from under her lashes, her long hair hanging around her in wet strands.

Nodding, I leave the room, just as my phone rings.

My dad.

"Hey, Papà. Give me five minutes and I'll call you back, okay?"

"Si."

I drop the clothes off in the laundry room and make my way to my office, where I've been keeping my things. The couch in here isn't the most comfortable one, but this cabin only has one bedroom, so until Gemma's better, it'll have to do.

Picking some gray sweats and a black T-shirt, I put them on and get into my office chair.

This cabin might seem like a normal—albeit large—cabin from the outside, but during the remodeling, I have spared no cost on the inside, or on the security of this place and the ten-acre property.

Once the computer is online, I check that lines are secure before I video call my dad back.

His face pops up on the screen, his dark oak office furniture behind him. "Come stai, figlio?"

I shrug. "Bene."

"How's the girl?"

"Alive." Even though he probably already knows that fact, I tell him anyway. I'm sure Luna has given him a play-by-play of everything she's seen and heard. That girl and gossiping go hand in hand.

"Keep her that way. The last thing we need is a feud with the Fiore family. They've got large amounts of money coming in from their underground gambling rings. It would be a waste to lose that."

"Of course." What the hell did he think I was planning on doing with Gemma? Letting her die on my watch, or worse, killing her myself? And I'm fully aware of the mutually beneficial business we have with the Fiores, which is probably why Lorenzo let Gemma stay with me in the first place.

He reaches for a bottle of scotch and pours himself a drink. He's the reason it's my favorite drink too. And it all stems from my great-grandfather being enamored with everything Scottish, for some strange reason. The love for scotch is all that's left of that.

Picking up the tumbler, he lifts it to his nose to smell it, then takes a sip. It's something I've seen him do hundreds of times over the years, but I still find it fascinating. It's taught me that there are things in life that deserve to be savored, that they're worth waiting for.

I watch his Adam's apple move as he swallows down the liquid.

Then his focus is fully back on me. "Word's gotten around about the work you've done with your team. It's been good for the family. Lots of people want to do business with us."

It was exactly what I expected to happen, so I nod. "That's good, Papà."

"How long are you going to stay?"

"Not sure yet. I want to make sure she's okay and her wound doesn't get infected."

I don't need to say her name. My dad knows exactly who *she* is. Normally the only female I talk about is my sister. And I'm not sure she's welcome here, not after she freaked Gemma out with her shopping spree. Maybe I should tell her to back off. Never mind, that might just make her meddle even more. There's no middle ground with *that* woman.

My dad swirls his glass in his hand. "I think it's time to come back to that break we talked about last year."

I shrug. "Why?"

He rubs a hand over his jaw. "I'm not going to pretend I don't need you here. You've achieved a lot with your team, but I'm worried about you. You've changed, especially since Tommaso died."

My lungs expand with an uneasy breath. "I'm fine."

"Matteo, you were gone for most of the last two years and just got back. On top of that, you've been consumed with finding your cousin's killer, and even though I'm still not happy you used Alessandra to get your way, you have to wait for Nikolai's move now. You might as well take some time off while you're at the cabin."

This is the main reason Luna and I usually do whatever our dad asks of us, because he always puts us first. When my mom lost her health battle, he promised to take good care of us, and he did. Still does. He's also right about playing the waiting game.

With that in mind, I tip my head toward the screen. "Fine. I can also still work on some accounts from up here. Luna set everything up, so I have remote access. I can do video calls too, if necessary."

He's quiet for a while, just staring at me the way he likes to do whenever he's trying to figure something out. It has made many people squirm before, but I'm used to it.

He taps his fingers on his glass. "How long are you planning on keeping her?"

Keeping her? What a loaded question.

I lean back in my office chair and shrug. "Depends on how things play out with Lorenzo, Toni, and Nikolai."

He nods. "I'll have Luna check you're all up to date with everything, just to make sure."

"Sounds good. Thanks, Papà."

"Salute." He lifts his glass toward the screen and ends the call.

I use the chance to catch up on the online accounts I do the laundering for, and the next time I check the clock, three hours have gone by.

Pushing out of the chair, I stretch my tight muscles before shutting everything off and closing the office door behind me. I double-check the keyless fingerprint lock activated properly then head into the kitchen.

I'm just about to open the fridge when a scream comes from upstairs.

CHAPTER 7
GEMMA

S trong arms squeeze me so tightly, I can't move. My breath feels restricted, and I try to gulp in a lungful of air, only to draw short. I gasp, my breaths accelerating alongside my heartbeat.

This time, I won't get away with only a scar on my stomach, I just know it.

This time, I'm going to die, just like my poor mamma. She bled out all alone because our attacker wouldn't let me go to her. Maybe I could have helped somehow, put some pressure on that throat wound or something. Instead, I was trapped in his arms, forced to watch my mamma's panicked stare and listen to her whispered, "Ti voglio tanto bene," while the life left her body. I told her I loved her so much too, but I don't think she heard it anymore at the end.

Despite what happened back then, I still claw at my attacker now, trying with all my might to get him off me. He shakes me, yelling something in my ear that I can't understand properly. Sweat runs down my back, and I tremble in his arms. I'm still clawing and pinching, trying to get my hands on anything I can. My legs lie immobile under one of his, but I'm happy with any damage I'm causing. The more damage, the better. A small opening is all I need to escape.

The man must have come to the same realization since I'm suddenly flipped over, and his whole weight collapses on me, his arms holding mine completely hostage. A sharp pain registers on my side, and I whimper. He already hurt me.

"Please don't." I try to buck up with my hips, but he remains unmoving.

He's talking again too, but I still can't hear him.

Something presses against my lips, and I try to recoil but don't have anywhere to go.

Now that he's even closer, I can smell him. Woodsy with a hint of orange.

So opposite of what he smelled like last time when he reeked of sweat and that terrible cologne I'll never be able to forget. It ruined anything vanilla-flavored or scented for me for all eternity.

A thought tingles at the edge of my mind.

Don't I know someone who smells like oranges?

Who was that again?

Pressure.

More pressure against my mouth.

The lips on mine become more persistent. They feel familiar. Why do they feel familiar?

And why did I stop fighting him?

I gasp for air, and the man uses that moment to delve into my mouth.

My eyes fly open, and tears stream down my cheeks as I enter reality.

It was a dream.

Only a dream.

And a vicious one at that.

I had them on a regular basis right after the attack, and I've had a random one here or there over the years, but never anything like this.

Matteo—it's only been Matteo this whole time—pulls back to stare at me with wide eyes in the moonlit room.

His thumbs brush over my cheeks, wiping away the wetness. "Fuck, baby."

Then he closes his eyes and leans his forehead against mine, taking deep breaths that I try to match in order to calm down my own erratic breathing.

I'm okay.

I'm okay.

I'm okay.

Then the pain in my side registers, and I groan.

Matteo is off me in a flash and flips on the bedside lamp. Darkness creeps over his eyes as he gives me a once-over, the vein in his neck throbbing violently the second his gaze stops at my side. "Shit."

Abandoning me, he walks to the door to turn on the big light, and I flinch as my eyes don't have any time to adjust to the harsh light.

Matteo makes his way back over to me, his angry footsteps sounding across the carpet. The covers are already down by my feet, thanks to my terrifying nightmare with my attacker. No, not my attacker, but Matteo. I can't believe I just fought with him like that.

It all felt so real.

What a mess.

Matteo is back by the side of the bed, pushing up my shirt

to expose my midriff. He takes his time to pull off the bandage, but it still aggravates the pain.

When it's off, he scowls at my waist and closes his eyes. "Don't move. I'll be right back."

I focus on my breathing to try and get rid of the aftermath of the nightmare. It's sticking to me like a dark cloud, and I hate the way it makes me feel. Like I can't escape this hell of anxiety and fear . . . like I'll never be okay again . . . like I should have died alongside my mom, or maybe instead of her.

"I need to wash off the blood to see the damage." Matteo's voice comes from next to me again, but it doesn't sound as clipped as it usually does.

I open my eyes and gasp at the sight of him. "Oh my gosh, I'm so sorry."

With a heavy feeling in my stomach, I take him in. There are scratch marks all over his hands, arms, and shoulders, even a couple on his neck with bloody streaks marring his beautiful tattoos.

His gaze flicks to me, then he focuses back on the wound. "Don't worry about it."

I flinch as he pours some water over my injury and dabs it dry with a washcloth. He's gentle and careful, and it hurts like a bitch, but my brain is still focused on his body.

How can he say not to worry about it? "I hurt you."

"Not as much as you hurt yourself."

"That doesn't make it okay."

"I'm used to a lot worse. A few scratches don't bother me." He gets closer to the wound. "The corner split open a bit, but the sutures are still in place. You should be okay as long as you take it easy. No more thrashing around."

I huff out a breath. "Trust me, if it was up to me, I'd never have this nightmare again."

He applies ointment and a new bandage, giving it one more soft press, then pushes to his full height again. His dark eyes bore into mine, and they're filled with questions I'm not sure I'm ready to answer.

So before he can ask anything, I say, "I don't want to talk about it."

He runs his hand through his hair. "One day you will. Now go to sleep."

Leaving everything where it is, he drags the blanket back up and turns off the main light and the small one on the nightstand.

I expect him to leave, but instead, the bed dips on the other side.

Careful not to make any sudden moves, I stay on my back and only turn my head in his direction, trying to see him. But my eyes haven't adjusted enough yet, so I just stare into the darkness. "What are you doing?"

"What do you think I'm doing?"

"I think you're in my bed."

"Technically, it's my bed."

I grab the edge of the blanket and roll it between my fingers. "Yours?"

"Yes."

"But you said it's my room."

"I did."

My chest tightens with every passing second of this conversation. This man is driving me insane.

"Matteo, can you please stop speaking in riddles and just tell me how it is?"

He chuckles in response. Chuckles.

I wish I could see what that looks like on his face.

No, no, no. Bad. He's not yours to marvel at.

"'This place only has one bedroom, and I gave it to you so you can heal. But seeing as you just injured yourself again, it's safer for me to stay here with you."

A noise comes out of my mouth. It's half-groan, half-snort. It sounds awful, but there's no way I heard him correctly. He totally did not just say he's going to sleep with me here from now on. In one bed. Right?

"Don't worry, passerotta. I told you earlier I wouldn't touch you again, so you're safe. Now sleep."

How on earth am I supposed to sleep with him right next to me? My brain doesn't even know how to properly process this new situation.

Also, did I imagine that earlier, or did he call me baby? Because in my head, he did.

I fiddle around with the blanket, my feet pushing against the bottom fabric.

Matteo exhales loudly. "Go. To. Sleep."

I huff. "I'm trying."

"Doesn't seem like it."

Suddenly something occurs to me. "Where were you going to sleep tonight?"

"On the couch in my office."

I tug at the collar of my T-shirt. "You didn't have to."

"Mmmm."

We stay quiet for a while, my brain going a mile a minute, a mixture of the aftermath of the nightmare, the fact that this man is lying so close to me I can feel his body heat, and this whole fucked-up situation in general.

My life was far from perfect before; in fact, I actually hated it, but now, I'm not even sure where left and right are.

At some point, my eyes got heavy, and when I wake up the next morning, Matteo is gone.

The next two weeks go by in similar fashion. I spend most of the day by myself, happy to not have any obligations or expectations on my shoulders, and at night, Matteo shares a bed with me. He never touches me and always lies on top of the covers. My nightmare has come back several times, but never as bad as that first time since Matteo has always been able to wake me up early on, calming me down with his arms safely around me, and I'm grateful for that.

The way he took care of me after that first nightmare, the way he called me baby, the way he was so caring and gentle with me and my body in the shower earlier that evening. And knowing he's only a few inches away from me in bed every single night. It's made all the difference, calming my anxiety and apprehension, and I'm thankful I've been able to sleep better due to him.

He's also turned me into a live wire, ready to jump him at any moment, so he can put me out of my sexually frustrated misery. But then I remember Ally and the engagement, and my libido is doused in cold water. Or at least that's what I tell myself.

Matteo and I spend time together but not too much. At first, I reveled in that fact. For maybe the first time in my life, I've been able to just be, and it's thanks to him kidnapping me and taking me out of the city.

But is it actually considered kidnapping if I didn't protest much, taking into account I was injured? Half-kidnapping? Maybe a soft kidnapping?

Whichever one it is, him bringing me here has, without a doubt, changed my life for the better. All I did that first week was read, eat, and sleep. Then one day last week, Matteo came into the bedroom in the late morning and told me we were going for a walk, and we've been doing that every day since. The property is expansive, and once around the perimeter takes us almost forty-five minutes. Which could partially be due to Matteo making me walk at a snail's pace, but I actually don't mind. It's nice to be outside and moving again.

That part of the day has quickly become my favorite, to the point where I'm enjoying Matteo's company, and the companionable silence, more than I thought I would.

I grab my hoodie from the armchair, accidentally pushing my book off the edge. It drops to the floor and lands half under the chair. When I reach for it, my hand bumps against something hard, a black box. Since my curiosity is piqued, I drag it out.

The lid is slightly dusty, and I gently lift it to peek inside. I'm not sure what I expected, but it definitely wasn't photos. Dozens, maybe hundreds, of them. Sitting on the floor, I pull the box on my lap to get a better look. My fingers brush over what is unmistakably a younger version of Matteo. A handsome teenage Matteo. An adorable toddler Matteo. A ridiculously cute Matteo at various ages.

One photo catches my eye, and I pick it up. Matteo's father can't be much older than Matteo is now, the two of them almost passing as twins. The huge grin on his face is directed at his family, especially at Matteo's face that's covered in something, and a young version of Luna who's laughing hysterically. The woman next to the kids glances at them with the same amused expression. But it's more than that, her gaze is adoring, like these kids, this family, are her world. After studying her more closely, it's easy to spot traces of Luna, especially the way her lips curve and her eyes shine.

Without a doubt, this family loves each other. It's so obvious in their beaming faces and the parents' affectionate touches on the children's shoulders and arms.

A sharp pain pierces my chest, robbing me of my breath.

"Luna's always been a nutcase."

I shriek, the voice behind me startling me so much that the box slides off my legs, tumbling to the floor, the contents spilling all over the carpet.

With a hand pressed to my racing heart, I stare up at Matteo.

But his gaze isn't on me, it's on the picture still in my hand.

I clear my throat awkwardly and swallow. "Sorry, I . . . uh, my book dropped, and I found the box under the chair."

"I forgot it was there."

I nod like that makes total sense.

He crouches and reaches for the photo, his fingers brushing along mine as he takes it. "Every year before Christmas, we'd bake cookies together. It was my favorite time of the year. That time, Luna thought it was hilarious to smack some dough in my face."

The expression on Matteo's face, his soft eyes and the way the corners of his mouth gently turn up, is so different from anything I've ever seen on him before that I don't dare make a sound.

I reach the point where I can't hold my breath any longer

and ask him the question I'm positive I already know the answer to. "Is that your mom?"

"She was an amazing woman."

His gaze finds mine then, and I'm sure he can see the million questions in my eyes.

"She got cancer and died when I was sixteen."

My breath catches in my throat. He lost his mother as a teenager, just like me.

But unlike me, he was loved, still is loved, by his family, his father.

Matteo picks up another happy family photo, and the ache in my chest grows. I drag my gaze away from him as a memory from my own childhood pops up in my brain. A memory of a time when I was younger and thought I might finally have a sibling because my mom was pregnant. But a few weeks later, she lost the baby. What I didn't understand back then was that it wasn't her first miscarriage. What I also didn't understand until much later was the meaning of the terms incomplete miscarriage, uterus infection, and hysterectomy.

My mind jumps back in time to that dreadful day at the hospital. My mom had been sick for a while after having a terrible infection that ultimately led to her hysterectomy. My dad had sent me away to get a drink, and just as I came back, his loud voice carried into the hallway through the slightly ajar door.

"I think I've been more than patient with you, Maria, even though it wasn't easy for me to watch you lose baby after baby. And now you're telling me you can't have any children at all anymore? What about my heir?"

My mom's voice was weak as she answered, "You have Gemma."

My dad scoffed. "You think I'd hand over my business to a daughter? You're both useless to me."

Hearing my mom's sniffles that followed my father's cruel words, twisted my heart in a way nothing before ever had. A minute later, my dad opened the door, gave me a disapproving glare, and left.

Everything changed that day. Before, my dad wasn't exactly the nice and heartwarming man you see portrayed in a lot of TV shows and movies, but we shared some meals and were together on special occasions. But from that moment at the hospital on, I barely saw him. My mom kept telling me he loved me, that he was just incredibly busy with work. She said that maybe if we could show him that I can be exactly the daughter he needs me to be, he'd spend some more time with us again.

She started crying then, and I promised her I'd help her. There was nothing I wanted more than to see my mom smile again. But she never did, not like she used to. All I could do was love her as much as I could and keep my promise because she was everything to me.

Something touches my arm, and I flinch away, staring straight into Matteo's questioning gaze. "Hey, you okay?"

I blink a few times and nod, noting the mess I made of the photos is cleaned up, the box pushed neatly back in its hiding spot.

I try my hardest to do the same with my memories and emotions.

Matteo straightens to his full height and after staring at

me for a few seconds, he grabs my hoodie and holds out a hand. "Let's get some fresh air."

Nodding, I let him tug me up to follow him through the house and out the front door.

The sun's out as we make our way across the property, warming my skin, trying to wash away the ugly feelings that are still clinging to me.

Eventually, it works. I focus on my steps, the refreshing, cool air around us, and the birds chirping in the trees.

Just as we make it to the end of the property, Matteo's phone vibrates, and he puts it to his ear, answering the incoming call. "You close?"

He listens to whoever is on the other end of the line and watches me. "Yeah, we're out for a walk and should be back in about twenty minutes." Another pause. "Sounds good."

He ends the call and puts his phone back into his sweatpants.

At least there's the small blessing of them being black today. Other days, I'm not so lucky and he wears gray pairs, which have to be part of some divine test I'm supposed to pass. I cannot think of a single reason why a man would willingly put his dick outline on display otherwise. It's madness. Pure temptation. And a distraction I'm not sure I welcome.

Matteo glances at me before focusing straight ahead. "That was Ash. He'll be here soon."

I smile at the news. "That's great. I'm ready for my clean bill of health."

"Are you getting bored?" He tilts his head my way, his brown eyes lighter than usual in the sunlight, almost like a warm honey gold. He lifts an eyebrow when I just stare at him like a moron.

I avert my gaze, trying to remember what he asked. Oh, if I'm getting bored. I think about that, tapping my fingers on my leggings. "I don't think I'm necessarily bored. It's more of a feeling that I should be doing more with my days. You know, now that I actually have the opportunity to be away from my dad and all."

He stiffens beside me. "He doesn't let you do what you want?"

I shrug. "Well, it's not like he locks me in my room all day. More like a schedule, I guess, with workouts, taking care of my appearance, spending some time in the kitchen, and learning everything I need to be a good wife." I pause. "It sounds weird to say it out loud."

Maybe it sounds weird because it is weird.

"Hmmm." He's quiet for a beat. "What would you do if you had the choice?"

I inhale deeply, enjoying the oxygen filling my lungs. "I'm not sure, to be honest. I've always wanted to go to college to explore my possibilities and see what would interest me, but my dad said I didn't need to waste my time or his money with that."

I glance at Matteo, watching the taut muscles along his jaw flex with tension.

He studies me, his eyes darker than before. Stormier.

Did I say something wrong?

I think back over our conversation, just as we make it back to the house and a sleek black car pulls into the long driveway.

Although it's Ash, the sight of someone else here, of someone invading my little bubble, is more jarring than I expected it to be.

We walk up to Ash, and Matteo welcomes him with a clap on the shoulder.

I lift my left hand in a small wave. "Hey, Doc."

The smile he gives me has my own lips tilting up at the corners. Oddly enough, I haven't smiled much in the last two weeks, but I've been happier than before when I had to plaster on fake ones every day for everyone.

"Gemma, how are you?"

I shrug. "Good, I guess? Matteo took out the stitches a few days ago, which wasn't pleasant, but it's a lot better than before."

Just then the passenger door opens, and I start. I was so focused on Ash that I didn't notice someone else in the car. Zero points for my observation skills.

The man who exits has me almost choking on my spit. Inky-black, disheveled hair and ice-blue eyes. I think my ovaries just celebrated and cowered in fear at the same time. He doesn't look at me, yet I've never been more intimidated in my whole life.

He and Matteo share the same thump on the back as Ash and Matteo did, but the man completely ignores me.

Ash sighs next to me. "Zeno, don't be rude. This is Gemma." He points at me. "Gemma, this is Zeno, a member of our team."

Zeno's gaze lands on me, and I feel the urge to hide behind Ash.

I have zero clue what team he's talking about, and I'm not sure I want to know.

"Hi." The word comes out all high and pitchy, and he doesn't seem impressed.

Ash chuckles. "Ignore him. He's hangry. Let's go inside

and check your wound, okay?" He walks to his trunk to get a small duffel, a medium-sized shipping box, and the same brown doctor bag he had with him last time.

Together, we head inside and go straight to the kitchen, where Ash washes his hands before he gets some gloves out of his bag and puts them on. Zeno didn't come to the kitchen with us—thank goodness—but I have no idea where he went.

"Gemma, turn toward the light and pull up your shirt so I can see your wound." Ash waits by the kitchen island with his bag.

"Of course." I walk over to him and do what he asked.

Ash prods around gently, then moves back and drags his gloves off. "It looks great. It's healing well, and the scar is nice and pink and will fade over time. We're talking about months and years here, but I'm sure you know that. Matteo did well."

Tugging my shirt back in place, I nod. "He did."

Matteo's leaning with his back against the fridge on the other side of the counter. "When can she continue with all activities?"

Ash throws the gloves in the trash and closes his bag. "There's no need for any restrictions as long as she takes it easy and listens to her body. No MMA fights or anything like that though."

He says that last bit to me and winks.

I hold up my hands. "No MMA fights, got it. I'll try my best, I promise."

"Good. Not that I mind taking care of you, but I'd rather not see you getting hurt again."

"Are you done chitchatting now?" Matteo barks at his friend, who only chuckles in response.

"Yes, boss. I'm ready."

Matteo tilts his head to the hallway where his office is. "Let's go then. Zeno is already getting started."

Ash grabs his bags and glances at me over his shoulder. "Are you going to watch these two idiots with me?"

Having no idea what he's talking about, I only stare at him.

Instead of replying, he walks back to me and takes my hand. "Come on, let's see if they need help before we make some snacks."

"You said she's fine, so she can walk by herself," Matteo calls from the hallway, his tone colder than I've heard it in the last few weeks.

Ash's shoulders shake, and he mumbles something that sounds like, "Too easy," as he drags me after him.

We walk down the hallway, past the door I know is Matteo's office, and to another door all the way at the end. Since I've spent most of my time upstairs, I haven't explored the house much and have no clue what's behind this door.

To my surprise, it's a staircase leading to where Matteo just went. My muscles tense before I can even think about this whole situation, and my steps falter.

Ash sends me a questioning look over his shoulder. "What's up? You don't want to watch?"

"Uh." I glance around uneasily. "What exactly is down there?"

His eyes widen with understanding. "You haven't been in the basement?"

I shake my head. "Nope. Didn't even know there was one."

He gives me his boyish grin. "What have you been doing here this whole time? Hiding upstairs?"

"Pretty much, yeah."

His smile drops. "Oh." His fingers squeeze mine once before he nods in the direction of the open door. "Well, you're in for a real treat then because Zeno will probably kick Matteo's ass."

"I can hear you." Matteo's voice carries upstairs.

Ash shakes his head. "I swear, that man is half vampire with his hearing."

At that, I laugh. It's not loud and doesn't last very long, but it feels good. Now I'm also curious. "Well, let's see this ass-kicking."

"Yes, let's."

Ash nods eagerly and lets go of my hand so I can hold on to the rail that leads down the wooden staircase.

What awaits me below is nothing short of phenomenal.

The basement is huge and filled with more workout equipment than I've ever seen. I'm usually more of a yoga and Pilates person, but even I'm impressed.

My mouth falls open a little the instant I see what's on the other side of the room. A freaking boxing ring. "Wow."

"Pretty cool, huh?" Ash takes my hand once more, since I'm still standing here like an idiot. "Come on."

He pulls me toward a set of couches that are placed around the ring at a safe distance, or at least I hope it's a safe distance. The last thing I need today, or any day really, is to get blood spatter all over me.

Ash puts his bags down on one of the couches before turning to me. "Want to stay here or get some snacks with me? These two need to warm up."

"Snacks?"

"Yes, everything's better with snacks, am I right?"

I bite my lip to hide my grin. How on earth is Ash friends with these guys? The few times I've seen him, he's always been friendly and happy, whereas Matteo is a grumpy ass almost nonstop. And Zeno? Well, I don't know him, but on first impression, he makes Matteo look like a total sunshine. Nothing makes sense anymore.

Ash and I make our way back up into the kitchen, where he moves around like he's done this a million times before. He opens cupboard after cupboard, getting things out so fast, I can't even see what it is until he puts it all on the counter.

I wipe my hands on my shirt. "Can I help with anything?"

He turns around and gives me several bags of popcorn and a bag of white chocolate chips. Then he places two large silver bowls on the counter and a small ceramic one that he pushes toward me.

"Okay, let's microwave the popcorn first, and once that's in the bowls, we'll melt the white chocolate chips in the microwave. Then we'll pour that over the popcorn and toss it all together with the crumbled Oreos. Sound good?"

I stare at him and nod.

"You like Oreos?"

"Yeah, sure."

"Good. Let's get going then, before the guys pummel each other while we're gone."

About a million questions pop into my head at the same time, and I ask the one that's been on my mind the longest. "How do you guys know each other? You seem very . . . uhm."

Ash regards me curiously. "Very what? Don't mince words around me, Gemma. No need for that, I promise."

I chuckle. "I wasn't going to say anything bad. I just noticed that you guys are very different, I guess?"

"We are, even more so if you throw in the rest of the group. But I think our differences are the reason that we make such a good team. You know, diversity makes us stronger and all that."

His gaze is on the Oreos in front of him and not me. For a moment, I only watch him as he puts a few cookies in the bag, then shoves one in his mouth, a few more in the bag, and another one in his mouth. A laugh bursts out of me at the sight, and he stops what he's doing to glance up at me with a proud smile and a mischievous glimmer in his eyes.

"What?" His smile gets even wider as he pops another cookie in his mouth.

"Nothing." I shake my head at him. "Absolutely nothing. Please continue."

Coming as no surprise, the Oreo package is empty now, and he crushes—or rather smashes—the cookies in the bag with a small mallet he got out of one of the drawers.

Shaking my head at him, I get started on the popcorn, and once that's in the bowls, I pop the white chocolate chips in.

When I carry it to the kitchen island, Ash stares at me expectantly. "Are you ready to be amazed?"

I snort. "Sure. Show me what you got."

He grabs the melted chocolate and drizzles it over the popcorn before dropping half of the Oreo crumbles on each one. After giving both bowls a good shake, he hands me one. "You're welcome."

I start to roll my eyes but catch myself halfway, my dad's words echoing through my mind.

No one likes a childish woman.

Since I already took a piece of the popcorn-cookie mix, I put it in my mouth, despite the fact that my dad just ruined my mood with a simple memory. My taste buds try to talk to me, and I half-heartedly realize how delicious it actually is.

Peeking up, I find Ash's waiting gaze on me.

He lifts both brows. "Aaaaaand?"

The corners of my mouth don't want to work properly, so I nod. "It's good."

His whole demeanor changes to match mine. "Hey, what's wrong?"

I shake my head. "Nothing, just thought of something."

He purses his lips but doesn't say anything, which I'm grateful for.

The last thing I need is for him to start asking questions.

What I need is a distraction. I think for a minute, remembering something he said earlier. "Before, you mentioned a team that includes you three guys and others. What exactly do you do?"

Eyes on me, he tilts his head to the side and regards me like he's trying to decide what to tell me. Then he pops a piece of popcorn into his mouth. "How much do you know about the business dealings and all that happens in and among the families?"

It takes me all of three seconds to think before I shake my head. "Not much. My dad thinks that the business isn't for women. My job is to look pretty, to be quiet, and to marry someone who can benefit our family."

The moment the words are out of my mouth, bile rises in my throat, and I cover my mouth.

La famiglia è tutto.

Family is everything, and once again, I'm a disgrace to it. If he could hear me right now, he'd shun me from my family, this time officially, and not just emotionally like he's done ever since my mom died.

He always wanted a son but got me instead, and no siblings followed due to complications. The only person who ever really cared about me was my mamma, and she died for it, something my papà will never forgive me for.

"You look like you could use a hug."

Ash's voice yanks me out of my thoughts, and when I blink back into the here and now, my eyes are burning. He's moved closer, one of his hands on my upper arm, like he wanted to make sure I don't fall over.

Not overthinking it, I take him up on his offer and close the distance between us. I exhale loudly, sinking into the comfort of the hug I hadn't realized I needed so badly. It's been way too long since I last had one, probably the day of the shooting at the club, and that was only a quick one from Ally.

I tilt my head to the side and press against his chest, my arms now tight around his middle. If it's awkward for him, he doesn't say anything. Instead, he cocoons me in his warm arms, and I soak it all in. The burning sensation in the back of my eyes comes back, but I don't even care.

Without realizing it, he gives me exactly what I need, refilling the part of me that craves human contact. The part of me that needs to be touched and hugged and loved, so I don't wither away.

When I pull back, Ash cradles my face in his hands. "You're not okay, are you?"

I blink as his thumbs brush away any moisture that might

have escaped my eyes. His hands are softer than Matteo's . . . what a weird thing to think. Matteo's also engaged to my cousin, as well as kind of an asshole half of the time, whereas Ash has been nothing but super sweet and kind to me.

Why can't he make me all hot and bothered?

Ash glances over my shoulder, his eyes widening. He pushes me to the side, just in time for him to be punched right in the face.

CHAPTER 8
GEMMA

Ash falls back from the punch he just took, taking one of the barstools down with him. Without thinking, I step in front of him, facing off with a furious Matteo. He looks like a bull ready to charge with his flaring nostrils and the tightness in his eyes. Again.

My dad's voice is in my head. *Go to your room, Gemma, and let the men handle this situation. It's not for little girls.*

But I ignore the words because I've got this. *I've got this.* So instead of cowering away, I straighten my posture and hold out my hand in front of me in a stopping motion.

Shaking my head at Matteo, I'm unable to hide my disbelief over what he just did. "What the hell is wrong with you?"

My voice has an extra bite to it that sounds foreign to my ears.

Matteo's body tenses even more at my question, and the vein in his neck pulses angrily. He scrubs a hand over his face before pushing into my personal space and bumping against my still outstretched hand. "What's wrong with *me*? He had his fucking hands all over you."

He glares over my shoulder at Ash, who's still on the floor but seems to be okay if his mumbles are anything to go by.

I swallow when I realize that my hand is firmly planted on his naked chest since he's only wearing workout shorts. His tattooed muscles ripple under my touch, the distraction of the visual paired with touching his warm skin sending sparks off in my entire body.

Even though my libido has been kicked into overdrive, my anger is impossible to ignore, so I lift my chin and glare right back at Matteo. "He did *not* have his hands all over me."

"Oh yeah? What would you call it then?"

"He gave me a hug."

"Why would he do that if it wasn't just so he could get his hands on you?"

My whole body quivers, and this time I yell, "Maybe because I needed a hug, you idiot."

I flex my hands, my nails biting into his skin, before I shove him. As expected, he doesn't move more than an inch, but it's enough to break our connection.

With a lump as big as an orange in my throat, I turn around and get on my knees next to Ash. "Hey. How bad is it?"

He grins at me like he didn't just get punched. "I'm all good, princess. Don't worry."

My brows pinch together at the way he's handling what just happened and the fact that there's blood on his hands and face, and his nose is already swollen.

Seeing his injury raises my blood pressure to new heights, and I huff out a breath, still furious at Matteo's behavior but trying to focus on Ash. "Do you think your nose is broken?"

"It doesn't feel like it. A few days of rest and some ice packs, and I should be as good as new."

Rubbing my forehead, I stare at him. "I can't believe you're acting as if this is nothing."

His mouth lifts in one corner. "Because it's not. It's how we sometimes handle things. No biggie. At least it's out now."

I tilt my head. "What's out now?"

Before he can say anything, loud footsteps echo across the floor, stopping somewhere behind me. "What the fuck is going on?"

Zeno. If he's getting in the midst of all this, we're all screwed.

"Nothing," Matteo spits out.

I spin around to glare at him some more, then point at Ash. "Matteo, this isn't nothing. Who goes around and just punches people in the face?"

Zeno's brows rise as he stares at me and Matteo, then Ash, who only grins at his friend. Zeno rolls his eyes at him. "Fuck, no."

Ash chuckles before wincing. "You better believe it. I told you."

Zeno groans and turns around, leaving the three of us in the kitchen. "I'll be downstairs."

Matteo comes closer to us, a little too close for my comfort. He'd better not punch Ash again, or that mallet Ash used to smash the cookies will come in handy when I hit Matteo over the head with it.

"What was that about?" Mr. Grumpy growls the words at his friend.

"What was what about?" Ash is so obviously feigning

innocence with his big doe eyes that even I can tell he's full of shit.

"Ash, don't test me. Was that one of your stupid bets?"

The doc purses his lips and shrugs, like what just happened isn't out of the ordinary.

"You're such an asshole. Leave Gemma out of your fucking games, are we clear?"

Matteo grabs my hand and pulls so hard, I practically fly straight into his arms.

He holds me close and stares into my eyes. "Stay away from him, understood?"

My body heat rises for more reasons than I'm willing to admit right now, but I'm crushed to his naked chest, for crying out loud. I'm caught in his stare, and even though I should probably run away from him as far as possible, I'm not sure I want to.

Whereas he's got a quick temper and has probably done things far worse than I could ever imagine, he also makes me feel alive. There's suddenly more than the slightly depressing state of acceptance I was in when my future only consisted of marrying a man my dad chose for me. The normally constant pressure I was feeling on my chest has now given way to this foreign sense of peace I can't remember ever feeling. Add the constant bouts of tingles rushing through my body every time Matteo touches me, and I'm pretty sure I've found my kryptonite.

Ash gets up, interrupting my spiraling thoughts.

He walks to the sink and turns on the faucet, probably to clean himself up. "Teo, it wasn't like that, I swear. I'd never hurt Gemma on purpose. You should—"

"Don't do it again." Matteo's voice is low, his tone threatening and final as his chest rises, his heartbeat thumping wildly against my shirt.

He turns around, dragging me after him, and we head toward the basement door, down the stairs, across the floor mats that line the entire floor of the basement all the way to a set of couches.

His grip is gentle, although it's easy to see how hard it is for him to keep his irritation at bay. In front of the couch, he nudges me until my butt hits the cushion. "Sit."

"I'm not a dog," I mumble at his retreating back. Now that he's not surrounding me with his all-encompassing presence, my anger finds its footing again, bubbling back to the surface.

"Good, because I'm really not into bestiality."

My mouth falls open at his comment, and I watch him climb into the boxing ring, where Zeno is hopping around in place.

Ash plops down on the other couch that's perpendicular to mine. He hands me a popcorn bucket and a water bottle, while he opens a bottle of beer for himself.

"Thanks."

He nods at me, still appearing his carefree self, regardless of what just happened in the kitchen. "Did he really just say he isn't into bestiality?"

Men. I'll never understand them.

"I think he did." I throw a piece of popcorn in my mouth and chew, my irritation slowly melting away with the sweetness. "Is it normal for him to punch people in the face?"

Ash swallows his popcorn and smacks his lips. "Not really. Only when you poke him the right way."

I'm trying to figure out if he's saying he made Matteo

mad on purpose, just as noise from the ring draws my attention away from Ash. Matteo and Zeno are now wearing boxing gloves and tapping them against each other in the middle of the space. Not even two seconds later, both are throwing punches at the other. I shift around, trying to see every move they make, but half the time, one of them covers the other or is turned away. Gloves hit abs, sides, pecs, chins, cheeks, and backs. Groans and grunts fill the room, and I can't remember the last time I was so mesmerized by something.

Ash chuckles. "You like that, huh?"

I nod, without looking at him, unable to tear my gaze away from the guys, even while they take short breaks between rounds.

This is clearly not the first time either of them has boxed. Their movements are smooth and strong, well-practiced, and I'm not sure if there's a clear winner. Zeno's definitely the more aggressive of the two though, and seems to have several pounds on Matteo, despite Matteo being a beast of a man himself.

In no time, sweat pours down their bodies, and their grunts become laced with pain while they keep landing more and more punches on each other. The skin on Matteo's entire side is an angry red, probably turning into one ugly bruise, and Zeno took a right hook to the cheek that'll probably be visible for a few days.

I swirl my fingers around the bottom of the popcorn bowl, just to find it empty. Wow. I was so mesmerized; I didn't even notice I'd already eaten it all.

It might only be my imagination, but it seems like the guys are slowing down. Not that I blame them. I probably wouldn't even last a minute in there, which is pretty embarrassing to think about.

What does it feel like to know how to fight, to be that empowered and confident?

My entire life, I've either been completely sheltered from violence, or protected by the men in my family. I've never even come close to a situation where I needed to protect myself. The scene at the bar was the only experience, other than the attack on my mom and me five years ago, where I barely made it out alive.

For a while after the attack—when I was able to push through my grief—I was so upset I didn't know how to protect myself or anyone else. If I'd known how to, maybe I could have saved her. Instead, we were like two innocent lambs offering ourselves to the big bad wolf on a silver platter.

Something about that idea has my chest fluttering, and I'm too antsy to sit. Planning on pacing around the ring to work off some of the nervous energy, I jump out of my seat.

At my movement, Matteo's head snaps around, his gaze finding mine immediately. Zeno uses that instant to catch him on the temple, and Matteo goes down like a sack of potatoes.

"Oh shit." I throw the empty bowl on the couch and rush toward the ring. "I'm so sorry."

Zeno taps Matteo's foot with his own.

I'm not sure if it's to gloat or to make sure his friend is okay, but I glare at him and climb into the ring through the ropes. "Will you leave him alone now?"

The mountain of a man only raises one brow before he stalks off toward the stairs, Ash following behind him.

I drop to the floor next to Matteo, my hands hovering all over his face and body, not sure what to do.

"That was a low blow." His voice is raspy, and his eyes slowly open.

"I'm really sorry. I didn't mean for that to happen."

"Are you sure about that?"

I lick my dry lips. "Well, you did kind of deserve it for hitting Ash earlier, but I still didn't do it on purpose."

"Mmm." He closes his eyes again and just lies there.

"I swear. I was just going to walk around a bit and didn't think about being a distraction." When he doesn't move or say anything, I continue, "That looked like a pretty nasty hit."

"Don't sound so happy about it."

I press my lips together. "I'm really not."

"Uh-huh, could have fooled me." He pushes himself up on his forearms, which brings him incredibly close to my face. "But if you really feel that sorry, I know how you can make it up to me."

Closing my eyes for a second, I gather my strength to resist this inexplicable connection I feel toward him. When I open my eyes again, he's still right there. "You're engaged, Matteo."

But Ally made it sound like her and the Russian might be involved.

Does that change anything about this engagement?

Matteo mumbles something, and his gaze flicks to my mouth. "What if I told you that—"

The door slamming upstairs and Ash calling my name breaks the spell between us. Matteo sighs and stands, offering his hand to me.

121

I gaze up at him, putting my hand in his and letting him pull me up. "What did you want to tell me?"

"Nothing. Come on, let's see what's going on upstairs."

My mind is still stuck on his unfinished sentence as we walk upstairs. He was staring at me with such intensity that it seemed like something important. Damn it.

We get to the kitchen, and the guys are standing next to the island, clearly waiting for us.

Ash points at the box in front of him. "Gemma, I forgot to give this to you earlier. Luna sent it for you."

"Really?" Warmth settles in my stomach at my new friend's kindness.

"Yup." He holds it out to me.

I grab it from him, surprised at how light it is.

Ash winks at me. "She said you should open it when you're by yourself."

Heat rushes through my body like a raging wildfire. Damn that woman and her big mouth. I bet she rubbed her hands together like an evil witch at the thought of having Ash tell me this, hoping I'd get embarrassed.

"Well, I better go then. Thanks for everything, Ash." Without glancing at any of them, I turn around and head upstairs as fast as I can.

After closing the bedroom door behind me, I sit on the bed and open the box. I take out the three books that are on top and feast my eyes on them. Witches and vampires. Very nice. Can't wait to get started on those once I'm finished with the others. I put them on the duvet and see what else is inside. The only thing left is something in nondescript wrapping paper.

I take it out, undo one of the corners, and slide my finger

under the edge to open it. The paper slips off easily, revealing a white-and-blue box. A personal massager, the same one I have at home, hidden way back in the bottom of my closet, just in case anyone ever snoops around.

Licking my lips, I shake my head at the heat that rushes back through my body. I should have known what was inside the moment Ash told me to open it by myself. Luna Lunatic strikes again. I swear that woman has no boundaries.

What was she thinking sending me a sex toy? She probably sent it as a joke to make me squirm, because when on earth would I even use it, especially now that Matteo is sharing my bed.

Speak of the devil, Matteo enters the room following a quick knock and a half-second wait. Because that would be so incredibly helpful if I was in the middle of changing or other . . . uh, things. My fingers are lightning fast, and I grab the massager and push it behind me under the pillow. The last thing I need is for Matteo to know about this sex toy. He'd probably tell me we should use it together just to mess with me.

Giving me a quick once-over, he averts his gaze to the bed. "Did Luna send you more books?"

I clear my throat and nod. "She did."

Good thing that wasn't a lie. I'm not the best at hiding my feelings, especially once any kind of connection is established with a person. My mamma used to say that I wear my emotions on my face and that it was one of her favorite things about me. As I grew older, especially after she died, I learned she was one of the only ones who believed it was a good thing. My dad, in particular, wanted me to hide my emotions and thoughts, arguing that people like us die if others can read us like an open book.

Since I couldn't just flip a switch and undo something I've done my entire life at that point, he decided hiding me was the best option, as he didn't have my mom to keep me "in check" anymore, and I was too old for a "babysitter." Just another reason to reinforce my belief that he never deserved my momma. To this day, I don't understand what she saw in him. When I asked her once, she said he wasn't always like this, but she never explained further.

Noise from the bathroom jolts me out of my thoughts. Yikes. I need to stop zoning out so much.

Maybe a little nap will help. There really isn't much a nap can't cure. Closing my eyes, I let myself fall back on the bed, only to have the vibrator poke me in the back. Damn you, Luna. But also, thank you, Luna. I admit that yes, it's been way too long without my toys, and I could really use an influx of endorphins.

Whereas I'm not sure I'll be able to do anything with Matteo here, it's nice to have just in case.

Mumbling comes from the bathroom. What is Matteo doing?

I turn toward the door, and I notice he left it slightly open.

I hear that same noise again, but this time it's accompanied by other sounds.

Curiosity gets the better of me, and once the box is put away, I tiptoe to the small opening in the door. It's just enough for me to see inside the space, specifically the shower, and holy shitballs, my breath catches in my throat.

Matteo's standing in the shower under the spray with the

water cascading down his muscular back and butt. His body resembles that of a Greek god: a narrow waist, defined leg muscles, broad shoulders, and well-developed arm muscles. His tattoos only accentuate his perfect physique, truly making him a sight to behold.

With his head leaning against the wall, and his left hand propped against the tiles, my attention shifts to his right hand because it's busy, and so damn full.

Full of his incredibly large erection. My eyes widen, and I swallow. Having a vibrator or even a dildo is one thing, but seeing a cock in real life, it's drastically different. Ally tried to show me some porn once since she thought it would be fun, but after two minutes of it, I was done.

If it had been something like this, I would have popped some popcorn and stayed for the show.

Without question, this is magnificent.

His penis is long and thick, with a perfect mushroom head. I can see the thick veins all the way from over here while he keeps pumping up and down his shaft, the pace slowly increasing.

My body feels a little feverish as I keep watching Matteo masturbate.

The forbidden aspect of watching him like this makes me feel slightly guilty, but it also sends an extra ache of pleasure through my entire body. Did he want me to watch him? Did he plan all of this and leave the door open on purpose?

My gaze travels up to his face, mesmerized by his profile. With his eyes closed, his lips slightly parted, and the sharp angles of his face, he is a masterpiece of masculinity. Breathtaking. And despite the fact that he often makes me angrier than I've ever been in my life, I can't deny my body wants him.

Every time he stares at me with that intense heat in his eyes, my ability to stay away slips a little more.

Every time he touches me, the yearning to give myself over to him grows stronger.

It's like he's trying to make me a junkie. Turning him into my obsession would be so easy, but it could also mean my downfall.

His hand pumps faster, the movement becoming more frantic and aggressive while his breathing grows harsher and louder. With his head now tipped back, his whole body tenses, and shudders of pleasure course through him. Big white spurts hit the tiles in front of him as he comes with a low groan.

I'm so captivated and consumed by him and this unexpected encounter that I almost miss him letting go of himself and opening his eyes. When my brain finally catches up with reality, I step away from the door and lean against the wall.

How will I ever look at him again after witnessing this sensual moment without wondering how it would feel to do it for him, or to sink to my knees in front of him and take him into my mouth? This reverie is both exhilarating and terrifying. I've never wanted to do this to a guy before, and now I'm consumed by this lust for the one I can't have.

Even if I could have him, I shouldn't want him knowing he's engaged to Ally.

But she made it sound like she's involved with someone else.

She did. And I also feel like there's something else going

on that I'm missing, something more than an arranged engagement.

Even then, would I act on my feelings for Matteo, no matter how unwanted they are?

My thoughts evaporate the instant the shower turns off, and my legs move toward the bedroom door. Following this little show I just witnessed, I can't stand here when he comes out of the bathroom. I need a few minutes to collect myself. I also need to change my panties, but that will have to wait until later.

Downstairs, the kitchen is empty, and I let out a sigh of relief. I'm assuming Ash and Zeno left, which is a godsend, considering it would probably only take one glance at me for them to know that I was up to something.

In an attempt to find my cool, I chug down a large glass of water, then open the patio door and step onto the expansive wooden deck. The afternoon sun warms my skin, and the view is absolutely amazing, with greenery and forest as far as the eye can see. Some of the trees are in the beginning stages of changing their color, and I can only imagine how breath-taking the fall foliage must be once it's completely changed.

Stepping up to the rail, I put my hands on the wood and close my eyes. Deep breath in, deep breath out. I focus on my breathing for a while until the patio door creaks open behind me. I'm frozen in place, unable—and unwilling—to spin around. I'm not ready to face him yet. My thoughts are still too jumbled when it comes to him, especially after what I just witnessed him do in the shower. It's messing with my brain, the lust for him overthrowing my logic more and more with each passing second.

His scent reaches me first, his bodywash serving as an

aphrodisiac. Does his scent seduce all women, or is it just me? Or is it because he's the first guy I've ever felt this attracted to, so it heightens everything about him? Why else would my kidnapper not only turn into my savior but also be the first man I crave? I certainly didn't expect for either of those things to happen.

He steps up behind me and places his hands next to mine on the rail, without actually touching me. "Why are you hiding out here?"

Focusing on anything other than jumping him is harder than it should be. It takes me a minute to collect myself before I swallow hard. "Who says I'm hiding?"

There. My voice sounded totally normal, right? Well, mostly, I hope.

Leaning in, he brushes his nose up and down the back of my neck. Tingles explode in my body, and like a helpless doll, I lean to the side to give him better access.

When he licks his way up, I can't conceal my whimper.

Regardless of how I feel about this man, my body is putty in his hands, no matter how much I want to be steel.

His tongue makes it to my ear, twirling around my earlobe before he gently sucks and bites on it. "I cannot wait to taste you; I just know your pussy will be exquisite."

With those words, the last bit of my logic flies out the window, and my knees go weak. Matteo catches me with his body, pushing me against the rail to keep me upright, which also means his hard-on is now pressed upon my lower back. How is he already hard again?

"You want me to fuck you?"

His words.

My clit pulses.

How is that even possible?

He grinds against my butt, and I press back.

I hate myself a little for that.

One of his hands goes to my throat as he licks and nips his way down and over my shoulder. He bites me, freaking bites me, and I moan.

Something is clearly wrong with me.

"Is that what you were thinking about when you watched me in the shower? About my cock deep inside your pussy?"

CHAPTER 9
MATTEO

I'm not sure who I'm torturing more, her or me?

My balls still feel heavy and ache, although I just came so hard in the shower I almost lost my balance.

Gemma's ass moves against me, her body craving friction with a desperation that rivals mine.

But she's more stubborn than I am, or maybe it's her loyalty and sense of right and wrong that makes her not want to give in. Which would be admirable in any other circumstance where my dick isn't begging to be inside her on an almost daily basis.

Nothing in the last few months, not even trying to find my cousin's murderer, has made me feel as alive as Gemma does. There's something about her that gets under my skin. It's more than her beauty, more than her sweet cunt that I want to make mine. Even though that's all I can think about right now.

Sliding the shirt off her shoulder, I lick her skin. "Tell me, did you touch yourself?"

I'm pretty sure I know the answer, but I enjoy playing

this game with her. If this tension between us drives her half as insane as it does me, she gets off on this push and pull just as much.

When I got out of the shower, I skipped my underwear and jumped straight into my sweats. Which now allows me to easily change my angle. After pulling back, I thrust forward again, but this time, I go lower, which puts me straight between her unspread legs, making this both a tight fit and an absolute godsend. Holy shit, the friction is unreal.

"Are you wet for me, baby?"

Push.

"I thought of you when I came all over my hand."

Push.

"About your pussy."

Push.

"And how much I wanted to be deep inside you."

Gemma moves back against me, and I'm so delirious, I'm about two seconds away from either yanking her pants down or ripping them apart at the seam, so I can fuck her.

"Oh my God, Matteo. Please." Gemma arches her back.

She grinds her ass against me, and I snap.

Tugging her back by the throat, I growl in her ear, "Please what?"

"I need to come," she moans and whimpers. "Touch me. I'm begging you."

I don't make her wait and shove my hand down the front of her pants. "Fuck. You're dripping, baby."

Gemma gasps and tilts her head my way, seeking my lips until she finds them. My tongue is ruthless and demanding, and she keeps up with every single stroke. The way she kisses me is laced with the same fire I see so often in her eyes. The one I'm guessing she's been trying to suppress for most of her life.

I drive a finger into her pussy, pumping in and out of her wetness, before circling her clit a few times. Then I slide my hand out and drag her pants and underwear down in one swift move before sinking to my knees behind her.

Gemma glances down at me, uncertainty mixed with lust.

I take hold of both of her ass cheeks and give them a firm squeeze. "Bend over the rail and spread your legs for me."

She obeys, and my cock jumps at her compliance. It throbs even more when I lick her all the way from the front to the back. She wiggles at the contact, and I grab her thighs to keep her still. Then I show her how good it can feel to be worshiped by a man.

After licking her pussy lips several times, I plunge inside her, first with my tongue, and then with my finger. I add another one, and she clenches around me as they press deeper inside her. The second my tongue makes contact with her clit, she moves against me, practically riding my mouth and fingers. I don't think she's doing it intentionally, which makes me even hungrier for her. One of her hands reaches back for me and grips my hair.

Fuck me.

This pussy is mine.

"Come for me, baby." I suck on her clit a few more times, and she comes so hard, I almost come in my sweats. Her moans are all I hear, and they're the hottest fucking sounds I've ever heard.

Her legs tremble around me, and I maintain a good grip on her, so she doesn't collapse. Once I'm sure she can stand on her own, I tug up her underwear and leggings and stand.

She slowly turns around and stares me straight in the eyes. I wasn't sure what to expect. Shy Gemma or confident Gemma. Seems like confident Gemma likes to be tongue-fucked.

Her tongue darts over her lips. "That was . . . uh . . . thanks?"

Insanely beautiful and shy is a dangerous combination, apparently one that definitely does it for me.

She takes a step toward me, and my hard cock greets her. It's straining against my sweats. Her hand reaches out, and she touches the fabric-covered tip, and I hiss in response. Damn this woman. She only has to touch me once, and I'm done for. It takes every ounce of my focus not to come all over her. If what I've heard is true and she's a virgin, this might very well be her first time touching a cock, and, for some reason, I want this to be good for her too.

She moves her hand down my shaft but stays over the top of my sweats. She explores more while I tilt my head to the sky and let out a heavy sigh. I've never had an issue holding back my orgasm until now. Until her.

She makes me want to lose control and just be in the moment with her. But bad things happen when I let go. We live in a world where a woman like her can be a weakness that can cause my destruction.

I find my control and snap it back in place. In a rush, I yank down my pants, ignoring the whimpering sounds my cock wants me to make.

Gemma's gaze drops to my dick, and fuck, the look of awe on her face, mixed with something that's similar to fascination, has me groaning. Anticipating her touch, I focus on my breathing, but it's a total waste of time. The second she touches me, my dick jumps in her hand, and when she swipes the drops of precum and spreads it all over my head, I pump my hips, needing and wanting more.

Her hand slips, but that doesn't deter her, and she instantly brings it back to my heated skin. "It's so big."

I shake my head at her innocence, and the fact that my cock pulses in her grasp. I've never begged anyone for anything, especially regarding women and sex. But fuck, the words are already on my tongue.

Gemma's hand circles around my length, and she moves up and down, the pace slow and torturous.

"Harder." The one word is all I get past my teeth.

Her grip tightens, and as if she can sense my desperation, her strokes come faster.

Once she has a good rhythm going, she seems satisfied enough to avert her gaze. Her gaze finds mine, and she licks her lips. I'm not sure if she's ready to put her mouth on my cock, but there are other things to do with those pretty lips.

Grabbing a handful of her hair, I drag her closer and crash my mouth on hers. She opens with a gasp, and I devour her, tease her. Worship her mouth like it's never been worshiped before, needing her to understand something important.

No other man will ever make her feel this good again.

No man will ever be able to make her come as hard as I can.

No man will ever make her go out of her mind the way I do.

I draw back but keep her close. So close our mouths are

only a breath away. Waiting.

When *she* closes the distance between us, I suppress a roar of triumph.

I want her to feel the same violent desperation and misery that's been building inside me from my need and desire for her because it's fucking with my head. *She's* been fucking with my head ever since I first laid eyes on her.

The mental image of her in her hotel room in only her wedding lingerie, mixed with the way she keeps pumping me, and her hot tongue in my mouth, swells my cock, and I come with a long groan. I keep coming, over her hand, her shirt, and my stomach.

"That was—" Instead of finishing her sentence, she stares at my cum, smearing it all over both of us.

I wish I could keep it on her like this forever, claim her in a way no one else ever will.

Capturing her face with my hands, I kiss her again. Not as aggressive as before but not particularly soft either.

She moans into my mouth, and my cock twitches in her hand. She's still holding it, like she doesn't want to let go.

I step back and out of her grasp, so I can pull up my pants. Then I take her hand and walk inside the house and to the kitchen sink. "Let's get you cleaned up, so I can get you all dirty again."

Her eyes widen as she stares at me. "Again?"

Fuck, I didn't think her innocence would be such a turn-on, but it is.

The look I give her is pure heat. "Did you think I was already done with you, passerotta? I haven't even begun with you."

I watch her swallow, getting a sick sense of satisfaction

from making her squirm like this.

Leaning in, I lick her from her collarbone all the way up to her ear. "I want to fuck that tight little pussy until you can't walk anymore."

At my words, her whole body shivers, and I chuckle. "You like that idea, don't you?"

Her answer is a barely audible, "Yes," but it's all I need.

"Such a naughty princess. Who would've thought?"

I give her some room to wash and dry her hands, holding mine out to her because I'm beyond ready to take her upstairs. I'm finally going to take what I've wanted for so long.

My phone chooses that moment to ring. I ignore it, but Gemma pulls away from me, untangling her hand from mine.

Letting her head hang, she avoids my gaze. "You should probably answer that. It could be about Ally."

Fuuuuuck.

I forgot all about my fiancée and that shitshow. No one else has ever distracted me like this woman.

She takes a step back, still not looking at me. "I . . . I'll give you some privacy."

With that, she turns around and walks out of the kitchen. I tighten my fingers around my phone as I get it out of my pocket and put it up to my ear.

"Yes?" I put every ounce of frustration into my voice, my footsteps loud as I walk to my office.

"Matteo, seems like I got you at the right time. You sound delighted to hear from me."

My steps falter at the deep voice and the Russian accent. "Nikolai."

He scoffs. "I heard you've been searching for me."

The fucking nerve of this man. After everything that's happened.

"Listen up, you fucking asshole. Stop playing innocent and give me Vladimir. He has to pay for what he did to Tommaso."

"He didn't do it."

"Oh yeah? And you just believe him, even though we have evidence?"

"He has no reason to lie."

I grip my hair, my calm long gone. "I don't give a fuck if you think that. He killed my cousin. I want his location, or I will kill every single one of you until I find him."

If I hadn't been traveling across the country with my team, I would have started my vendetta months ago. When my dad told me what had happened, it gave me something to focus on that wasn't work.

He exhales loudly and doesn't say anything for at least a minute. But I give him the time. I've been trying to find him and/or Vladimir for months now, and this is my best shot.

"I'm not just going to hand him over like that, but I have a deal for you."

"I'm listening."

"I need all the details of the murder, and then I'll prove to you that Vladimir didn't kill Tommaso," he pauses, "under one condition."

Despite the grim conversation, I smile.

I am ninety-nine percent sure that Vladimir killed Tommaso; he left a handwritten note for fuck's sake, so Nikolai can run in circles to prove me otherwise for all I care. All I want is to get my revenge. The Mafia families have been civil for the majority of the past few years after coming to a mutually beneficial agreement regarding the districts. But the most basic rule still counts: an eye for an eye.

Cooling my expression, I swallow, not wanting to give away anything. "And what would that be?"

"Stop insulting my intelligence, durak. We both know your engagement to Alessandra is a sham. Call it off."

I ignore that he just called me an idiot because, motherfucking, yes, I got him. Hook. Line. And fucking sinker. "Or what?"

"Or you'll never find Vladimir."

"Deal."

"Good."

"When can I expect the information?"

"In two weeks."

My breath catches in my throat. "Two weeks?"

"Yes."

"Why not sooner?"

"Because I . . . just because."

"I see." I wouldn't believe it if I hadn't just heard him hesitate during his answer. He isn't ready to send Alessandra back home. I'm surprised he's sending her back at all, but if I had to guess, that might be Alessandra's doing.

"Stop gloating or the deal is off."

"Ditto."

"I'll send the details for the exchange. Let me know when you've done your part once she's back, and I'll do mine."

The line goes dead before I can reply, but I let it slide. I've given my life to this mission for most of the last few months, and I'm finally going to get my revenge.

With my mood in the sky, I call my dad and update him on what's going on. He wants me back in the city in a week for a meeting, which means I have one week left with Gemma up here. And I plan on using every single second of it to my advantage. Preferably spending it inside her.

I jog up the stairs just as my phone rings again. I stop to answer it. "What?"

"Santarossa, is this a bad time?"

I can't place the voice, but it sounds familiar. "Who's this?"

"You wound me. It's Frederico."

"What the fuck do you want?"

"I want Gemma back with her family where she belongs."

That little shit. "Did Lorenzo put you up to this?"

I can totally see how Gemma's dad wouldn't want to cause unrest himself and instead has someone else do his dirty work.

"Does it really matter?"

Not exactly an answer, but I guess he's right. In the end, I don't really give a fuck who calls me. I don't appreciate it, no matter what. And it's not like any of them deserve Gemma anyway. The woman I first met was merely a ghost of the person she could be. Married off to someone who wasn't a great guy, but who was obviously chosen for her by her family. The least they could have done was show her some respect and pick someone decent.

"Santarossa, are you still there?"

God, even on the phone he's annoying the shit out of me.

"Yes."

"So you agree?"

"Agree to what?"

He sighs like I'm the stupidest person he's ever talked to,

and I vow to myself to teach him a lesson about respect one day because he clearly has none. "We want you to bring Gemma back."

"We'll be back in the city next week."

"We want her back before then. She belongs with us."

"Well, tough shit, since she's with me right now."

I almost said, *No, she's mine*, but I swallowed those words before I showed my hand.

"Don't push your luck, Santarossa." He growls the words through the line.

I tighten my fingers into a fist. This guy needs to learn who's higher up the food chain, considering it's not him.

"Or what, Gallo? Are you gonna run to Lorenzo?"

"I wouldn't want to find out if I were you, stronzo."

The line goes dead, and I stare at the phone. He just hung up on me. After calling me an asshole. That motherfucker.

His words echo in my head. *I wouldn't want to find out if I were you.* He didn't even threaten me directly like so many do. If he so much as touches a single hair on any of my family members' heads, he's a dead man. I don't care what family he belongs to, or that he's Gemma's cousin, no one crosses a Santarossa and lives to tell the tale, not as long as I'm alive and breathing.

With my body as tense as a bowstring, I walk up the rest of the steps and pause a minute in front of the bedroom door to get my thoughts in order.

First, I want to make sure Gemma's okay. I can figure out what I'm going to do about Frederico later.

After taking a few breaths to calm down, I open the door and stop short when I see her.

CHAPTER 10

GEMMA

S trong arms nudge their way under my body to lift me out of the chair. I'm disoriented for a moment but relax against the warm body the instant I smell Matteo's woodsy orange scent.

My eyes flutter open, but I'm greeted with darkness. "Matteo?"

"Shh, go back to sleep."

He gets on the bed with me still in his arms, the mattress dipping under our weight.

"What time is it?" My voice is all raspy, which isn't too surprising when I try to swallow with a dry throat.

"It's almost ten. Sleep."

I'm still tired, so I close my eyes again until my bladder complains. Once I feel like I need to go to the bathroom, all bets are off, and there's no way I can go back to sleep.

Wiggling in his arms, I try to pull back, only to find his arms caged tightly around me. Almost like he doesn't want to let go of me.

That possibility sends a quivering feeling to my stomach,

but I stop it before it can go any further. This is Matteo we're talking about here. There will be no sappy emotions from this man.

But he's called you, baby, more than once now.

Now that I think about it, wasn't that always when shit was going down, so almost like a knee-jerk reaction?

My thoughts are all over the place to the point where even I have trouble following them in my still-sleepy state. Although it sounds like my subconscious is having a field day with my drowsy conscience.

With my hand on Matteo's chest—his very naked chest, I might add—I push back as far as I can go. "I need to use the bathroom."

He grumbles, the noise vibrating under my palm. "Fine."

I tighten my hand on his skin before relaxing it, enjoying the feel of it under my fingertips. I even like the feel of his coarse chest hair, which is something I never expected to like.

He opens his arms for me and rolls aside. "Hurry back, so we can go to sleep."

I don't respond but rush toward the bathroom. Albeit I do need an extra couple of minutes to take care of the mess I made of my hair. Falling asleep in the armchair with a towel on my head wasn't ideal, but it's too late to fix it now. I brush through it at record speed before throwing it up into a bun on top of my head.

Then there's the issue of still wearing the bathrobe and not having any pajamas or even a shirt lying around.

Walking back into the dark bedroom, I clear my throat. "Can you turn on the light, please, so I can get something to wear from the dresser?"

"I got something over here for you."

"Oh." After more than two weeks in this room, I can mostly navigate it in the dark without any issues, at least the path from my side of the bed to the bathroom and back. Since there shouldn't be anything in the path to Matteo's side I can bump into, I slowly make my way over there to get my clothes.

"Take off your robe. Just leave it on the floor."

I hesitate but then do it anyway. I won't be naked for long, not that he can see me in the darkness anyway.

The robe quietly floats to the floor, and I feel my way around the bed to get to the top. I touch Matteo twice but ignore him and keep moving.

"Almost there." His voice is close. "Just a little more."

I hold out my hand so he can give me my clothes, but the next time I make contact with him, it's his face. There's no mistaking his stubble and that delicious mix of soft and rough, depending on which way you touch it, or where it touches you.

He leans his face into my touch then turns his head and kisses my palm. I start, ready to yank my hand back when he grabs my arm with his fingers, kissing his way up my hand to my wrist. He lingers there, as if it's a special spot. Which it's definitely not to me. I'm about to ask him if he might have a wrist fetish, just as he licks the spot he just kissed.

Well, shit. If he continues like this, I'll be the one with the wrist fetish in no time.

By the time he stops, my breath comes out in quick bursts, and my heart is beating like it's trying to create a new rhythm that's just for Matteo.

Why does it need to be this man who makes me want to throw all caution to the wind?

Why does he have to be the one who makes me want to disregard all the rules?

He isn't the one for me, not the one I'm supposed to marry anyway, yet I've never craved another man this much. My body has never reacted to anyone like it does to him. This pull inside me, this need to connect, never existed until him.

He's everything I shouldn't want; everything forbidden and wrong, yet here I am, aching for his touch like I've never ached for anything else in my life.

His fingers slip off my skin, and my first instinct is to whimper, but I keep it in. I won't whimper for him. I shouldn't whimper for anyone.

"What's going on in that pretty head of yours?" His hand grazes the skin on my waist before brushing it lightly down the curve of my hip and thigh.

I'm delirious from his touch and unable to form a coherent thought.

How am I ever supposed to marry another man, to allow his hands on my body, after knowing what it means to be touched with so much reverence?

"I . . . I shouldn't like this so much." The words fall from my lips, and I don't regret them. The darkness knows no difference between truth and lies, it only knows words. And I want to say them.

"Like when I do this?" Matteo's hand goes back up my outer thigh and hip before making a detour to my stomach, where it slowly traces over my marred skin.

He touches my scar with such tenderness that I never want to leave this darkness with him.

"Yes." My voice is barely a whisper in the otherwise quiet room.

"What about this?" His fingers move higher, brushing over the underside of one breast before doing the same to the other one.

His touch feels exquisite, and my lips part in response.

It's not too late to stop.

Pinching my lips together, I hold back the groan.

I really shouldn't be doing this.

What if the roles were reversed and I found out my cousin did this with *my* fiancé?

Shit.

Talk about an ice-cold bucket over the head.

I'm a crappy friend and a crappy cousin.

I truly am.

What was I thinking?

Apparently, I have no self-control around this man.

"Matteo." I place my hand on his, enjoying his warm skin on my body for one more second before taking it off. "I . . . I can't."

I was weak when he found me on the deck, the lust swirling in my head too strong to ignore after I watched him masturbate. But I can't let anything like that happen again, not if this entire situation remains the same.

He lets me take his hand off but doesn't let go of it. "Is this about Ally?"

"Mostly, yes." There's so much more than just Ally, but she's definitely the biggest issue of them all, no doubt about that.

He yanks on my hand, and I have to take a step forward to catch myself. His soft breath hits my stomach a moment later, and I draw in a sharp breath. The fact that I can't see him makes everything so much more intimate and intense, yet also liberating.

Then his breath is gone, and he shifts around on the bed. When he's back, his breath moves up my body like a gentle breeze, caressing it without ever touching me.

He doesn't stop at my breasts but continues until he's right in front of my face. Letting go of my hand, he cups my face. "What if I told you I'm going to break things off with Ally?"

Hope flares inside my chest, and I immediately hate it. Because, where there's hope, there's also the chance of pain. And I don't want to feel any more of it, I really don't.

Licking my lips, I try to compose myself, to find that spot inside me that's stronger than my desires. "I'm not sure I'd believe you."

One of his calloused thumbs brushes over my cheeks, and I love the contrast of it on my skin.

He pauses. "Good. I know words don't mean as much as actions, but I want you to know anyway."

"You're really going to call off the engagement?"

Another rough caress over my cheek. "I am. I talked to Nikolai earlier, and he'll bring Ally home in two weeks, as long as I end things between us."

A sudden lightness starts in my chest and spreads throughout my body. "She's really coming back?"

"Yes."

"Thank you." I don't think, I just act and throw my arms around his neck, pressing my naked body against his. "Thank you."

"It was in my best interests."

That statement triggers something in my brain, the conversation I overheard on our drive up here last month. I'd forgotten about it, writing it off as one of those things you imagine while you're half asleep. "You want Nikolai, not Ally."

"Yes." There's no pause before he answers, and I'm surprised he admits it without any hesitation.

My brain is spinning in circles until it connects some dots, and I gasp. "Was the whole engagement a setup?"

"Yes."

I draw back. "Why?"

"Business."

I imagine him shrugging, since that's a nonchalant thing he'd do, as if we're talking about something mundane like the weather.

"Business?" I peel myself out of his arms, wanting to create some distance between us. I can't think this close to him.

Matteo is quiet, without further explanation. What a surprise.

"What does Ally have to do with your business?"

He sighs. "Honestly, nothing."

My mouth opens and closes, not that he can see it. I couldn't have possibly heard correctly. "You're saying you have some kind of business beef, or whatever, going on with Nikolai, and Ally got caught in the crossfire, and now you're using her as leverage to get what you want?"

"Yes and no."

I ball my hands into fists and I growl. I legitimately growl into the darkness. "You're driving me insane. Just spit. It. Out."

A noise comes from him at my outburst. If I didn't know any better, I'd say he just snorted, but not Matteo. Right?

"Calm down, passerotta. Even though I have to say it's hot when you're angry."

If he continues like this, I'll have steam coming out of my ears soon. "Hot?"

This time, he most definitely chuckles. "You don't believe me?"

"Pffft, of course I don't."

He grabs my hand and drags me closer. Holy shit. He's a vampire who can see perfectly in the dark, while I can barely see my own hand in front of my face.

My fingers touch something hot, and my scattering thoughts disappear. It's something smooth yet hard. Rock-hard, to be exact. Matteo's fingers are on top of mine, and he puts our joined hands around his massive erection.

He groans as we pump him up and down, once, twice, and that snaps me out of it.

What the hell is happening? This man has bewitched me with his dick.

I jerk out of his grasp. "I can't believe you."

"Maybe you should have more faith in me. If I say something, I mean it. And you're hot when you're angry."

I fold my arms across my chest, my still very naked chest. This is definitely the most awkward conversation I've ever had, no doubt about that. And, apparently, Matteo likes awkward to the point that it makes him hard. Just great.

After taking several deep breaths, I'm willing to give him one more chance. "Could you please tell me what's going on? And in more than just one or two-word answers?"

"Your cousin has been secretly seeing Nikolai."

Time stands still until a million things flood my brain at once.

"No. That's impossible." The words rush out of my mouth.

"I have proof." Matteo's steadying hand is on my elbow, lightly caressing my skin with his thumb.

Well, shit. My head turns fuzzy at the edges, and I plop onto the edge of the bed. "I can't believe it. How?"

"I don't have all the details about them, but I know they've been seeing each other for several months at the very least."

I rub my hand over my forehead. "I can't believe this. And she never told me." Then something else occurs to me, and I turn to him in the darkness. "And you let me believe you were really going to marry her?"

Matteo's quiet as if the question warrants some deep thought. "I honestly didn't think that far ahead. I've been trying to back Nikolai into a corner for so long, I had to take the chance when I found out about him and Ally."

"What did he do to you that you want him so badly?"

A heavy sigh hangs in the air between us, and just when I think he won't answer, he says, "He's hiding someone who killed one of my cousins."

My heart skips a beat at the news. That was not what I envisioned after the whole business beef conversation we had earlier. I was thinking of something more along the lines of owing money, or something simple like that. But losing a loved one is a totally different ball game, and it can do crazy things to you, I know that firsthand.

"I'm sorry about your cousin."

"Thanks. I'll be able to sleep better once the person responsible for his death has paid for it."

Can I really fault him for that?

He didn't choose for my cousin to somehow be involved in all of this. He saw an opportunity to get closer to his goal, and he took it.

My mind keeps spinning, trying to fit this new piece into a puzzle that's shaped completely differently. I think about Ally and the last few weeks and months with her. Should I have noticed something changed? There *were* moments where she quickly put her phone away before I could get a look at it, and times where she seemed uncomfortable whenever I asked her questions about where she'd been or what her plans were. I thought it was just a mixture of all of my wedding stress and a bad case of life. And now this?

What a little minx.

She has some major explaining to do, that's for sure. And possibly groveling.

Not that I blame her for hiding it from the rest of the family. Her dad would forbid it, or maybe even worse. Marrying someone who isn't Italian might as well be considered treason in our circle.

But hiding it from me too? It stings a bit.

On the other hand, Matteo opened up to me, which I really appreciate. Even if I don't necessarily like the news, I'm glad to be more in the loop.

"What . . . what happens now?" My voice sounds distant, even to my own ears.

"Now, I'm going to fuck you."

CHAPTER 11

GEMMA

L aughter bubbles out of my mouth, and I can't stop it. In the last month, my life has turned into an absolute circus, and the man in front of me never ceases to surprise me. I'm not sure if he's incredibly cocky or slightly delirious. Maybe both? If he expected that line would work on me, he's sorely mistaken. After everything he just told me, having sex with him is the last thing on my mind. Okay, maybe not the last thing, but it's definitely not at the top of the list.

Still slightly wheezing, I take my chances and fumble my way around in the dark. I bump into furniture a few times but make it to the dresser at last. I grab the first thing I can find in the top drawer and put it on. Anything's better than nothing. Then I shuffle around until I'm on the other side of the bed. *My* side of the bed.

Unless he's as quiet as a ninja, Matteo hasn't moved much or left the bed since his ridiculous statement.

When I'm under the cover, he says, "I take it that's a no?"

I only huff, pretty sure that's answer enough.

He clears his throat. "I'm not going to apologize for what I did."

The sigh that leaves my lungs is long and frustrated. Because what other reaction is there really? This whole clusterfuck deserves a sigh and so much more. "What exactly are you *not* apologizing for, Matteo? That you took something from me on my wedding day that wasn't yours to take? Or that you stole something from me at the bar three weeks later that wasn't yours to take either? Right before your engagement to my cousin was announced, no less, which turns out to be a sham. Then I got shot, which I suppose actually wasn't your fault—on second thought, maybe it was—and last but not least, you carried me off to your home, had me stitched up, and kidnapped me."

My mouth feels dry, and I'm out of breath. Apparently, being irritated takes up a lot of energy and lung space.

"I didn't kidnap you." His voice is closer than before.

I turn toward him, and the little bit of moonlight shining through the windows allows me to at least see his faint outline.

"Debatable."

"You can go home if you want to."

"Mmmm."

"Do you want to go home?"

Shit. That was the wrong question for him to ask. But I don't really want to get into *that* with him right now. "Why wouldn't I want to go home?"

He scoffs. "Maybe because they treat you like a piece of meat and you hate it there?"

The heat behind my eyes from earlier comes back with a

vengeance, and I rub at them furiously. I hate that he's right, that he already knows me so well.

When I put my hands back down on the comforter, Matteo's hand is there to grasp mine, his tone softer than before. "You're too good for them."

Damn him, he makes it hard to keep the tears at bay.

We're silent for a while, and he continues to hold my hand.

"I don't have a choice." The words escape my mouth before I can stop them. They aren't very strong though, they're barely a whisper, but they're the most honest ones I've ever spoken. I feel them to the depths of my soul, and I'm afraid they have the power to break me from within.

"You always have a choice. It just might not be an easy one."

Maybe he's right about that. It sure doesn't always feel like it.

"I don't think my family would let me go, even if I wanted to. Not to mention, I have nothing in my name, no possessions or money, or a place to stay. Plus, my dad's too obsessed with marrying me off for his own gain. He hasn't been happy since what happened to Luigi."

Matteo doesn't say anything, but his grip tightens on my hand.

"Matteo?"

"Yeah?"

"Did you kill Luigi?"

"No."

I swallow. "Oh."

"I didn't come to your wedding to kill him, no." He

pauses for a beat. "But the second I laid eyes on you, I wanted to."

"Why?"

"Because he was a greedy bastard who didn't deserve someone as beautiful as you."

My chest tightens at his words, and I press my lips together.

Who is this guy? He makes me absolutely furious one minute before soothing my anger with his words the next. I'm not sure I'll ever be able to fully understand this man and the way I react to him.

That reminds me of what Ash told me earlier, which adds another layer to who this man is. Since honesty seems to be what we're giving each other at the moment, I take advantage of it. "Ash said something about you guys being a team?"

"Ash is terrible at keeping his mouth shut."

I shift around under the covers, freezing when I touch his warm skin by accident. For some strange reason, I don't move back though, and just stay where I'm at. "What kind of team are you?"

"A clean-up team."

"Clean-up?"

"Yes."

"Matteeeeeeeo."

"You're relentless."

"You're insufferable."

He bumps his leg against my foot. "Do you talk like this to everyone, or just me?"

That question gives me pause. Am I talking differently to him than how I usually do?

I just called him insufferable; I keep asking him direct

questions, probing him to spill more details. I talk to him without thinking, without filtering, like I'm just me. The same way I talk to Ally, like I'd talk to friends.

"Is that what we are? Friends?" The rumble of his voice drags me out of my thoughts.

Shit. Did I just say that last part out loud?

I lick my lips. "I don't know. Are we?"

"Every time I see you, I want to lick you from head to toe until you scream my name, before fucking you so hard you can't ever look at another man without thinking of me deep inside you. So, you tell me, passerotta. Is that something friends do?"

Heat rises in my cheeks at his crude words, but that's not the only place heating up. "So dirty."

"And you love every single word of it, don't you?"

I never would have imagined that dirty talk could turn me on, but he's right, it does. So very much. Because of that one sentence alone I want to rub my thighs together to find some relief. I didn't even know it was possible to feel like this.

Willing some of my brain cells to stop malfunctioning, I focus back on the conversation we had before we got off track. Which seems to be something that happens quite often with us.

I clear my throat. "Mmm, so . . . you're part of a clean-up crew?"

He clicks his tongue, and I have the inexplicable urge to put my hand on his chest, or anywhere really, to soothe his frustration. Somehow, I've come to like touching him, being with him.

If my father knew.

The things I've done.

Nope, not thinking about him now. Not. At. All.

He's an issue I'll have to deal with later.

"There has been a lot of unrest amongst the Italian Mafia families over the last decade. Things have changed exponentially with technology, and quite a few people thought no one would notice if they took a little more money than they deserve. Some turned into moles or worked for someone else on the side. It's gotten pretty messy, and as such, the heads of the biggest families decided to put together a group to clean house, so to speak."

"You cleaned up every Italian family?" I pull back, astonished by this.

"Yes, all of them across the United States. Took us two years, and a lot of work, but it was worth it. There will always be a few black sheep in some of the families, but we took care of the ones who were damaging to the business."

"All of them?"

"The ones we were able to uncover. A lot of them fled since they got wind of what we were doing. Others needed some more convincing to leave the family business."

"Wow."

His thumb brushes over mine. "I'm guessing your dad doesn't talk business with you?"

"Never. Every time there was a single flicker of business talk going on, I had to leave the room. Not that we spent a lot of time together to begin with, but that destroyed any that was left."

"That sounds like a princess being confined to her ivory tower."

A heavy weight settles on my chest. "Pretty much. I had everything I could need in regard to food, clothes, books, school items, tutors, or whatever else I needed for hobbies, but friends or freedom definitely weren't on the list. Which is why I've always thanked the universe for Ally. The fact that she's family allows me to see her more than anyone."

"But she didn't tell you about Nikolai."

Way to shove the knife deeper into my heart, Romeo. "She didn't."

"She was probably concerned about your safety. The moment more people get wind of their relationship, shit will hit the fan."

I shudder at the thought of our family finding out about Ally and Nikolai, let alone other families. "It won't end well."

"No, it won't."

"Will you . . . do you have to . . . I mean—" My lungs constrict, and I suddenly feel like I can't get enough air.

"Will I tell anyone about it?"

I nod then remember he can't see me. "Yes."

"I won't. So far, it's been working in my favor, more than anything else would have. If it becomes an issue, we'll have to handle the situation one way or another."

The implication that not everyone would get away unharmed if it came to a blowout hangs unspoken in the air. "That's fair, I guess."

We're quiet after that for a few minutes until my eyes become too heavy to keep open, and I close them. Just for a second.

When I wake up again, I'm in Matteo's arms, my cheek on his chest. I snuggle closer, feeling safe with him surrounding me, and go back to sleep.

The next time I wake up, it's morning, and I'm alone.

Sunlight filters through the windows, and I blink against the intrusion.

I stretch my limbs, feeling a little sore between my legs.

Is that normal?

We didn't even have sex.

But what we did was absolutely incredible.

My sleepy mind gets lost in what happened yesterday. How Matteo was on his knees behind me, making me see stars.

It was strange, at first, especially being in such a vulnerable position, but once Matteo started licking me, I couldn't focus on anything else. It wasn't anything like I expected it to be; it was an absolutely earth-shattering experience.

If my dad ever finds out about this, we might both be killed.

That possibility extinguishes some of the warmth in my body, but not the lingering energy of reliving the sexy times in my head, as well as the conversation we had last night. The way he opened up to me was surprising, but in a good way. I'm elated I got some answers, and it's comforting to have someone else on my side.

Ally has been my only friend, my only companion and confidante for so long, that it's still unfamiliar territory for me to suddenly have another person in my life who isn't there due to my dad's orders.

Tears burn the backs of my eyes, but I shake my head and slide the covers back. It's too early for a meltdown.

Instead, I hop out of bed and go through my morning routine in the bathroom. Most of my hair has fallen out of the bun overnight, so I fix it and tie it in a new one before getting dressed in leggings, a tank top, and a hoodie over it. The fall weather has officially arrived, so mornings and evenings have mood swings and can get a bit frosty.

I remember I wanted to check my phone, so I grab it from the dresser. My heart beats a wild tune when I see a message from Ally. That witch. I still can't believe she kept such a big secret from me.

ALLY

Niko said I'm coming home in two weeks.
Can't wait to catch up. Miss you. Xoxo

Niko, huh?

Little liar.

I dial her number, but it sends me straight to voicemail after one ring. A couple of seconds later, a text message pops up.

ALLY

Sorry, I can't talk right now. Too many ears listening.

ME

You have some major explaining to do, Ally. If what I heard is true, you're in so much trouble.

I'm just about to leave my messages, as three small dots dance across the bottom of the screen.

My heart skips a beat as another message pops up.

ALLY

I'm so sorry. It's such a mess and so beyond complicated, and I didn't want to drag you into it.

ME

You owe me a minimum of ten pounds of chocolate for this.

ALLY

I'll buy you a hundred as long as you forgive me. I'm really sorry.

I inhale deeply. I know she wanted to protect me, that's Ally in a nutshell, so I can't hold this against her. At least I can try not to.

ME

I know you are.

ALLY

Did Matteo tell you?

ME

He did.

There's really no point in lying to her about that.

ALLY

Are you doing okay? He's treating you well, right?

Am I okay? And is he treating me well? Why do those questions feel so loaded?

ME

A lot has happened, but yeah, I'm okay.

ALLY

Good, I'm glad. I'd hate to have to kick his ass otherwise.

> **ME**
>
> I'll kick his butt if he misbehaves. I watched a boxing match, so I've learned a thing or two.

Ally replies with about twenty laughing emojis, and I have to chuckle.

That did sound a bit ridiculous, but only reinforced my previous idea of wanting to learn how to fight.

Another message from Ally pops up.

> **ALLY**
>
> I really can't wait to see you again. It's been too long.

> **ME**
>
> I agree. You'd tell me if you needed to get out of there, right?

> **ALLY**
>
> Absolutely. None of this is ideal, but I'm glad I got this time here.

That's what I gathered from the way she talked, but it's good to hear it anyway.

> **ME**
>
> It's definitely complicated.

> **ALLY**
>
> So much. It's a constant battle to talk him out of starting a war between the families.

> **ME**
>
> Did you know he was going to get you?

ALLY

Oh my gosh, no. It wasn't supposed to happen the way it did either. Someone messed up, and he paid for it.

ME

And you didn't know about the engagement to Matteo either?

ALLY

Absolutely not. I still can't believe my dad did that. There's no way I'm going to marry that guy. Not in a million years, trust me.

ME

Okay.

ALLY

Okay? Sounds like I'm not the only one who's got some explaining to do.

ME

Maybe.

ALLY

Well, well, how the times have changed. Catching up will be so much fun. But I've got to go now, Gem. I'll try and contact you again when I can. Love you.

ME

Sounds good. Love you too. Take good care of yourself.

I exit out of my conversation with Ally and into the one I have with Luna, sending her a quick message.

ME

You're in so much trouble. Sending sex toys with Ash? What if your brother sees them?

Her reply is almost instant.

LUNA

Tell him you have needs.

My mouth opens and closes as I stare at her words. Maybe she's on drugs.

ME

You're crazy.

LUNA

Maybe.

I laugh and type out one more message.

ME

But thank you for sending something for me. I really appreciate it. I love the books.

LUNA

You're so welcome. Let me know if you need anything else.

Smiling at the phone, I'm about to put it back in the drawer just as the screen lights up.

LUNA

Also, please let me know if Matteo needs something. I'm not sure if he's told you about the last few months, but I've been worried about him, we all have. Anything either one of you needs, just say the word.

ME

Sounds good. I'll keep an eye out.

LUNA

Thank you. I'm glad you're there with him.

Since I'm not sure how to reply to that, I put the phone away and leave the bedroom in search of a certain someone.

The noises coming from the basement lead me down the stairs to find a shirtless Matteo in the gym.

He doesn't stop when he sees me, but the corner of his mouth lifts.

With his hands in gloves and positioned by his face, he's in a fighting stance in front of the heavy bag.

I sit on the workout bench, my pulse speeding up as I watch him. Every time he makes contact with the bag, a thundering crack fills the room. Sweat pours down his tense muscles, and right now, he strikes me as someone who'd be capable of taking out every single one of his enemies barehanded.

I want that.

Badly.

I want to know what it feels like to be strong and powerful.

To be able to defend myself.

This need I feel isn't based on fear, it's built on a hunger to build a stronger me. It's a gut feeling inside that believes it will somehow help me escape my gilded cage, or at the very least, make my life easier.

Once Matteo's done hitting the bag, he kicks it. Low kick, high kick. Low kick, high kick. He does that several times before taking a short break, just to do it over again and again.

To say I'm mesmerized is an understatement.

I've always worked out, something my father insisted on to keep me healthy—his way of making sure I stay in shape to be marriageable—but I've never done anything as intense as this.

Watching Matteo now, and him and Zeno the other day, has started this fire, this hunger in me that hasn't dissipated. I want to feel like that: invincible, powerful, knowing that no one could ever force me to do anything against my will.

When he's finally finished, he takes off his gloves and tosses them to the floor before grabbing his towel to wipe off the sweat. Then he picks up his water bottle and drains half of it, his Adam's apple moving in a way that shouldn't be appealing, yet it is. The whole time his eyes are on me, like he's quietly trying to figure out what my deal is. I probably look like I'm high on something with how inexplicably excited I am.

He straddles the workout bench opposite me and glances at me with such a heated expression, I feel its warmth humming throughout my body.

Before he can get a word out, I open my mouth. "I want you to teach me how to fight."

Both of his eyebrows draw up as he takes another swig of his water. "Do you now?"

"Yes."

"Why?"

I hold up my hands as if that explains it all.

"That's not good enough." He brushes his hand through his damp hair, making sure to get it all out of his face.

Leaning forward, I scowl at him, trying to appear fierce. I need to convince him since there's no one else I can ask, no one else I'd feel comfortable enough to ask. Considering I do feel secure enough with Matteo is something to revisit at another time. "Do I really need a reason?"

"Normally not, no, but I'm curious."

I wrinkle my nose, some of the earlier excitement fading.

"If you must know, I've wanted to learn how to fight ever since the incident with my mom, but my dad thought I was being ridiculous. Now all this crap happened, and I hate feeling like I can't protect myself. Watching you and Zeno fight reawakened that desire of wanting to learn, I guess."

What I don't tell him is that I want to feel more confident, capable of doing things for myself, something that might help me escape not only my metaphorical cage at home, but also the cage in my brain. With each passing day away from my dad, one thing becomes crystal clear: he's brainwashed me, to the point I didn't even notice it anymore. Or maybe it was just easier to ignore. Did I know he was grooming me to marry me off for his own gain? Yes. But there was this little part of me that was still hoping he was doing it because he cared about me, and because he wanted to pick a man, a husband, who'd take good care of me.

Matteo stares at me without saying a word. If it wasn't for him blinking every once in a while, I'd have said he's a robot.

Getting up, he nods and says, "Okay."

I shoot up too, my brain taking a minute to switch back to our conversation. "Okay?"

"Yes."

"Just like that?"

"Just like that."

"Huh."

"Are you complaining? Did you want me to say no?"

"What?" I stare at him with wide eyes. "No, no, no, of course not."

"Could have fooled me."

"I mean it, obviously I wanted you to say yes. I guess I'm just surprised." I brush my hands on my pants, trying to calm my nervousness. "But not in a bad way, you know? And I promise I'll be an excellent student."

"Gemma?"

"Yeah?"

"Shut up, I already said yes."

"I know, I know. Sorry. I'm just super ex—"

His lips smash on mine, his tongue demanding entry, which my mouth immediately gives. His lips are warm and soft, such a contrast to his whole demeanor. His kiss is something in between, soft yet demanding, and my body molds against his without any demand. My new curves—thanks to a few weeks of regular eating, without my dad's strict meal plan—fuse with his hard planes like they were two pieces made to fit.

His hands circle around my body and grab two handfuls of my ass, and I'm about to jump into his arms and demand he put me out of my misery. But I don't. Instead, I let him grind his hard-on against the seam of my yoga pants while I shamelessly rub against him.

I'm so in the moment, I have to blink several times to shake out of my daze when his lips and hands leave my body and he carefully puts me back on the floor. He steadies me with his hand on my elbow, which I'm grateful for, because I most definitely need the assistance.

His other hand brushes a strand of hair off my face. That quick and dirty make-out session did a number on my already messy bun, and I can feel it falling apart on all sides.

He kisses my nose. "Let's wait for a while longer before we start on the fight training. You're not supposed to overdo it."

One of his fingers presses against my lips before I can

protest. "Buuuuut I was planning on teaching you something else, so we can focus on that in the meantime."

I tilt my head. "What is it?"

After throwing on his shirt, he reaches for me. "Come on, I'll show you."

CHAPTER 12

GEMMA

With my hand firmly in his, Matteo leads me upstairs, out the front door, and toward the large shed that's nestled on the side of the property partially hidden behind the trees.

Clueless to even begin guessing what we could be doing out here, I stay quiet. I'm a bit disappointed that I have to wait to learn how to fight, but I'm also curious to see what Matteo wants to teach me. And the fact it's something *he* wanted to do with me, without me asking him first, has my blood pumping a little faster. The closer we get to the shed, the more I second-guess my excitement.

After unlocking it and flicking on the light, Matteo holds the door open for me and waits for me to step inside before turning the lock behind us. I study him suspiciously since him bringing me out here and locking us in makes no sense. My curiosity is still there, but now so is my anxiety.

The shed is filled with a variety of tools. I'm no expert when it comes to such things, but it seems like there's something for everything—the garden, the house, or whatever else might need fixing or need to be taken care of.

My excitement lessens with every step. "Are you going to teach me how to build something? Or are we going to mow the lawn?"

Matteo chuckles. "Do you want me to teach you how to build something or mow the lawn?"

Peeking up at him, I wrinkle my nose. "Not particularly. I mean, I can watch you build something if you want, or mow the lawn, but I don't think craftsmanship or gardening is really my thing."

All of a sudden something happens I'm not prepared for: Matteo laughs. My mouth falls open, and I gawk at him, my mind completely blown. His white teeth are on full display as a deep rumble leaves his mouth. The laugh lines at the corners of his eyes make him so much more attractive, my heart skips a beat before speeding up.

His features relax again, yet I'm still staring at him completely flabbergasted.

Grumpy and growly Matteo is a sight to behold and absolute fire, but laughing and happy Matteo is blindingly gorgeous. Whereas the first version of him can get my panties wet with a glance, this new version of him dissolves them into thin air.

His free hand reaches for my face, his thumb brushing against my lips. Tracing them, seducing them, taking ownership of them like he has every right to do so.

My body tingles, anticipating a kiss that never comes because he stops his delicious assault.

Instead, he turns me toward one side of the shed and points at the gray container sitting right there.

I tilt my head and stare down the length of it. "Is that . . . is that a shipping container?"

"Yes."

"Why on earth do you have a freaking shipping container in your shed?"

He shrugs. "I don't want anyone knowing it's here."

"Does that actually make sense to you?"

"Yes."

Blinking at him, I shake my head. "Okay. So what did you want to show me?"

He points at the shipping container.

I still can't believe there's a fucking shipping container in here. Who does something like that?

"You wanted to show me the container?" I'm getting more confused by the minute. And slightly annoyed too, but that might be due to not having had any food or caffeine yet.

The look he gives me is his pissy, *Stop being stupid* look. Maybe I deserve it, maybe not. Or maybe Matteo can work on his communication skills. Now there's a great idea.

"Come on." He pulls me after him once more and opens the door that leads into the container.

I dig in my heels and stare at him when he turns around. "You're not going to lock me in there or do something equally creepy, right?"

"I don't remember you being like this in the morning."

"Like what?"

Ignoring me, he yanks me into the container with a hard tug.

The lights go on automatically, and it takes me a moment to scan our surroundings because, holy crap. "Is this what I think it is?"

Matteo huffs. "If you think it's a shooting range, then yes."

"Wow." I do a three-sixty, still unable to believe what I'm seeing.

"Right?" He gives me a knowing grin before he jerks his chin toward a small sectioned-off area on one end of the container. "Okay, let's get you all set up."

I follow him and watch him boot up some kind of system for the range on a computer, before getting two guns out of a gun safe. This man is full of surprises.

Once he has everything he wants, he gestures for me to come closer. "You've never shot a gun before, have you?"

"How did you know?"

He purses his lips. "Just a guess, being the Mafia princess in her ivory tower and all."

Ah, that again.

Well, he's not wrong.

I still have a hard time keeping the bitterness away. "Sorry to disappoint."

Taking a pair of black earmuffs from the desk, he puts them around my neck. Next are safety glasses he places on top of my head. "You'll wear both while you shoot. But first, some basics. Most is common knowledge, but better safe than sorry."

"Okay." I nod. This is definitely not something I want to screw up, so I stay quiet and give him my full attention.

"Treat your gun like it's loaded, even if it's not. Which means, always point it in a safe direction and not at anyone. And keep your finger off the trigger until you're ready to shoot. We'll start small with a twenty-two, since it only has a light recoil and is relatively quiet too." He stares at me. "You ready?"

"Mmmm." I rock back and forth on my heels, wondering if the excitement or the nervousness in my blood will win out. It's a lot to take in.

Putting both weapons on the desk, he walks over to me and grabs my face in his hands. "Can you do this for me?"

My eyelashes flutter out of rhythm. "For you?"

"Yes."

"Why?"

"Any time I'm with you, no one will ever get close to you, but I want to know you're safe no matter what." His chest lifts as he inhales. "And I think it would be good for you to feel safe too."

All the air in my lungs dissipates at his words, and I gasp. When was the last time anyone ever thought about what I wanted or what was good for me?

I swallow and fresh oxygen rushes through my body. "Okay."

His thumb caresses my cheek. "Good girl."

Then he leans in and presses his lips to my forehead. I close my eyes and bask in his gentleness.

Thankfully, he pulls back before I embarrass myself because I'm weak in the knees for him.

"Let's do this."

He walks me through the whole process, showing me how to hold the gun steady, how to aim, and how to shoot. Then he demonstrates how it's done, and I watch him in amazement.

His posture, his stance, those tight muscles while he focuses on the target. Is this supposed to turn me on? It's like this man has spiked my drinks and food with endorphins for all the ways he makes me feel alive.

Once his magazine is empty, he sidles up next to me. "Your turn."

I blow out a loud breath.

"You've got this."

My slightly shaky hands say otherwise, but I nod anyway. I step on the spot he showed me, with my feet shoulder-width apart, find the right grip with both of my hands and align the gun at the right level for the target. Or at least what I think is right. I pull the trigger, surprised when my finger hits the trigger break Matteo told me about, but I push past the pressure point. The gun jolts a little to the side as it fires, and I almost drop it. Well, now I know what to expect for next time.

I catch Matteo's gaze, and he winks at me.

With renewed determination, I turn back to the target and try again, and again, until there are no more bullets left.

Matteo puts both of our guns on the desk and activates the target retrieval system. With his earmuffs around his neck, he steps next to me. I slide mine down too, and wait for the papers to reach us. My whole body is tingling, and I'm two seconds away from bouncing on my toes. This nervous energy that's running through my veins from shooting a gun is definitely unexpected.

The papers reach us, and I stare at them.

"Well," Matteo clears his throat and hands me the paper, "you hit it a couple times."

"I did? I did." I grin because I really did hit the paper . . . twice. The holes are so far on the outside they barely grazed it, but they're there, and that's all that matters to me.

Matteo's eyes are on me, but I'm too giddy to directly look at him. I don't want to see any disappointment in his eyes and ruin this moment for me.

"Eyes on me, passerotta."

Tightening my grip on the paper, I lift my gaze and meet his dark one.

"You did a good job."

I blink at his compliment. "Thank you."

His eyes darken, and he takes a step closer, his intense gaze never leaving mine. "That was also." Another step closer. "The hottest thing." And another step. "I've ever." Stop. "Seen."

Then his hands are at my nape, and his mouth crashes on mine.

I'm not sure if it's the adrenaline pumping through my veins from shooting, or something else, but the paper slips out of my fingers and lands on the floor. My hands find their way into his thick hair, and I grab it, unable to calm my frantic heartbeat while we desperately devour each other, unable to tell where one ends and the other begins.

It's messy, it's rough, and it's the best kiss I've ever had.

This man just did something for me that no one else has ever done in my life. He thought about me, about what I wanted and what would benefit me. He might as well have doused me in pure endorphins for what that did to me. Best aphrodisiac ever.

His hands move around my hips, and he squeezes my ass in such a firm grip, I lift one leg at a time to twist around his waist. Doing that brings my core closer to his hard length, and my body rocks against him before I even make a conscious decision to do so. It's like a certain part of my brain is still stuck on our mini make-out session at the gym earlier, ready to pick up right where we left off.

"Fuck, yes, baby. Don't stop." Matteo walks me backward, and I hit the cool wall of the container. He takes his hands away from my butt after another hearty squeeze and wanders around to my front.

His fingers immediately go for my breasts, massaging them until I'm writhing even more.

"Those tits are so fucking perfect. I need to feel them." He takes hold of the top of my shirt with both hands and rips it clean completely down the middle.

What the ever-loving Hulk?

My sports bra becomes visible, and he groans in frustration. Yeah, we're not just shredding that one. Together, we manage to get it off me, both of us groaning the moment he finally has access to my breasts. His mouth closes around one taut nipple, sucking and biting while his other hand grips my other breast, massaging it before tweaking the hard tip.

Unable to keep my eyes open, I close them and let my head fall back against the wall. This feeling, all of these sensations. It's like someone poured gasoline all over my body and is setting me on fire. It's too much. My heart beats thunderously, and I feel like I'm about to have a heart attack.

With one hand still kneading my breast, he presses harder against me so he can kiss me again. At this point, I almost feel like I'm having an out-of-body experience. It's the most exquisite sensation I've ever felt.

Since I'm only wearing my yoga pants, and his dick is hard, he hits my clit every single time. It's pure torture, and my entire body is buzzing, so much so I'm considering ripping my pants off so he can push right into me. I'm slightly delirious at the thought of him entering me, of us having sex.

"I need—"

Whatever other words wanted to leave my mouth die on my tongue because he reaches for my butt once more and increases the pressure of his movements against my core.

"Guardami, passerotta." He says the words through clenched teeth like he's trying to stay in control, but he's extremely close to losing it.

The fact that he wants me to watch him shoots another round of pleasure straight to my core, especially when he says it in his commanding voice. It makes every single touch that much more intense.

"Oh my God." Tingles spread from my clit, and my whole body tenses.

Matteo and I move almost in sync until I contract so hard, I think I can't take it anymore. It's at that moment that all the tension releases, pulsing through the nerves in my body, and I come with such a force, I can't hold myself upright.

Matteo cradles me against him, his harsh breathing right next to my ear. "I got you."

With my eyes closed, I lean on his shoulder, incapable of even lifting my head.

"Hang on, baby." Matteo walks a few steps and perches my butt on something.

I open my eyes to watch him pull his white T-shirt off. After flipping it around, he puts it over my head and drags it down as far as he can, before he also drapes something soft over my back. A few seconds later, my eyes are closed once more, and we're back on the move.

Cool air hits my neck and face, and I don't need to look to

know he's carrying me back to the house, and I'm more than okay with that. As amazing as the orgasm was, I'm probably going to feel it in my back tomorrow. Definitely not the best place for intimate acrobatics.

The feeling in my hands and legs is slowly coming back, and I tighten my limbs around Matteo in hopes of making it a little easier for him to carry me. Thankfully, it isn't far, and he walks up the front porch in no time.

He steps inside with me still attached to him and closes the door behind us. Suddenly, his phone goes off with a steady alarm.

Matteo stiffens around me, and his hands come to my waist. "Baby, can you stand? I need to check the security system."

That immediately snaps me out of my exhausted state, and I slide down his body to stand.

Matteo reaches underneath the entryway table and takes out a gun. He checks it and hands it to me. "Stay here. Shoot anyone who isn't me, you hear me? I'll be right back."

His lips meet mine in a quick kiss, and then he's gone.

What happens in the next few minutes is a blur: a thump on the front door, a gunshot, Matteo calling my name, his loud footsteps, and so much blood.

CHAPTER 13
GEMMA

"Thank God, you're here." I step back into the house, throw the door closed behind me, and jump straight into Matteo's arms, almost toppling both of us over. My whole body's trembling, and I'm clinging to Matteo with all my might, not quite ready to let go of him.

His hands roam over my back and neck, hugging me to him before he pushes me back to give me a better once-over. "Fuck, baby, where are you hurt?"

"I'm not. I'm okay."

"You're covered in blood." He's staring at the front of my shirt.

I don't blame him for thinking the worst. I probably look like a total monster.

Images of what actually happened pop into my head, and I draw in a shaky breath. "I . . . I . . . there was a thump in front of the door, and I heard a whimper. I peeked out the window and saw the bunny on the front porch, and it . . . The poor thing kept whimpering, so I wanted to check on it. And then . . . and then . . ."

I stop as a lump in my throat prevents me from talking.

Matteo rubs his fingers over my hands. "Shh, baby, I'm here. What happened then?"

Pressing my lips together, I keep the tears from spilling over. "I had to check on it. I . . . I didn't see it was bleeding so badly until I picked it up."

Matteo nods, his whole body going rigid. Then he cradles my face and forces me to gaze at him. "Listen very carefully right now, okay?"

I jerk my head up and down as much as I can in his tight grip. "I need to get my keys and wallet, so we can get out of here."

I swallow. "Okay, I'm coming with you."

He retrieves a gun from the back of his waistband, takes off the safety, and clasps my hand. "Stay behind me."

We head toward his office, where he finds his keys and wallet, and shoves them in the pockets of his sweatpants. He turns my way again and grasps the bottom of my shirt to lift it up and over my head. Goosebumps spread across my body, my exposed nipples turning into hard peaks. From a bag in the corner, Matteo snatches a T-shirt and holds it out for me to put my head and arms through. A hoodie is next, and I welcome the warmth and comforting scent I've gotten so used to.

He leans down to eye level and catches my gaze. "You okay? Ready to go?"

I lick my dry lips. "What about my things?"

"We can replace everything back home."

I hesitate but then open my mouth anyway. "My phone."

He tips his chin. "I secured the house. Get it quick."

There's no surprise on his face at the mention of the

phone, which I'm guessing means he knew about it all along. Since I want it, I run upstairs and grab it. I hate leaving everything else behind, but he's right, it's all easily replaceable.

Matteo's waiting for me by the bottom of the stairs and rushes me into the garage and into his SUV. I'm barely buckled when he backs out of the garage, spins around, and speeds down the driveway. He reaches over and puts his gun in the glove box and then takes out his phone.

He taps the screen a few times before holding it up to his ear. "Hey. We have a situation at the cottage." He listens for a moment before he says, "Yeah, she's okay." Another pause, then, "Yeah, call Luna to get access and report back." He ends the call and slides the phone into the dashboard dock.

I stare at his profile. "Who was that?"

"Ash."

We drive in silence for a while, our fingers intertwined, as Matteo rubs soothing circles over my hand. I'm still trying to process what happened, the gruesome scene on repeat in my head.

When his phone lights up with an incoming call, he nods toward it. "Could you answer that, please?"

"Uh, sure." I swipe the screen, jolting back as Ash and Zeno appear on it. I guess we're doing a video call.

The guys are wearing matching frowns, and Ash is the first to talk. "Hey, Gem. Are you okay?"

I nod. "I'm fine."

Zeno's frown deepens as he continues to stare at me.

Ash comes closer to the screen. "Is that blood on your face?"

"What?" My eyes widen, and my heartbeat picks up. I disentangle my hand from Matteo's and yank down the sun visor to stare at the mirror. Crap. I do have blood on my face. Just as I try to wipe at it, I see the smears on my hands too. I turn to Matteo and glare a hole in the side of his head. He could have at least told me I look like this.

"Did you see anyone, Gem?" Ash asks the question, and I focus back on the screen.

Sighing, I shake my head. "I didn't. I wouldn't have gone outside if I had. I peeked out the window first, and there wasn't anyone."

Remembering the small black bunny on the ground brings back the heaviness in my chest. New moisture builds in my eyes, and I swallow several times until the sensation subsides. I'd rather not cry in front of these guys.

Closing my eyes, I turn my head to the right.

The guys talk for another minute, before hanging up, and then it's just Matteo and me again.

He brushes my arm when he reaches behind my seat to get a blanket. "Here. Why don't you try and sleep?"

I don't think I'll be able to but nod anyway.

The next time I open my eyes, we're driving into the same underground garage as last month after the shooting at the bar. It feels like a lifetime ago. Matteo parks in his spot, and I yawn so much, my eyes tear up.

"Hey." Matteo caresses his thumb over my cheek, and I automatically lean into his touch. "Let's go upstairs and get you cleaned up."

"Okay." My voice is scratchy, my throat dry.

"Thirsty?"

"Yes."

He cradles my cheeks in both of his hands and presses his lips against mine, staying there for one, two, three seconds.

Then he gets out of the car and comes around to open my door for me. I take his hand and climb out, then together, we walk to the elevator that leads us straight into his penthouse. Once the security door closes behind us, I let out an unsteady breath.

You're okay. You're safe now.

At least until you have to go home.

Matteo pulls me down the long hallway toward his bedroom and into the large en suite. The last time I was here, I was in the makeshift patient bedroom. I don't have the energy to pay much attention to my surroundings; it's something I can explore at a later time.

In the bathroom, Matteo leads me to a chair that's against the wall and faces me. "Are you okay by yourself? I just want to grab a trash bag for your clothes and some water."

I nod, and he squeezes my hand before leaving. Taking advantage of being alone, I use the toilet, and Matteo walks back in just as I'm stepping out of my sneakers. He hands me a water bottle, and I guzzle it down all at once.

Matteo walks to the shower and turns it on. "Let's get you under the water."

My knees are still slightly wobbly, but I manage to take off my socks while still standing. I don't want to get any bloodstains on the chair; it's bad enough that I probably made a mess of the car.

My shirt comes off next, and I don't protest when Matteo helps me out of my pants, sliding down the underwear with them. I don't need to peer down to know my skin is sticky from where I held the sweet little bunny to my chest.

Matteo's eyes are on me, and I feel both the concern and the heat radiating off him. I'm not sure if I should be annoyed

183

or flattered that he's capable of even thinking about anything other than what happened, but then again, this might be nothing to him. Just another bloody day at the office, so to speak.

"The water should be good now." Matteo takes my hand and helps me into the shower. "I'll be right back, okay? I need to quickly call Zeno back."

"Okay." I step into the heat.

He closes the shower door but makes no move to leave. His eyes are on me, his gaze a tender caress that I know can turn into a wild inferno in an instant.

Focusing on him almost makes me forget what happened. Almost.

"Matteo?"

"Yes, baby?"

Baby.

Something to worry about later. Or never to think about again.

"There was something I didn't tell you guys. It's probably silly and not important, but—"

"What is it?" He steps closer and opens the glass door a fraction, so there's nothing between us.

My body is so aware of him that I notice my reluctance to cover up. I want him to see me. That realization stuns me until I remember what I wanted to tell him.

"Umm, the bunny . . ." I swallow hard.

"What about it?"

"Like I said, it's probably not important and a total coincidence, but that bunny resembled the one I used to have when I was younger. It even had the same bell around its neck."

He takes in the information, his brows furrowed. "What happened to your bunny?"

I open my mouth, then close it again. "He . . . he got killed during the home invasion too."

His eyes narrow, and his jaw tightens so much, I'm not sure how I don't hear any bones splintering under the pressure. "The one where your mom—"

"Yes." I don't want him to say it. I know it happened, and I can't change it, but hearing it and being reminded of it, always makes it worse.

He purses his lips and leans in. "Are you sure?"

I nod.

His gaze never leaves mine, and I'm not sure if that's comforting or a reason to freak out. If Matteo is concerned about something, it's probably not a good sign.

Without giving anything away, he taps his fingers on the glass door twice and closes it. "I'll be right back."

The water cascades down my body while I watch him throw my clothes in the trash bag and leave the bathroom. Once I'm alone, it's like something snaps inside me, and I rub my hands all over my body. I need to get the blood off me, need to be clean of all the evidence of what happened today.

Maybe then I can pretend it didn't happen. Or, maybe I'll wake up soon, and this whole day will all just be another crazy dream. Except, I wouldn't want to forget a single second of what happened with Matteo today.

We'll figure this out; we have to before I go crazy with worry, because lately, something else seems to be lurking just around the corner, something new to spin my life into yet another direction I wasn't prepared for.

If I could, I'd never go back to my old life again, that

much I know, but I'm also not sure if I'm fit for this kind of roller-coaster life either.

The shampoo and bodywash get a good workout, and I use both several times in a row. Once I finally feel like I'm somewhat clean, I turn off the water and reach for the two fluffy towels on the rack. One for my hair and one for my body.

When I'm all dry, I leave the towel on my head and slip into the big, fluffy robe that hangs on the back of the door. I almost disappear in it, which feels somehow comforting. Matteo is still nowhere in sight, so I stand here, not sure what to do. Eventually, I climb into the huge king-sized bed with my knees tucked up as close as possible and close my eyes.

The next time I blink them open, it's dark.

"Matteo?"

"Shhh, baby. I'm right here."

My mind spins immediately, everything that happened earlier coming back in a flash.

"Did Zeno find something?"

"Not really, which says a lot since he's one of the best trackers I know. Whoever did this knew what he was doing and didn't leave a trace."

"I see."

"We'll try our best to catch the bastard who did this. If anyone can find him, it's Zeno."

I close my eyes, wanting to forget what happened so badly.

"What . . . what happened to it?" The words are hard to get out, but for some reason, I need to know.

"Zeno buried it behind the house."

That reply surprises me enough that I turn around and face him. "He did?"

"Yeah. Zeno is a good guy."

At that, I snort. "Sure. If by good guy you mean serial killer."

Matteo chuckles. "I'll let him know you said that. You'll probably make his year with that comment."

I relish the sound then ask, "Is that good or bad?"

"Definitely good for him. I know he can be a little intense sometimes, but I promise, he really is a good guy. Saved my ass plenty of times over the years."

"I'll file that information away for later." I rub my forehead. "Will you tell him thanks, please? It was a very nice thing to do."

"Sure."

Matteo's hand comes up to my face, his fingers brushing over the side of it. It's a kind and even loving gesture, one that suddenly sets off sparks in my body. What happened earlier was absolutely terrible, but even knowing someone was out there doing it, I never felt unsafe . . . because Matteo was there.

At the first sign of danger, he got me out of there.

He put me first.

Something flutters in my stomach and spreads to my chest.

His thumb moves over my lips, and that feeling extends downward, turning into an aching need for this man.

I slide closer to him and press my lips to his. This isn't the first time I initiated contact, and a little thrill runs through my body when it still feels the same as before—bold, powerful, and arousing. My thoughts go back to the moment he made me come so hard in the shed, after teaching me how to shoot. Was that really less than twenty-four hours ago?

My body craves him. *I* crave him.

I nip at his lip, eliciting a deep rumble from his throat, right before he presses me on my back and covers my body with his.

He's hard, pushing against the material of my robe. It's not enough. I need more of him, more of us. I want to lose myself in him completely, letting him erase all the bad memories, until all that's left is this burning fire between us.

Reaching amidst our bodies, I brush my hand alongside his cock once, twice, before untying my robe. I shove it aside, opening myself up to him, offering myself to him on my terms. The towel on my head comes off next, my wet strands billowing out around me.

"Fuck, baby." Matteo rocks against me, devouring my lips.

The friction of the fabric against my naked skin has me trembling, and I gasp when he scrapes along my throat and lets out a low groan. An inferno ignites inside my body at the noise, and I dig my fingers into his back. His skin is warm under my touch, his muscles flexed and hard. Powerful. Sexy.

From the way he looks at me to the way he actually sees *me* and my needs.

Before him, I wasn't sure I'd ever feel wanted or cherished. I'd hoped, but that hope had vanished the second my papà introduced me to Luigi, my then future husband, who dismissed me after a once-over, treating me just like any other possession.

"I need you inside me." The words are out of my mouth

before I can truly think about them, but there isn't a trace of regret in my mind.

"Are you sure?" The question comes out as a half growl, as if he's having trouble controlling himself.

"Yes." If he's not inside me soon, I might implode from this incessant need that's been building under my skin ever since I first saw him.

Matteo slides off me, exposing my body to the cooler air. My nipples are hard and aching, especially as I remember how good his mouth felt on them earlier. No man had ever done that, and I didn't know it could feel like this. I didn't know any of this could.

Just another thing I had resigned myself to out of duty. Out of a promise to my mom to put family first. Taking this next step, letting Matteo take my virginity, will break more barriers than just one. It will ruin my worth to my father, and that knowledge feels oddly satisfying. Giving my body away is my personal act of defiance, one I will enjoy until I can't stand anymore.

Matteo walks around the room, and a lamp on the other side of the bed flicks on, bathing a naked Matteo in soft light. He's a true work of art with muscles lining his body from top to bottom, showcasing his strength in the most delicious way. The tattoos on his arms and upper body only emphasize his appeal. My gaze lands on his erection that's proudly leaning against his stomach. I swallow at the size of it. How on earth is that supposed to fit?

Matteo walks to the bottom of the bed and touches my ankles, caressing his thumbs over my skin. "Open your legs, baby. Show me that pretty pussy of yours."

Pushing away all my doubts, I close my eyes and let my

legs fall open. My stomach flutters at being so exposed to him, but the low string of Italian curses that leave his lips settle them a little.

His fingers brush over my left foot before he takes it in his hand. Then his lips are on my ankle, slowly inching up my leg. By the time he reaches my knee, I'm squirming, unable to stay still any longer. When he gets to my inner thigh, I'm shaking.

The tingles and pleasure multiply the moment his tongue hits my core. I'm panting at the way he licks all the way up to my clit, my back arching off the bed while he eats me out like a starving man.

He thrusts a finger inside me, then another and sucks on my clit, and I grow feverish.

"Oh my God."

Matteo goes back to licking, and I glance down at him. It's incredibly intimate, and my stomach tightens nervously, because holy shit. The way he's staring at me is so intense, the eye contact so deep and prolonged, I can't look away, even if I wanted to. I'm utterly mesmerized. His fingers keep pumping in and out of me several more times before he rubs my clit in firm circles.

"I can't wait to fuck this tight pussy. Be a good girl and come for me, passerotta. Now."

The combination of his dirty words and skillful ministrations is too much, and I fly over the edge without a safety net to catch me. My whole body quivers, and I moan my way through an earth-shattering orgasm.

Matteo softens his touch but doesn't stop until I'm done shaking. The grin he gives me is so full of satisfaction and hunger, I swallow loudly.

Even though I'm still high on my orgasm, I'm aware enough to feel the knot in my midsection over what comes next. "Mmm, so . . . are you sure you're going to fit? I've never . . . uh . . . this is my first time, so I just want to make sure."

The second the words are out of my mouth; I cover my face with my hands. Who says stuff like this? Especially while they're naked in bed with the man who just gave them one of the best orgasms they've ever had?

Matteo chuckles against my skin while he kisses and licks his way up my stomach, stopping at my breasts to lavish them both with attention too.

He makes it up to my throat and face and nudges my hands away with his nose. Not that I put up any kind of fight.

"If you keep saying stuff like that, my ego might not fit in the room anymore." The corners of his mouth lift, and he stares down at me. His pupils are dilated, and his hair is disheveled. It suits him. "But don't worry, I'll fit. And I promise I'll take good care of you."

His mouth descends on mine, and the first thing I taste is myself, which isn't as strange as I expected it to be. My thoughts are fleeting with the way Matteo's rubbing his thick cock along my pelvis.

He groans against my lips, and I open my legs wider in invitation. Despite my apprehension, I'm ready for him, more than ready. I want him to claim something that no one has claimed before and no one ever will again. It's mine to give and his to take.

Telling him I'm a virgin wasn't just for my sake but also because I wanted him to know he'll be my first.

Going on his knees, he leans over to the nightstand, and I stop him with a hand on his arm.

"Are you clean?" My voice is strong, and I'm grateful for that.

Matteo's surprise clearly shows on his face. "Yes. I've always worn condoms, and I just got tested when I got back to the city and haven't been with anyone since."

He already knows I have an implant, since he was there the day Ash went through my medical history.

Determined, I nod and pull him back so he's flush upon me.

Then I whisper against his lips, "I want to feel you without anything between us." When he doesn't respond, I quickly add, "Only if that's something you want too, of course."

He quiets me with a kiss and lines up against my core.

CHAPTER 14
MATTEO

The need to thrust into her hard is almost impossible to ignore, but I promised her I'd take good care of her, and I meant it.

So I do the next best thing and kiss her the way I want to fuck her, with a desperation that's threatening to tear me to shreds from the inside out.

With my cock lined up at her entrance, I move forward and feel a slight resistance. My kiss gets more out of control, but Gemma seems to like that. Despite the fact that she can't hide the slight body tremor, her hands are fisting my hair, her fingers clawing at my neck in a frantic rhythm.

With her lower lip between my teeth, I draw back and let it pop free. Then I kiss my way along her jaw and over to her ear. She moans when I lick down her throat, her upper body arching. I push in a couple inches, past the barrier, the head of my cock now engulfed in her tight heat.

Fuck, that feels good.

She whimpers, and I palm one of her perfect tits, rolling her hard nipple between my fingertips.

"Matteo." Her eyebrows draw together, and her grip on my neck tightens.

I shift back but don't get far since she digs her heels into my ass.

Lowering myself, I cage her in with my elbows and smooth out her frown with my thumb.

I'm lost in her gaze while she rocks her pelvis. The movements are shallow since I'm still on top of her, but I have to bite my lip to keep from groaning. My cock slips in a fraction more each time as she stretches around me. The pressure is so intense, I nearly come.

"Kiss me." Her words are a hot whisper against my skin, and I can't help but grind against her.

Her mouth is ready for me, and I take over. I love how she's this mix of yielding and demanding, always giving as good as she gets. It gets me harder than anything else.

The tension eases in her body, and I use that chance to slip farther inside, so much easier now than before. Her inner walls contract around my cock, and she lets out a loud moan.

"Keep going."

With her approval, I thrust until I'm fully seated, and she bites my lip to the point where I taste blood.

"You're so fucking tight." I lean my forehead against hers, because fuck, if I don't get a grip on my control, this will be over in an embarrassingly short amount of time. It's so much more intense without a condom. For a few moments, I stay still and we just share the same air. "You okay?"

"Yeah, I think I'm good." As if to make a point, she moves her pelvis against mine.

I pull out before driving back in. It gets easier with each

thrust, and I'm soon breathing hard whilst my spine tingles with the orgasm that is building up quickly.

Putting my weight on one arm, I reach between us to rub her clit. My arm shakes, and it takes every ounce of my concentration to focus on her face, to see what feels good for her. The second I increase the pressure, her lips fall open, and she moans. Bingo. Thankfully, it doesn't take long until she tenses around me because I've reached the point of no return. I need to come right fucking now.

"Fuck." She's still clenching around me, and I continue to pump into her, my balls throbbing and tightening from within. The intense sensation reaches my cock, and I explode, feeling every pulse and surge as I empty myself inside her.

Our ragged breaths fill the space between us while my brain is trying to process what just happened.

I study her serene expression, and the need to kiss her consumes me. Our lips meet, and I know immediately this kiss is different. It's softer and laced with something else I can't pinpoint. When I draw back, I kiss her nose and study her face once more.

"Hey."

She gives me a lazy smile and nods. "Hey, yourself."

"You okay?"

She hums in response.

Then my cock twitches, and her eyes widen. Although I'd love nothing more than to go for round two, especially since I now know it feels like absolute heaven, she needs some time to recover. She's probably going to be sore enough tomorrow.

So I do the responsible thing and pull out of her. She winces at the movement but gives me a reassuring smile.

"I'll be right back." I walk to the bathroom and glance back as I reach the doorway, satisfied to find her gaze glued to my ass.

With a wink, I disappear into the bathroom and close the door. Then I shake my head at myself. Since when do I wink?

I wet one of the washcloths to wipe my blood-smeared dick off before using the toilet. Then I make my way to the bathtub to turn on the water. After pouring a large heap of the orange liquid my sister gave me into the running water, I go back to Gemma.

My plan was to carry her from the bed directly to the bath. Instead, I'm faced with her rushing around the bed.

My eyebrows draw together. "What are you doing?"

She freezes at my words, and I take in the scene I just walked in on. Her back and that shapely round ass of hers facing me, and I'm definitely not complaining about the view. What doesn't sit right with me though, is the fact that she's clutching the bedsheets in her arms.

Her shoulders slump a little, but she makes no attempt to face me. "I wanted to clean up the mess before you got back."

"Mess?"

"Yes." Still holding the sheets in front of her, she turns around and stares anywhere but at me. "You know, there's all of the . . . the stuff on it."

Raising one eyebrow, I stare at her, waiting for her to say more, but she doesn't. "You mean the cum and your blood?"

She sighs and stares at the bundle in her arms. "Yes."

"Does it bother you?"

This time, her head whips up. "Me? I thought it would bother *you*."

I take slow steps toward her, a burst of irritation leading me there. "Did I give you any indication it would bother me?"

Gemma shakes her head, and I'm right in front of her.

My muscles are tense, and I wait for her to look at me. "Don't assume, passerotta. I can go down on my knees right now and lick your cunt clean to prove my point."

"Wh-wh-what?"

"I don't do things I don't like. *You* shouldn't waste your energy on it either."

Her cheeks flush pink. So fucking beautiful.

The sheets fall to the floor when she drops them to point at me. My little bird has a fire burning inside her. Maybe it's time for her to rule the flames rather than letting them consume her.

"Don't be a jerk, Matteo. Some people don't have a choice." She pokes my chest harder with every word, and I snatch her hand.

With my other hand, I grab her chin, clasping it tightly until I'm sure I have her full attention. "Some people don't, but most do. Life is riddled with choices, a careful assemblage that can often fall apart at the barest of touches. You might have been led down the wrong path, but you still chose to continue walking it. Don't take the easy way out because the right path isn't simple or pretty."

Her mouth falls open before it closes again. I know I hit a nerve, and that this is about more than what just happened, but we both know what I said was the truth. And for some reason, I want to push her. I want her to stand up for herself, to rebel against the bonds she let her father put on her.

Since she's probably going over the multitude of options of how to kill me in my sleep, I bend down to hold on to her thighs and throw her over my shoulder.

Gemma squeaks before she hits my back. "What are you doing? Let me down."

My hand meets the soft flesh of her ass in a satisfying slap.

She stops her assault for only a second before she continues. "Bastardo."

I turn my head to the side and bite her hip.

That keeps her quiet all the way to the bathroom where I let her down in front of the bathtub.

She gazes at the water that's almost overflowing with hundreds of bubbles. "You got this ready for me?"

"Yes. And now I'll get us something to drink." I leave her standing there with a dumbfounded expression and go back to the bedroom to get some sweats and my phone, before making my way into the kitchen.

I missed a message and a phone call.

The message is from an unknown number, saying two words: **Front desk.**

My muscles tense, and I stare at the words. Then I pull up the front desk contact on my phone and swipe the dial button.

"Signor Santarossa, I was just about to call you again. A courier dropped off an envelope for you."

"I'll be right down, Stefano. Thank you."

"No problem, signore."

I hang up and walk back to the bedroom to get a T-shirt. Once it's on, I peek into the bathroom to make sure Gemma is okay. Her whole body is submerged in the bubbles, with only her head above the water. With her eyes closed and her head leaning back against the bathtub edge, the curve of her jaw and throat is exposed in the most sensual way. A true masterpiece.

As if she can sense me, her eyes open, her gaze instantly connecting with mine where I lean against the doorframe.

I get sucked into this moment until my phone vibrates in my pocket.

Damn it. It's so easy to forget my surroundings when she's around.

I press off the doorframe and clear my throat. "I'm going to the front desk to pick something up. I'll be right back."

She nods, the previous fight in her eyes almost gone. "Okay."

With that, I leave, not sure what else to say after our altercation, or whatever you want to call it.

She needs to understand her world doesn't have to be the way it is, that it's in her power to change it. If I need to push so she can realize that, then so be it.

A few minutes later, I reenter my penthouse with the courier envelope in my hand. Ever since Stefano gave it to me, it's been like a heavy weight between my fingers. Despite the security being top-notch in this building, no system is ever one-hundred-percent impenetrable. Hackers constantly hone their skills, my sister being a prime example of that. For that reason alone, I would never open something in the elevator that could potentially be incriminating, no matter how badly I want to.

I make it to my office where I rip open the envelope, dumping the contents on my desk. The second my gaze lands on the first picture, my blood boils.

Pictures of Gemma and me, most of them upstate at the cabin. Gemma leaning over the rail of the deck while I ate her out from behind. The next one is Gemma staring up at me with my cock in her hand. The two of us taking a walk together on the property, with Gemma pointing at something in the sky while I continue to stare at her.

The next one has my stomach churning. Gemma on the front porch with the bloody bunny clutched to her chest.

My anger turns to rage, and I grab the nearest item from the desk and fling it against the wall. It explodes into hundreds of small glass pieces on impact, the light shining through the window reflecting in every piece like a rainbow exploded. Shit. This will be a pain to clean up.

But none of that matters right now. What does is that someone had the guts to not only follow me and Gemma around, but to also take photos of us and to send them to me. Who'd be so callous, who'd have the balls to do something like this? It must be someone with a death wish because whoever's behind this won't live for much longer.

I stare at the pictures again, picking them up one by one, needing a closer inspection, no matter how blood-tainted my vision is from the rage I'm feeling. The first image is the one of us on the deck, and it's easy to tell that it was taken mid-orgasm. Gemma's eyes are closed, her mouth parted, and her hands clutching on to the rail like she's seconds away from breaking it. She's absolutely magnificent, and the fact that someone intruded on this very private and intimate moment has me seeing red.

I flip to the next one, where our roles are reversed, and notice something I missed before. I was so focused on Gemma, I didn't see my eyes are crossed out. Not just crossed out, but someone—the motherfucker behind all of this—seriously X-ed out my eyes with something sharp, leaving the photo paper half cut.

With the push of a button, the computer screen comes to life, and I log in with my fingerprint. While it starts the security program, I'm lost in the other pictures, confirming what I already knew. My eyes are crossed out in every single picture, but never Gemma's. When I get to the last picture, the one of Gemma and me on the deck, there's a circle drawn around her whole body with the words *She's mine* written right next to it.

Fucking hell.

I pull up the security camera feed for the building—my sister's hacking skills can be incredibly useful at times—and rewind it. I spot the delivery truck parking at the curb and pause it, then hit play again and watch the delivery guy in a brown uniform bringing in several boxes and envelopes. I pause and hit play. Both the truck and the guy appear to be a regular courier service. Damn it.

Grabbing my phone, I dial Zeno.

He picks up after a few rings. "Hey, boss."

"Seems like our situation just got a lot bigger." I relay the details to him before hanging up and calling my sister.

"What's up?" Luna's cheery voice comes through the speaker, loud pop music blaring in the background.

"Luna." I put as much annoyance in my voice as I can muster, and it works. The music shuts off.

"God, you're such a party pooper, I swear. Mom definitely dropped you on your head a few times as a baby."

"Luna," I say her name again, but this time, there's a bite to it. Despite being such a ray of sunshine, she's been

201

working in the business long enough to know when it's serious.

"What happened?"

She's quiet as I repeat the events once more, only to huff out a breath once I'm done and to mutter, "Son of a bitch."

"Zeno's on his way to you." I pause and inhale deeply. Then I lower my voice. "I want you to watch every bit of footage you can find to figure out who's doing this, are we clear? Find me this motherfucker, so I can make sure he's never going to see another day again. No one fucks with what's mine."

"Understood." She's in business mode, already clicking away on the keyboard in the background. "You can count on me."

"I know I can. Let's make him pay for what he did to Gemma."

"Oh, he—"

"What's going on? Who's going to pay for what?" The female voice comes from behind me.

I close my eyes and slowly turn around.

Fuck.

Gemma has one towel wrapped around her torso and one around her head, her brows tightly drawn together.

As expected, she doesn't just stand by idly to wait for an answer from me. She takes a step into the room, then another, before I finally snap back into action and hold my hand out in front of me, indicating for her to stop.

Surprisingly, she does. But now, her gaze roams around the room, and I know exactly what she sees. The broken glass pieces all over the floor and a bunch of photos on the table. I want to rush and hide them all so she can't see them, but, at the same time, I also know she can take it. She isn't the incapable, flowery girl her father has made her out to be. The one who isn't good for anything but being married off for his benefit. She couldn't actually be farther away from that type of woman.

"Matteo." Her throat works hard and she swallows, trying to peek around me to catch a glimpse of the photos.

"I've got it handled, passerotta."

She slides her gaze to me, her eyes full of questions as she tugs on her bottom lip with her teeth. But I can't give her any answers, and frankly, I don't want to.

"Are those photos?"

I nod.

"Of me?"

Another nod.

"And of us?"

One more nod.

She licks her lips and bobs her head several times, like this is exactly what she expected me to say, but she's still trying to come to grips with the new information.

A noise coming from the desk tugs at my concentration, and I whip my head around. The phone. Damn it. Luna's still on the line, listening in on us this whole time.

"Seriously?" I reach for the phone.

My sister clicks her tongue. "It's not my fault."

Her tone is nonchalant, and I can totally picture her with her little pout and shoulder shrug.

"Hey, Luna." Gemma uses this opportunity to come closer.

"Hey, Gem." Luna's voice is noticeably warmer while she talks to her new friend. "Don't worry about anything, you hear me? I'm going to figure out this whole mess. You just stay with my brother, so you're safe."

Gemma's eyelashes flutter, and she blinks at me, mere inches separating us now.

Her "okay" is no more than a whisper, and it barely registers that she says goodbye a few seconds later before Luna hangs up.

Seeing her slumped shoulders and her blank features tugs at something in my chest. It urges me to say something that'll make her smile, do something that'll take her mind off this newest obstacle in her life.

I'm incapable of resisting her, the pull I feel toward her too strong, just like the ocean is powerless to withstand the moon's pull.

Having her in my life seems to come with a bunch of complications, adding even more to my plate, but whenever I look at her, the only thing that matters to me is keeping her safe.

"I want to see them." The words come out strong and sure.

I don't answer her. Instead, I study her then step aside.

Her choice, not mine.

Her eyes widen, like she actually didn't expect me to let her have this, and that knowledge uncurls the anger that's continuously been building toward her father. That man clearly doesn't believe his daughter is capable of much else than he wishes her to be, and he's been keeping that role for her very narrow and beyond powerless.

The more she relies on him, the less likely it is she'll step out of line.

Gemma's towel brushes against my arm as she walks to

the desk. She's motionless for several moments, just taking in the sight in front of her. Then she picks up one picture after the other. Her breath hitches a few times—especially when she gets to the one on the deck, where she's mid-orgasm and the words *She's mine* are scrawled over her body. Her chest rises faster than before, but other than that, she shows no emotion. No reaction.

That is until there's only one photo left. It's turned over, so she hasn't seen it yet.

I know which one it is though, and I can't help but put my outspread fingers over it. "Maybe you should skip this one."

She blinks but shakes her head. "Let me see. I have to."

I don't know why she feels the need to torture herself with these, but I take my hand away.

Her throat bobs, and she picks up the last one to stare at it for a very long time. It's the one with the bunny. The asshole wrote *Oops* on it next to her crumbling body.

She moves the pictures around in her hands, shuffling them into a neat pile of fucked-up grotesqueness.

After placing the stack on the desk, she faces me with her chin tilted up. At first glance, she appears hardened and tough, but I still see the hint of softness in her eyes. Although she grew up in this world, she hasn't seen much of it, always having been kept away from the business dealings. Sheltered from the violence.

"I obviously know there are bad people out there, but I've never wanted anyone to die until now. I don't know why he's doing this, but the thought that he finds pleasure in doing these kinds of things to others makes me sick."

Lifting my hand to her chin, I cup her jaw gently

between my fingers. "We'll get this bastardo. He will not get away with this."

Her tongue darts out to lick her lips, and she gazes up at me. "Promise?"

I nod before I even think about her question. "Promise, passerotta. No one messes with what's mine and gets away with it still breathing."

There's a gleam in her eyes, like she's trying to conceal she actually enjoyed what I said as if she's not supposed to like that I'm going to kill the person behind all of this.

Because they will pay with their life.

I touch the curve of her bare shoulder, following the slope down her arm. Goosebumps follow my touch, and I revel in the knowledge that she reacts like this to me. When I make my way back up her arm and trail along her collarbone, Gemma barely suppresses a shiver.

My fingers wander down, the tips grazing over the swell of her breasts just as my phone rings.

I want to ignore it. I'm going to ignore it.

But then Gemma gasps, and I follow her gaze to the phone screen. It's her dad. Shit.

The ringing feels suddenly deafening, and I stab the green accept button.

"Lorenzo." My voice is sharp, my tongue like a whip as I enunciate each syllable.

"Matteo, I hear you're back in the city." He sounds almost chipper.

"Yes." Irritation crawls at my insides as a result of him knowing about our whereabouts.

"Great, great." He pauses. "Listen, I need Gemma back."

"No." The word shoots out of my mouth like a bullet.

Gemma's sharp inhale has my gaze snapping to her wide eyes.

I'm not sure what Lorenzo was expecting, but it seems like it was a different response than the one I gave him, since it's easy to hear his quiet curses through the line.

After several more seconds, he chuckles awkwardly and says, "Oh no, I think you misunderstood."

I once overheard a conversation where a group of men spoke highly of Lorenzo Fiore, but I find him utterly lacking. He might bring in good money from the underground gambling, but he's a complete asshole, only caring about his bank account and nothing else. That's the only reason he wants his daughter back, but I won't let him have her.

I raise a brow. "Did I?"

"Si, si. I remember our agreement of Gemma staying with you until Alessandra is back, but something came up with the family business, so I need to talk to her . . . in person."

"We can meet at one of my family's establishments. I'll let you know the details."

I'm about to hang up when he says, "Please tell her to dress for the occasion, it's going to be a surprise for her."

Gemma hears his words and immediately turns away from me, shielding her face in the process.

Without another word, I push the end call button and grab Gemma's wrist. "What's wrong?"

She shakes her head. "Nothing."

I pull on her arm, spinning her around.

Her hand flies to her towel, clutching it at the front to keep it together.

I have the urge to rip it off her, to bare her to me in more ways than one, but I don't.

Right now, I just want her to open up to me, to tell me what made her want to flee from me. Especially after she shocked the hell out of me with her reaction regarding the photos. The only thing that happened between then and now is the phone call with her father.

"What did he say that got you so upset?"

All emotion, all life is gone from her eyes as she utters her next words. "The last time he said he had a surprise for me, he told me I'd marry Luigi, and we both know how that ended."

CHAPTER 15
GEMMA

T toss and turn all night. The prospect of my father marrying me off again has driven my anxiety through the roof, and my mind is incapable of calming down enough to sleep. But Matteo doesn't complain. He actually doesn't utter a single word.

Instead, he wordlessly pulls me against his body and holds me so tightly, I almost can't breathe. Somehow, it does the trick, and I finally fall into a deep slumber until the sun is high, and the bright daylight shines through the bedroom window.

The space beside me is empty, probably has been for a while. After sharing a bed with him for almost a month now, I know one thing: Matteo is an early riser, and a grumpy one at that. The few times I managed to drag myself out of bed early because I couldn't sleep anymore, or needed something from the kitchen, he pretty much glared at me from over the rim of his coffee cup. Which suits me just fine, since I don't even want to be awake at that ungodly hour.

I stretch in all possible directions, enjoying the way the

tension leaves my body and how it softens my muscles. Then I throw back the blanket, cursing the much cooler temperatures outside my fluffy heaven, and swing my legs over the edge, my feet landing on the soft rug.

Following a quick bathroom break to pee and brush my teeth, I trudge into the kitchen.

What awaits me there stops me mid-step.

Matteo's behind the kitchen island, a spatula in one hand and a pan in the other. His naked upper body is on full display, his *glistening* skin fully capturing my attention. His tattoos are breathtaking, and every time I see them, I notice something new that must have escaped me every other time.

The tribal art on his pec and shoulder is stunning, and the wings tattoo that wraps around his other shoulder and bicep is my favorite, I think, but there is also something that keeps drawing me to the large dragon eye right below the wings. Maybe because it feels like it's always staring at me, like nothing can take its focus off me.

Is it wrong to like that? Is it wrong to want to be this man's focal point?

Or maybe my anxiety is screwing with my brain, and my fear over what today's meeting with my dad will bring is taking over. Or it could also be the fact that I've never felt as free as I have been with Matteo.

At the same time, if I'm honest with myself, that feeling sprouted the second he touched me in that dim hotel room on my wedding day. The second I *let* him touch me on my wedding day, even though he wasn't my new husband. Far from it.

Whatever he unlocked from deep within me doesn't feel as foreign as it maybe should. That might be the scariest part of all of this. While it feels a little strange, it also feels familiar, like it was a part of me this whole time and I just wasn't aware of it. I just needed the right person to help me find it.

"Are you hungry?" His gaze hikes up slowly. He stares down at my legs then my torso, and I'm highly aware of the tiny pajamas I'm wearing. If you can even call the silky spaghetti-strap top and boy shorts pajamas.

This is the first time I'm wearing this little while we're not in bed or ripping our clothes off elsewhere.

His gaze finally reaches my face, and the corners of my mouth lift the tiniest amount.

"Yes, please. I'm starving." I have to focus on putting one foot in front of the other, but somehow, I manage to make my way over to him. I pause on the other side of the island, peeking at the eggs and vegetables he's cooking in the two pans. "It smells delicious."

"Thanks." He shifts his attention back to the food, which allows me to watch him some more.

Despite having no issue getting in my face, and having a fairly large presence and frame, he's also rather composed and reserved. He doesn't talk because he likes the sound of his voice or because he thinks everyone should constantly listen to him like my father does. He's quiet, only talking when he really has to, like he knows every single one of his words matter.

I grab one of the barstools opposite him and watch him while he works. "Where did you learn how to cook?"

"My mom."

I remember our conversations about her and how she got sick during his teenage years. "She taught you how to cook when you were younger?"

211

He nods. "She did. She said it was important that Luna and I knew how to be self-sufficient."

The opposite of me. Everything was done for me, especially after my mom died, no matter how often I asked my dad if I could learn how to cook. The only thing he taught me was how to manage the kitchen staff since that would be one of my responsibilities as a wife. He said he didn't want me to get my hands dirty, but I assumed he was trying to make things easier for me. Now I see that it was just another way of controlling me, of keeping me dependent on him.

Matteo turns off the pan with the vegetables and tosses them into the egg mixture, his lips curving in a smile. "Honestly, I think she just didn't want us to be spoiled. She was a very hands-on woman and didn't like to have too many people help around the house."

"I wish I could have met her." The words slip out of my mouth without thought, but they're true.

Matteo sprinkles cheese over the scrambled eggs and vegetables before raising his gaze to meet mine. "She would have liked you."

His words settle in my chest, depressing yet soothing, as he pushes one of the plates over to me and hands me a fork.

Since I'm practically salivating, I take a big bite. The food hits my tongue, and while it's still way too hot, the flavors explode in my mouth. "Oh my gosh, this is so good."

"Thank you."

A low chuckle comes from his direction, but I'm too busy eating. Now that I'm shoveling food in my mouth, I actually can't remember the last time I ate. So much has happened so fast that I've been losing track of time. Everything meshes together into one big block of time with Matteo. That's how

I'll remember it when I'm not with him anymore. An escape from real life, my own personal bubble of freedom and peace.

The notion is sobering, the looming possibility of not being with him anymore suddenly unpleasant. Or maybe it's not so sudden? Didn't I just acknowledge that he unlocked something inside me the very first time we met? The moment where he wiped the blood from my skin and sucked it off his finger. Who does something like that? And who likes a guy who does it?

"You're thinking way too hard again." He points at my plate with his fork, at the food I abandoned mid-chew, because my brain got too loud. "Eat."

"Sorry."

He pokes his fork into the last bite of eggs and puts it into his mouth, his lips rolling over each other like they don't want to miss a single morsel of flavor. Then he nudges the plate away and leans forward with his elbows on the dark-gray island. "Are you worried about the meeting with your dad?"

I chew and swallow before answering, "I'm trying not to be, but it's pretty much impossible. You'd understand if you were around him for a while."

"How so?"

I shrug. "He likes to spring things on people, often without any kind of warning. I think he likes that it throws people off, which often works to his advantage."

"Mmmm." His eyebrows crease deeply, but he doesn't share his thoughts.

"He wasn't always like this. Nothing was the same after my mom died." I think back on all the years with my dad and how things changed. I'm not even sure why exactly, just that they did. It's not like he ever talked to me about her or what was going on with him.

I swallow. "I'm not saying he was an angel before either, but I'd like to think the dad from back then wouldn't have sold his daughter off for his own gain. His only daughter, his only child."

Matteo watches me, his silence oddly comforting. It brings back that piece of strength, of determination I've discovered since I've been with him.

A sigh escapes me as that familiar numbness comes back, which is exactly what I need to face my dad. "When are we meeting with him?"

Matteo purses his lips. "Five o'clock."

My mouth falls open. "Today?"

"Yes."

Damn it. I was hoping I'd have a few more days before I had to face him.

My gaze flickers to the clock on the wall. Since I slept in, it's already nearing noon. "What time do we need to leave?"

"Half an hour before then."

"Sounds good." I eat my last bite and stand, taking both of our plates and putting them in the dishwasher. When I walk to the sink to take care of the pans, he stops me with a hand on my arm.

"I've got it."

"I don't mind."

"Neither do I."

"Okay, thank you."

"No problem."

I turn away from him, but his hand slides down to grab my wrist, hauling me back to him. My body smacks against his, my hard nipples aching at the contact, longing for more.

He keeps hold of my wrist with one hand and shoves the other into my hair, half of his palm cradling my cheek. It's possessive yet gentle, and I gaze up into his dark-brown eyes.

"I don't want you to worry about anything today. I won't let anything happen to you, and you *will* be coming back home with me."

"Why?" The question is out of my mouth before I can think it through. Do I even want to know the answer?

He told me the whole thing with Ally was a sham to lure out Nikolai—one that will most likely not go down well with either my father or my uncle—and that he doesn't want her. He never said he wants me, at least not long term.

Yes, we've been playing house, and I've enjoyed a level of freedom and comfort I never had before, but I don't think the same can be said for him. First, he had to take care of me and my injury, and then I brought trouble to his front door, quite literally in the form of a dead bunny. Now he's getting pictures sent to his home with his eyes crossed out.

Instead of wanting to protect me, to promise me the safety and freedom I long for so dearly, he should be eager to drop me back off at my father's house.

Yet he isn't.

But why?

He still hasn't said a single word, his gaze never leaving mine, but seeming to have turned inward. His thumb glides over my cheek, the contact barely noticeable. But I catch it, just like everything else about him.

I don't do things I don't like. You shouldn't waste your energy on it either.

His words from before rush to the forefront of my mind. While he flung them at me in a heated moment, nothing he said was untrue.

As if he can read my thoughts, he comes closer, and in a voice that has an awfully wistful tone to it, he says, "Because I want to be there when the sheltered princess explodes into the fiery queen she's meant to be."

My heart stutters before picking up its pace. Unable to help myself, I lean forward, wanting a taste of him, needing it even. He's made me hungry for a lot of things, things I assumed I might never have, but right now, I'm only hungry for one thing. Him. He's the one closing the gap as he tilts my head the way he wants it and crashes his lips on mine.

His tongue delves into my mouth, his hand sliding from my wrist and up my arm, leaving a trail of goosebumps behind.

With that one touch, that one caress, that one kiss, I'm putty in his hands once more. Or rather, I turn into someone who's foreign even to me. This sexual side of me is new, and it's tenacious. Sometimes I'm hesitant, not wanting to make any mistakes and embarrass myself, yet at the same time, I'm starving for him, eager to explore and learn, to enjoy this kind of pleasure I was deprived of for so long.

Matteo moves away from my mouth and kisses along my jaw. "I cannot tell you how badly I want to lay you out on the kitchen island and have you as my dessert, but unfortunately we don't have time for that."

My pussy throbs at his words, at the promise of pleasure, while my mouth opens to tell him we have plenty of time. But the doorbell rings before I can get a single word out.

Matteo ignores it and presses me against the cool material

216

of the cabinets, his hard cock rocking against my pelvis and my clit. The moan that comes from between my lips is more of a whimper. It's needy and greedy, and I want nothing more than to fall into this man's arms for the next hour or two and explore this sexual connection that's got me all worked up.

The doorbell rings again, at the same time Matteo's phone goes off on the counter behind us. He pulls back and closes his eyes. I listen to his deep breaths, each one a little slower and longer than the previous one. When he opens his eyes, the heat in them is gone. The calculated man I've come to know so well is back.

His phone goes off once more, but this time, he answers. I barely pay attention to the conversation but walk with him while he makes his way to the elevator.

"Zeno is waiting for me to let him in."

"Oh." I grimace. "I better go then. He doesn't strike me as the kind of guy who likes to wait."

"I don't give a fuck. He's going to have to wait until you get your half-naked ass behind closed doors." To make a point, he grabs a handful of my flesh and squeezes. "It's mine to see, not his. Now go."

He sends me off with a slap on my butt, the implication that my body is only his to see still circling around my mind long after I close the bedroom door firmly behind me.

I curl up on the couch and get lost in my book, reluctantly putting it away a few hours later since it's time to get ready.

Once the shower is on in the bathroom, I slip out of my pajamas and step under the hot spray. Gosh, I love this shower. The water pressure is just right, the temperature is perfect, and I want to stay in here for hours. I enjoy the heat raining down on me for some time, then wash and condition my hair. Next is the new oversized loofah that Matteo—or probably Luna—got me, which almost feels too good on my skin. Together with the bodywash, it forms a layer of bubbles all over me, and I love how my skin feels all soft and smooth.

I want to be there when the sheltered princess explodes into the fiery queen she's meant to be.

Matteo's words pop into my head just as I glide the loofah between my thighs. That man says things to me no one else ever has. Things I need to hear. And he believes in the words, in me, which is as mind-boggling as it is exhilarating.

It's also a complete turn-on.

My clit tingles while I brush the webbed material over it, so I do it again. Back and forth, back and forth.

Once it doesn't offer the pressure I need anymore, I abandon the loofah and use my fingers instead. I push two deep inside me, caressing my inner walls, before drawing out enough liquid to spread around my clit and lips. Holy hell, that feels good.

I go back to my clit with my fingertips, making tight circles while also tilting up my pelvis to increase the pressure. Oh my God, yes. I smooth my other hand over my stomach to my breasts, squeezing one, then the other. The first moan escapes me when I pinch my nipple, the sensation shooting like lightning through my body and straight to my clit. My insides tighten, and I know I'm close. While I masturbated before I met Matteo, it's never felt as intense or as satisfying as it has since I met him. This intense sexual desire yet another thing that's awoken at his hands, slowly developing with each passing day.

Suddenly, something makes a noise, and my head whips around.

Not something, but someone.

Matteo stares straight at me from a few feet away, an inferno in his eyes as he yanks down his shorts and boxers in one go, kicking them to the side once they hit the floor.

"Show me how you touch yourself whenever you think about me, passerotta."

His long, hard cock bobs against his stomach, and he grabs it, squeezing the head once before stroking it all the way down. "Show me how you cream yourself for me."

A rush of white-hot desire burns in the pit of my stomach, his challenging look only stoking the flames.

I watch him, the rhythmic motion of his strokes incredibly erotic. And then my fingers move again. It's slower than before, less sure, because I've never done anything like this.

I don't want to make a fool of myself, but then he groans and says, "Yes, baby, just like that," and my movements become frantic and my breaths choppy.

My orgasm crashes into me like a wave, swallowing me whole, and my eyes close on instinct, unable to hold Matteo's intense gaze any longer.

Without warning, the shower door opens behind me with a squeak and Matteo slips inside. "Turn around. Now."

I'm so stunned at his command that I simply obey, turning my back toward him.

"Lean against the wall."

Again, I do as he asks, not bothered by his demands since they're such a turn-on.

In all the time we've been together, he has never failed me in any way. The fact that he always makes me feel good, even when I'm unsure about a certain position, helps too.

The slap on my ass comes as a surprise. The area stings for a moment before he glides his smooth palm over it, still stroking himself.

"Oh fuck, I'm almost there, baby. I'm going to come all over you. I want to watch my cum drip off that perfect ass of yours."

I suppress a shiver at his words. There's this little voice in the back of my head—one that sounds awfully close like my dad's—mumbling, *Shouldn't you feel disgusted by him talking to you like this? It's filthy.* But then I feel my body respond to every one of Matteo's dirty commands, lighting me up from the inside, and the appalled voice vanishes. It's like a secret language I didn't know I could understand, but now that I do, I can't stop thinking about it and want more.

Matteo's breathing picks up, as does the tempo of his strokes. Unable to help myself, I peek at him over my shoulder, and my breath stalls in my throat. His face is laced with pleasure, the vein on his neck thick and pulsing wildly as he pumps his cock almost violently.

The roar he lets out when he comes echoes around us, adding even more of a thrill to this encounter. Thick spurts of cum shoot out of his mushroom head, all of them hitting my ass. Matteo strokes himself one more time, all the way to the tip, where he holds his cock and stares at his handiwork.

Then he lets go of himself and smears his cum all over my lower back and ass. His other hand joins in, and soon, he's rubbing and massaging my ass cheeks, pulling them apart. I whimper, not in pain, but because this is unchartered territory for me, and my brain doesn't know what to do with half of the things it's being exposed to.

"Shhh, baby. I'm just looking." As if to make up for it, he moves one of his hands between my legs from behind, running his fingers through my cum this time, before he cups my pussy. "Did you enjoy fucking yourself, passerotta?"

My breath hitches at his touch, the oversensitivity of my clit fighting with my renewed arousal, and heat spreads up my neck and into my cheeks at his question. But I manage to whisper, "Yes."

"Such a good girl."

Those two words have me pushing back against him.

His fingers brush through my folds, and I close my eyes.

"I can't wait to fuck you tonight." With that, he switches the angle of the showerhead, washing off the evidence of our impromptu shower masturbation session.

I turn around to face him and go up on my toes. "I can't wait either."

After giving him a quick kiss, I once again pick up the loofah and give my body another quick washing. Matteo grabs his shampoo and cleans up as well, his gaze never leaving me.

I know I should get out and get ready, but I like being with him here. The warm water also feels too good on my skin. Once he's done, he finally convinces me to get out too, making me promise to get ready while he catches up on some business, which I do.

He walks in five minutes before we have to leave, just as I slip into my black heels and finish putting on my hoop earrings. A quick glance in the mirror confirms what I already know: I'm made up perfectly. My makeup is flawless—

elegant with a touch of seductiveness—and my hair falls around my shoulders in soft waves. Exactly the way my father has groomed me to look, with the help of stylists as well as makeup and hair artists.

"You are stunning." Matteo walks toward me, perfectly complementing my black sheath dress with his charcoal suit and white shirt underneath. He takes my hand and draws it up to his mouth, pressing a lingering kiss to my skin.

My heart races behind my rib cage, just like every other time this man is near me.

"Turn around, passerotta."

I comply with his gentle demand, unsure of the reason.

"Lift your hair for me."

I swallow but do as he says, right as cold metal touches my collarbone, and my chest expands at the contact.

Matteo's hands leave my skin, and I turn toward the mirror, grasping the small pendant between my fingers. My throat tightens as I inspect it and realize what it is: a small bird in a cage.

It takes several long breaths, and every ounce of self-control I can muster, to keep the tears at bay. This damn man. Why would he give me something like this?

Raising my eyes, I meet his gaze in the mirror. "Thank you, it's beautiful."

He studies me, putting his hands into his pockets. "It opens."

I tilt my head in confusion. "What opens?"

"The cage. You can open the cage and let the bird out, set it free."

"Oh."

"Sometimes we need a little help to be free from the bonds that hold us hostage."

My eyes prick, the swell of emotion in my chest expanding so rapidly, I'm not sure how to contain it.

"Let's go." Matteo reaches for my hand and tugs on it, his fingers interlaced with mine.

We reach the bedroom door, and I halt, my thoughts clouded, and I jump into action before I can change my mind.

Raising up a finger, I say, "One second."

Then I kick off my black heels and slip into my gold ones, right before I rush to the mirror to pick up the red lipstick that was calling to me earlier, but I decided I should go with the regular nude one anyway.

I'm back by Matteo's side in a heartbeat, his curious gaze on me.

This time, it's me who says, "Let's go," before I change my mind.

To everyone else, these small changes might seem peculiar or like nothing special, but to me, this is the bird edging closer to the cage door for the first time, which is exactly how I need to face my father and whatever surprise he has in store for me.

CHAPTER 16

GEMMA

As soon as the driver pulls up at the back entrance of the restaurant, I'm ready to jump out of the car and bolt in the opposite direction. But I know we have to do this, that there's no way I can avoid my father forever. And, this time, I'm not alone because Matteo is by my side. At least for the time being, which comforts me. He promised me this meeting would end with me going back home with him, and I believe him.

Matteo opens my door, holding out a hand to me. I inhale deeply one more time before taking it.

Once I'm next to him, he squeezes my hand once and drops it.

We meet four men at the door, all dressed in black suits, and after Matteo talks to them, they follow behind us. We make our way into the restaurant through the kitchen where some of the staff nods at Matteo and greets him, but most keep their heads down. My heels click on the tile floor, the rhythmic noise following us into the dining room, where my dad is already seated in one of the large corner booths.

I haven't been in this restaurant before, but it's charming with its typical red-and-white checkered tablecloths and a lot of rustic furniture. The exposed brick wall gives it a unique and almost homey feel that adds to the overall allure.

When I see who accompanied my dad, my steps briefly falter, enough for Matteo to reach out and steady me. I didn't expect him to come by himself; he's not stupid, but I'm still surprised. I expected my cousin, Frederico, to join him, since he's deep in the family business, as well as two other cousins for protection and probably intimidation. Though I'm surprised to see my father's best friend, Emilio Moretti, sitting opposite him.

He used to be at our house all the time, but I haven't seen him since I was ten or so, and he moved to Italy to take over the family business overseas.

"Ah, la mia bellissima figlia." My father's voice booms through the room, and he gets up to open his arms.

The urge to run the other way presses heavily on my chest. I never minded it much when he called me his beautiful daughter in front of everyone, but for some reason, it encourages a little seed of irritation to grow inside the pit of my stomach today.

His gaze roams over me as I walk to him, and it's impossible to miss the slight tightening of his eyes, or the way his smile almost turns into a grimace the instant he notices my shoes and lipstick.

It takes all of my willpower to keep the pleasant and demure smile on my face, whereas a full-blown grin is dying to take over.

Gotcha, Daddy.

He envelops me in his arms, but it's brief with a clap on the shoulder and that's it.

Frederico walks up, almost shoving my father out of the way to get to me. He bends down to kiss my cheeks, and I return the gesture.

"Ciao, bellissima. How are you? It's been forever since I've heard from you."

He sounds different than usual—his tone the tiniest bit harsher—and I wonder if something happened? I've been gone for a while now.

I nod. "Yeah, I know. My phone got lost during the attack at the bar, and I realized I barely have any numbers memorized."

I don't tell him that I have a new phone, or that I never even had the desire to call anyone other than Ally and Luna.

He leans in and lowers his voice. "How have you been? Are you all right?"

His gaze goes over my shoulder, his eyes narrowing.

Is Matteo still behind me? I didn't notice him moving anywhere else.

I'm not surprised Matteo's getting some nasty looks, everyone's probably irritated with him for keeping me away from the family. They don't know about the whole situation with Nikolai or that the engagement to Ally is a total sham. My family will flip a lid when they find out. Although it might not be half as bad as if they heard about my cousin being involved with someone from the Russian Mafia. If that came to light, heads would be rolling for sure.

Frederico touches my arm, and I start. He frowns at me.

I laugh it off, because what else am I going to do or say? Please don't touch me since the only man who's allowed to touch me is the guy who's engaged to my best friend and cousin, and who's kind of been keeping me hostage until she's back, even if he actually never did anything to keep me from leaving? Oh, and I've also had incredible sex with him and can't get enough?

Yeah, that wouldn't go over well.

So I laugh some more and shake my head like I'm just being silly. "Of course, sorry. I was just lost in thought. But I'm okay, promise."

"Are you sure? You aren't hurt or anything, right?"

I shake my head some more. "No, he's been very good to me."

Frederico stares at me, his eyes turning into tiny slits.

I clear my throat. "You know, after the shooting and all . . . with my injury."

His jaw muscles flex before a tight smile takes over his face, without ever reaching his eyes.

"Gemma." Matteo's voice brings my attention to the table, where he's waiting for me. "Come sit."

He stands behind a chair, his fingers biting into the high back of it as he waits for me to take a seat.

I look around, momentarily confused by the fact that my family occupies the booth, and that there isn't another chair around. Matteo continues to stand behind my chair, the one that's situated right at the head of the table, with everyone staring at me. It's almost like I'm their queen and they should bow down to me.

A surge of something strong flows through my body at that image, something electric, the feeling unfamiliar yet comforting. It has me straightening my spine and lifting my chin a little higher.

The feeling mostly dissipates the instant my father opens his mouth, but the smallest particle remains, allowing me to meet my father's gaze head-on.

"Well, Gemma, Emilio and I have a surprise for you. We've been keeping it a secret because we were hoping to do it with the entire family gathered around us, but we couldn't have predicted the circumstances, and Emilio is needed back in Italy to handle an emergency situation over there."

The two of them lock eyes and grin, while I'm trying my best to keep the contents of my stomach inside my body.

Frederico shifts in his chair too, his eyebrows in a deep furrow. He doesn't know what's going on either?

That can't be a good sign.

"But when Emilio is back in two weeks, you're going to marry him. And afterward, he'll take you back to Italy with him. The whole family will be so proud." My dad rubs his hands together like this is the best news, or at the very least, like this is the best contract he's ever signed, which might as well be true.

Frederico rises to his full height, which is impressive, considering he's in the back of the booth, while my brain is trying to process what was just said. My wide-eyed gaze locks with his for a moment, and I watch his nostrils flare and his lips curl. The suffocating pressure on my chest grows with every passing second.

A few minutes ago, I heard every single word that came out of my father's mouth. Now, everything around me sounds muffled. My brain wasn't willing to handle any more, so it just shut down.

I blink, then I blink again.

Nothing changes.

As if we're in a movie, I watch Frederico's face turn red. He says something to my dad, and tight lines form around his eyes. Then he glances at me and shakes his head, as if to say, *Don't worry, I'll talk him out of it. You won't have to marry this sleazy, old man who was always a bit too friendly to you when you were a child.*

Now that I think about it, wasn't it actually Frederico who once dragged me away from Emilio as he was trying to make me sit on his lap? Gosh, I haven't thought about that in so long, since Emilio left for Italy shortly after anyway.

Hands land on my shoulders, but I can't move. A sudden feeling of coldness expands in my core, the heaviness of it shocking my entire system. My whole body freezes into one solid piece, and I'm unable to do anything about it.

My breaths come out quick and shallow, and two hands push their way under my body—one under my knees, and the other behind my back—and I'm hoisted out of the chair and pressed against a strong chest.

I manage to close my eyes, almost grateful I'm stuck in this bubble and can't fully make out the chaos that's happening around me. The faint sound of shouts is merely background noise in my brain, and I'm sure Matteo's men have stepped in so we can get out of here.

I'm jostled as Matteo tries to get into the car, still holding me. He ends up lifting me into the car first, before getting in himself, and cradling me back on his lap.

The driver speeds away while Matteo brushes over my hair in a soothing motion, constantly muttering things like, "It's okay, baby, I've got you." "I told you I won't let anything happen to you." "I'm right here, and I'm not going anywhere," and "He's not taking you anywhere. You're mine, passerotta."

"You're mine, passerotta."

My broken brain probably misconstrued that last one, but I keep repeating it in my head and focus on Matteo's heart beating steadily under my ear until my breathing finally evens out.

At least I can hear him, even if it still sounds so far away.

Tucked into my safety bubble that is Matteo's chest, I slowly drift off to sleep, my mind completely shutting down. At some point, I rouse with a start, but that familiar woodsy scent, with a hint of oranges, allows me to go straight back to sleep.

The next time I wake up, I'm in Matteo's bed, covered up to my chest with the blanket. I move around in the dark, immediately bothered by the tight confines of my dress. A quick glance at the clock informs me it's three in the morning.

Yet, the bed beside me is empty.

Even though there's this vague memory of him putting me down and hugging me to his chest when I drifted back to sleep.

After he took care of me and got me back home like he'd promised.

Home.

His home.

The place that feels more like my home than my father's house ever has because it comes with the man who's done so much for me.

Which is the opposite of what can be said about my dad. My father. The man who sells off his daughter—his own flesh and blood—like she's some goods he needs to make the highest possible profit on. For the second time.

Disgusted doesn't even begin to describe how I feel about

all of this. Moment by moment, my brain and body work more, my pulse speeding up in line with the rise of my anger.

I grind my teeth as I replay what happened today. No matter how often I think about it, it all seems surreal. Maybe I lack the capability to think the way my father does, to care that little about someone's life—your own daughter's life—that you'd not only be okay, but delighted, to marry her off for your own personal and professional gains.

Anger swells in my gut, and my chest burns, heat spreading outward into every single one of my cells, until I feel like I'm about to burst into a million drops of scalding lava.

The dress suddenly feels way too tight, and I need to get out of it. I tug on the zipper, and it rips straight off. For fuck's sake, seriously? I let out a groan of frustration and walk to the door. I yank it open and stalk down the hallway, heading straight for the kitchen island. The room is illuminated by the moonlight shining through the floor-to-ceiling windows, making it easy to navigate my way around. After turning on the dim light above the stove, I go back to the island and pull out the top right drawer. Bingo.

The scissors are heavy in my hand, the plastic handle smooth around my fingers as I hold it upside down in front of me.

"Passerotta."

I lower the scissors and watch Matteo walk toward me, his movements smooth and assured. The low lighting makes him appear otherworldly, larger than life, like a king, or a Greek god, someone who can't be rattled by anything.

His fingers wrap around mine, taking the scissors from me. "What are you doing?"

I huff out a breath. "I need to get out of this dress, but the zipper broke, so I was getting some help." I point at the scissors and shrug.

"Sounds familiar." His teeth bite into his lower lip, dragging it into his mouth.

I don't know if it's a subconscious thing or what, but damn it, it's hot. It's also incredibly distracting.

His reply finally sinks in, and I cock my head to the side. "Familiar?"

"The night we met."

"Aaaaah." My wedding night. Precious. I usually try to block out that time in my life, but he's right, it was when we first met. And I'm so glad we did, despite the crazy circumstances. "Well, I might have an undressing problem sometimes."

"It seems like you do." He does his lip thing again, but this time, the corners of his mouth twitch too. "Good thing I'm an expert at undressing."

I groan but spread my arms out to my sides. "Well, have at it then. Do your worst."

"Feisty."

I shrug. "Sorry, I guess that happens when your dad is marrying you off . . . again, and it feels like there's a heavy weight sitting on your chest."

His gaze darkens, and any playfulness that was just there is gone now. "He's not marrying you off again. I promised you that."

"There isn't really anything you can do about it."

Before he can say anything, I lift both of my hands and point at my chest. "Can we get me out of this now, please? I feel like I can't breathe properly."

Without another word, he situates the open scissors at the top of the dress and cuts an almost straight line down the middle. The cool blade of the scissors glides down my body, easily sliding over my heated skin until he reaches the bottom. He cuts through the thick hem with one more snip, and the dress falls completely open.

My chest expands, and I take several deep breaths, the fuzziness in my brain immediately feeling better. Sadly, the anger and irritation brewing inside me are still there, steadily growing.

Matteo puts the scissors behind him on the counter and leans so close to me that I instinctively move back and bump against the kitchen island. "Passerotta, you can be sure of one thing. There are a lot of things I can do to keep you from marrying that bastardo."

His breath is a whisper of air on my ear. "But I never said you'd like any of them."

I'm still processing his words once he steps back and walks to one of the cabinets.

I snort. "There isn't much besides keeping me here forever or marrying me yourself."

The words came out of my mouth so fast, they didn't have time to go through any filters.

I can't believe I just said that. Even if it's the truth, and I wasn't this irritated and appalled by my father's behavior, I'd normally never say anything like that. To anyone, especially him.

He places the glass he got from the cabinet on the kitchen island and grabs the scotch from the tray to pour himself a drink. By now, I know he adds a little water to the amber liquid, something about amplifying the flavors he once explained to me.

Watching him prepare it doesn't have the same calming effect today as it usually does.

He picks up the glass when he's done, but instead of putting it to his lips, he holds it out to me. "You might need it more than me."

I eye the drink but shake my head. It's not what I want or need right now, not that I know what *it* is. I huff out a breath and pace around the open living space. The cut-open dress sways around me, and I probably look ridiculous, but I don't care. I'd feel more awkward in only my underwear. My whole body is so tense, it has my muscles quivering, and all I can think about is my father and the insanity of this whole situation.

The day he told me I'd be marrying Luigi, I wasn't jumping for joy, but I was at least somewhat prepared for it. I'd accepted that fate long ago, and my mom had helped make it seem less like a bad situation by telling me things had worked out well for her with my father seeing as she got me. The best thing that had ever happened in her life. And I'd have that too one day, not just a husband, but a family. We'd sometimes go through my baby and childhood pictures and have a lot of fun together. My mom looked so happy in them, and the few that had my dad in them, he did as well.

Or that's the memory I've hung on to for so long, the way I wanted to remember things. Whenever I really think about it now, I realize it was a long time ago, not to mention, I was young and impressionable. My mom was my whole world, the person I loved the most. I wanted to be her when I grew up. Then she died, and I clung to my admiration of her, to the things she promised me I'd one day have, just like her. Even if the circumstances weren't the best because I'd have to marry someone I didn't want to marry.

Had I been home this whole time with my father after the shooting, instead of spending the time with Matteo, I probably would have put on a fake smile and gone along with the marriage to Emilio, focusing on that special future, where I'll have my own little person to make it all worthwhile, just like my mom had promised.

But I wasn't with my dad. I wasn't sheltered from a normal life or from other people. Ally was the only person I saw or talked to, every once in a while, who wasn't brain-washed by my father and the business.

I can't do it anymore. I just can't.

The veil got ripped off my eyes, and now I can never go back to how things were before I had a clear view of how it could be.

"Passerotta." Matteo's fingers move over my hands, holding them still. "Take a deep breath."

I do as he says, the air quivering as it leaves my throat a moment later.

"Now open your hands." His thumb brushes over my knuckles.

I frown at his request. "My hands?"

"Yes."

When I open my hands, they sting. I hiss at the unfamiliar pain, surprised to see small crescent shapes all over my palms.

My gaze flies up to Matteo's, my eyes wide as I stare at him.

His expression is soft. "You were storming around the

room with your fists clenched by your sides for the last few minutes."

I swallow, almost closing my hands again on instinct, needing an outlet for this blazing rage inside me.

The corner of his mouth tips up. "Don't get me wrong, it was a sight to behold with your hair flaring behind you and your billowing dress adding to the effect. You looked regal, like a queen."

I gasp at his words, remembering exactly what he told me before.

"I want to be there when the sheltered princess explodes into the fiery queen she's meant to be."

Is this what he was talking about? This seething fire inside me that's trying to take control of me? It certainly feels like a living, breathing thing, reddening my vision to the point where I can't see clearly, and consuming my mind in a way that makes me question everything.

"But you can't hurt yourself, I won't let you." He lifts one of my hands to his mouth and gently presses his lips to my palm, before wrapping it in his and pulling me.

I stumble after him, not really paying any attention to where we're going until we stop in the doorway of a room, and he turns on the light.

The gym.

He hauls me over to the bench and gently pushes me onto the seat. Then he's gone. A second later, warm hands tug on the straps of my dress. It slides off with ease, and Matteo slides a T-shirt over my head. It's one of his faded black ones that's cut off at the shoulders. I don't even need to stand to know it'll almost reach my knees, while also exposing the side of my torso.

Next, he grabs one hand at a time, inspecting each before picking up a roll that reminds me of gauze and wraps my hand. He covers my palm, my wrist and my thumb, then the spaces between my fingers. The wrap feels taut as he secures it, but not too tight. Then he repeats the same process for the other one.

When he's satisfied with his work, he steps around me, gathering all of my hair and tying it with a hair band. Even though it's such a mundane task, it's oddly intimate, and my heart doesn't know what to do with itself, first skipping a beat before picking up its pace.

Next are his clothes. It's the first time I notice he's still in his suit. The jacket is gone, but the dress shirt and slacks aren't. As if he doesn't have a care in the world, he slowly unbuttons his shirt before slipping it off his broad shoulders. The pants are next, sliding down his muscular thighs. He picks them up and puts them on the bench beside me alongside his shirt.

The bulge in his boxers is impossible to miss, but he doesn't say anything about it. My mouth waters, and I'm not sure if that's something I should feel embarrassed about or not.

The little voice in the back of my head shames me, telling me how wrong all of this is, and how disappointed my dad would be if he knew what I'd been up to with Matteo. And the fact that I'm not his precious virgin daughter anymore. I inhale deeply and growl at the voice, listening with satisfaction as it disappears.

Matteo raises a brow at me as he reaches up to get something from a shelf. "Did you just growl at me?"

Damn it, did I seriously just do that out loud? Heat spreads up my neck and into my cheeks.

I shake my head at him. "Sorry. That wasn't supposed to be out loud."

He nods like that makes total sense, going back to what he was doing before, but I'm pretty sure I saw his mouth twitch.

I'm a nutcase.

"Come here, passerotta."

Pushing off the bench, I stand and join him in front of the cubbies that are on one side. From what I can tell, they're filled with sports equipment.

Matteo holds out a boxing glove for me. "Left hand."

I shove my hand in before he grabs the other glove, repeating the same with my right hand. He ties them both for me before getting another set of gloves, or whatever they're called, with a pad on one side to hit.

He gives me a once-over, a deep, satisfied sigh leaving him, before he lifts his chin to the opposite side of the room. "Get on the mat."

I dart out my tongue to wet my lips, the rumbling tone of his voice going straight to my clit. Standing a little taller, I thrust out my chest and say, "Yes, sir."

He moves in, his body almost touching mine, and says, "The faster we're done with this, the faster I can fuck you."

CHAPTER 17

MATTEO

"Don't just use your arms to punch. You need to use your whole body. Turn into it and use the speed from it to hit as fast as you can, so you don't lose any of the power." I turn around and show Gemma what I'm talking about, so she can see it in action.

When I face her again and tilt my head in a questioning manner, she nods like she's got it. Then she shows me she actually did. This girl is a fast learner, and not too shabby in gloves either. Definitely not what I expected from a first-timer.

"Good job. Do you need a break?"

Sweat drips down her brows, but she shakes her head. "Again."

Her jabs have already slowed down, but I admire her tenacity. Not to mention, the reason I dragged her in here in the first place was to let off some steam, instead of keeping it all inside, or worse, hurting herself like she did earlier. Yes, cutting her palms open with her nails might not be that big of a deal, but it's still something that can easily be avoided. This right here is way healthier and more productive too. She wanted to learn how to fight anyway, so fight she will.

Most of the tension from earlier has left her body since we started, her shoulders more relaxed, but there's still some of that fire in her eyes that wants to seek and destroy. Not that I blame her. Her poor excuse of a father is selling her off to yet another guy. And, this time, to someone who lives on a completely different continent. What the fuck is wrong with him? All he cares about is money in his bank account, and it doesn't matter how he gets it.

What a pathetic excuse for a human being.

The force against my mitts has me staggering backward to find my footing, and my eyes widen as I take in her smug face. "Well, well, passerotta, look who's come out to play."

Seems like it's time to get out of my head and pay more attention to Gemma's punches again.

She lifts a shoulder. "That's what happens if you have an asshole for a dad and a pig of a future husband to give you enough volatile fuel for a lifetime."

"I already told you: you are *not* going to marry him." The words fly out of my mouth, low and menacing.

Her eyes turn into slits, and her lips press together into a tight line before she spits out, "Well, good, because I really don't fucking want to."

Then she holds up her hands in front of her face, exactly like I showed her, and I barely have enough time to lift my mitts before she makes contact with them again.

Damn, she's much stronger than I expected her to be. A magnificent tiger hidden beneath the shell of a sphinx.

She grunts in frustration. "It's my damn life. Mine."

Punch.

"I."

Punch.

"Do not."

Punch.

"Want."

Punch.

"To marry him."

Double punch.

Then she hits the pads with quick, hard jabs, letting out so much of that anger and frustration that has been eating her up from the inside.

Watching her dispel some of those demons is absolutely mesmerizing, and also incredibly hot.

When she stops, her arms fall limply to her sides, and she sinks to her hands and knees, her whole torso heaving from her fast breathing.

I rip off my mitts and throw them behind me. Then I grab her by the shoulders and flip her onto her back. I straddle her, untie her gloves, and take them off. The wraps are next, and I make quick work of them, throwing one away, while bunching the other in my hand.

Grasping both of Gemma's hands in mine, I kiss one, then the other. While keeping an eye on her and her expression, I use the wrap and bind her hands together.

"Hurry." Her lower body wiggles underneath mine, like she's rubbing her thighs together to alleviate some of the ache between her legs.

My dick is so hard from the way she punched, I want to sink into her right this second. Watching her beat the crap out of some of her demons was a major turn-on.

I put her hands above her head, and she whimpers, so I

bend down to capture her mouth and make it mine. I could feast on her soft lips, or suck on her tongue, for hours. Every time we kiss, she becomes bolder and more playful. Denying me my kiss, just to snatch my lips between her teeth a moment later.

Next is her shirt. It's so old and flimsy, it doesn't take much to rip it in half, right down the middle.

Gemma gasps at the action and arches her back. Her tits press against the constraints of her bra, so I free them and lower my mouth to suck on one hard nipple then the other. The brown tips are slick and salty, mixed with Gemma's own scent. It's perfect. *She's* perfect.

She tilts her head back and opens her mouth to let out a low moan. I love hearing her without any restraint, to know she drops her timid public mask for me and doesn't pretend.

"Matteo, please."

"Please, what, baby? You want me to fuck your pussy, or do you want my cock in your mouth?"

A small shiver runs through her body at my question, and she rasps out, "Both."

I get up to take off my boxers, taking care of her panties while I'm at it, pulling them down her legs before bunching them in my hand. Then I wrap them around my cock and give it a few strokes.

Fuck.

Everything about this woman is a damn turn-on, a thrill that's deep in my blood and has me so hooked, it's on the way to turning into an obsession. Or maybe it already has.

I wasn't lying earlier when I said she's not going to marry that old fucker. Or anyone else for that matter. I'm going to kill each and every one of them if it means I get to keep her.

I toss the panties on the floor and straddle her again. This time, I move closer to her face, my knees almost next to her ears. Gemma wets her lips while she stares at my cock, and it twitches in anticipation. Then she darts out her tongue to lick my tip, and I groan loudly at the contact.

Leaning over her, I snatch the discarded shirt and put it under her head as a cushion.

She whimpers again, this time definitely rubbing her thighs together.

"You want me to feed you my cock?"

Her eyes fly up to mine, and while keeping eye contact, she nods. "Yes."

Shit, she really is perfect.

I inch closer, palming my cock right in front of her lips. "Open wide, baby, and take me like a good girl."

Her warm lips wrap around my cock as I push in, sucking on it while her tongue glides along the underside of my cock in a way that has me pausing to enjoy this sensation some more. I rock halfway into her mouth several times until I can't wait any longer and shift forward.

Her eyes tear up as I hit the back of her throat, holding myself there for a few seconds, before pulling back to thrust in over and over. My balls grow heavier and tighter with every thrust, and when she moans around my cock, I almost shoot my load right there. But I want to come deep in her pussy, so I pump a few more times, then slip out of her mouth.

I trail my hand down her body, squeezing her breasts several times before I reach behind me for her pussy. She's wet, and I sink two fingers inside before spreading her arousal around her lips and clit.

A guttural moan escapes her mouth the moment I circle her clit, and she bows off the floor as much as she can with my weight half on top of her.

"Do you want me to eat that pretty little cunt, passerotta?"

She lifts her head and bites her lip. "God, yes. Please."

I chuckle at her enthusiasm then climb off to reverse our positions.

After lying down, I help her onto me with her still-bound hands behind my neck and grab her ass to drag her close enough for me to reach her pussy.

She shudders at the first swipe of my tongue to her clit. I draw back and do it again, and again, switching between sucking on it and applying pressure to it with my flat tongue.

"Matteo, please."

She barely moves, and I hate that she still doesn't seem comfortable enough to do whatever she wants, but she'll get there. I'll help her get there.

"Be a good girl and ride my face. I want your cum everywhere."

Her breath hitches, her chest rising a little faster than before.

For a split-second, I'm not sure she'll do anything, but then she comes closer, shifting her weight onto all fours. The new angle gives me a different kind of access, and I take full advantage of it, not wanting to waste any time. I leap up just as she lowers herself onto me.

I hug her to me, wanting to take from her as much as she gives, and after I suck at her pussy lips and show her with my tongue exactly how I want to fuck her with my cock, her weight increases on my face, her movements getting more demanding by the second.

Letting her take the lead, I follow her movements until her legs quiver around me and her whole body shakes above me. She cries out, riding me harder than before. Then she slows down and abruptly sits up, probably too sensitive for any more stimulation.

I close the gap she created and lap at her once more. Gemma gasps, and I can't keep the satisfied smirk off my face.

Clasping on to her waist, I steady her and let her take her hands from behind my head. With my hands securely on her, I roll us around and hover above her. My cock nudges against her pelvis, and she opens her legs. They fall to the side as if that's all she has the energy for, and it might as well be. Not only did she just work out like a machine, but she also rode my face as if she was a professional bull rider.

A few strands of hair stick to her face, and I brush them back, repeating the motion when Gemma closes her eyes and hums.

"You're so fucking beautiful. I could spend all day, every day, worshiping you and your body the way you deserve."

Her eyes fly open, and she gazes at me, her eyes shiny. "I want to stay with you."

Her words are barely audible, but I hear every single one of them as they slice my chest wide open.

Leaning down, I capture her lips and kiss her slowly, thoroughly. There's no rush, nothing that could tear me away from this woman who has, somehow, crawled her way under my skin without me even realizing it.

I lean my forehead against hers and fill my lungs with our

mixed scent. "I'll kill whoever tries to take you from me." Then I sink into her wet heat. "You're mine, passerotta."

She arches her back and gasps. I'm not sure if it's from my words or my cock sliding in and out of her pussy, but I pretend it's both while I fuck her with slow strokes that drive me to the edge of insanity.

After devouring her mouth once more, I get on my knees and drag her pelvis against mine, my movements becoming more desperate while I continue to slam into her. Gemma's whimpers fill my ears, and while I rub her clit with my thumb, she moans long and loud, pulsing tightly around my cock.

"Fuuuuuuck." Two, three more pumps, and I still, coming so hard my legs shake and my vision turns blurry at the edges.

My breathing comes out in loud, harsh breaths, and I catch myself with my hands on the mat. My whole body is buzzing like there's static under my skin.

"I can't move. I think you broke me." Gemma's eyes are closed, her words mumbled.

I huff and slowly slide out of her, watching the cum drip to the mat in odd fascination.

"Water."

Gemma's croaked plea snaps me out of it, and I scramble up to get a bottle from the fridge and some towels. Back by her side, I help her sit up and open the bottle to place it against her lips. I tip it back, and she gulps down almost all of it. Some of the water doesn't make it into her mouth, and the drops slide down her cheek and throat.

She signals that she's done, so I remove the bottle and drink the rest in one gulp. Then I unbind the wrap from her hands, taking each one in mine and massaging it gently once they're free.

Gemma sighs and leans her head against my shoulder. She yawns loudly and snuggles closer, shivering as both of our bodies cool down. It's been a long day.

"Come on, baby. Let's take a quick shower and go to sleep."

She hums in response, so I pull her up with me and pick her up, cradling her against my chest like the precious jewel she is.

"I'll take good care of you, I promise," I whisper into her hair, not sure if she's still awake or already asleep.

In the bathroom, I step into the shower with her, turning away from the spray so it won't hit her directly until it's heated up.

"Baby, can you stand?"

I keep my hands on her, only letting go once I'm sure she won't topple over. After getting her hair and body wet, I lather up the shampoo and soap and clean her. I use her products in the order she showed me before, and once I'm done with her, I wash up too.

I get out first and dry off. With a towel wrapped around my hips, I grab two more and dry off Gemma's hair first and then her body. Her hands hold on to my shoulders, and I make my way down her body with the towel, gently rubbing it over her skin to soak up the moisture. Warmth radiates through my chest like every other time I take care of her and she lets me.

Not bothering with any clothes, I climb into bed with her.

"Matteo?"

"Right here, baby."

Gemma turns around, and I drag her closer. She curls her hands under her chin and snuggles against my chest. The same way she sleeps when she's by herself. Like she feels safer all curled in on herself, comforted by the position. It makes her look smaller than she is, less intimidating too.

But she's a force to be reckoned with. I was sure of it before, but watching that fiery side of her come to light today, breaking out of that shell she's built around herself, was a sight to behold. And I'm going to feed that fire as much as I can, so it can continue to grow.

"Aren't you a ray of sunshine today?" Ash chuckles, like he just made a joke.

My punch hits his pad so quickly, I'm a little disappointed he's not stumbling backward. And the fucker knows it too, his grin growing.

He lifts his padded hands. "Okay, okay. I got it. I'll try to give you some quiet time."

Thankfully, he actually does shut up, and we continue with our workout. Normally, this is more Zeno's thing to do with me, since he's had a lot more training in boxing, as well as several different martial arts practices, but he had something come up this morning and sent Ash in as his replacement.

I regret ever opening the door for him.

With Zeno, things are easy, especially when I don't want to talk. Ash, on the other hand, doubles his efforts to try and make up for my nonexistent words by talking twice as much. That's the last thing I need today.

We go for several more rounds until we both have sweat pouring down our faces and the room is filled with our harsh breathing.

Ash grabs a couple of water bottles, and we crash on the mats. I gulp down my water before I close my eyes and just lie there for several minutes.

Apparently, that's all Ash can take, since he's shifting beside me and clearing his throat in a very inconspicuous manner.

Without opening my eyes, I sigh. "What is it?"

He huffs. "I just want to know what's going on, that's all. I expected to get here and find you extra cheery because Gem's still here. What I found instead is your extra grumpy ass."

I groan.

"So something *is* going on then?"

"Ash."

"What is it? Do I need to call in reinforcements? Zeno? Or your sister? Who do you need?"

This time, I open my eyes, just so I can glare at him. "What the fuck is wrong with you?"

One of his shoulders goes up and down. "Just wondering."

"Curiosity killed the cat, you know?"

He presses his lips together to keep the mouth twitching at bay. "I'm aware."

"In case you were wondering, you're the damn cat."

He nods once. "Aware of that too."

I exhale harshly, and he gets the signal and lies down beside me.

We both stare at the ceiling for a while, or at least I think Ash is too. Maybe I got lucky and he fell asleep. I don't want to look over and encourage him.

Probably better if he didn't witness my struggle anyway. "I haven't thought about Tommaso in days, maybe even weeks. Not once, Ash. Not one single time. He was my focus for so long, getting revenge for him my driving force for months. Then suddenly, nothing."

It's silent for so long, I believe he really fell asleep.

But then he inhales and exhales loudly. "Don't feel bad for living your life, man. I'm glad you finally reached a turning point. We were all worried about you, so this is a good thing. Not to mention, your cousin wouldn't have wanted that either, definitely not the old Tommaso."

"Mmm."

Now that I started thinking about him and the whole situation again, I can't stop.

"You know," Ash pauses, something that isn't a good sign for him, "I was getting a bit worried about you for a while there. You became pretty obsessed getting revenge for him. And don't get me wrong, I'm not saying the person who's responsible for his death shouldn't pay for what they did, but you were incredibly intense about it. It was the only thing you talked about for weeks, hiding behind the computer or phone every spare minute you had trying to find his killer. Barely anything mattered but his death. Complete tunnel vision where you barely spent time with us either. I think I've seen more of you in the last few weeks than I did in the few months prior."

I nod and gnaw on my lip, thinking about the last few weeks, months, years.

"Do you remember when we hung out with Tommaso all the time?" I pull up my left leg to stretch, just so I have something to do.

"Yeah. We were all together constantly. Until . . ."

I swallow. "Yeah, until . . ."

Ash sits up and stares down at me, his brows furrowed. "Is that why you got so obsessed with his death? Because you still feel guilty?"

I shrug. "I should have tried harder."

"Teo, he didn't want our help. We all tried our hardest, but his addiction was stronger." He brushes a hand through his hair. "I know the drugs weren't what killed him in the end, but we lost him a long time ago. I know you wanted to help him, but he was no longer the same person we used to know. There isn't anything you could have done differently."

I switch legs, the lump in my throat growing. "Maybe."

"Are you still going to meet with Nikolai?"

I nod. "Yeah. I started it, so I want to see it through."

"Just promise me not to get killed in the process?"

I huff out a small laugh. "You think I'm an amateur?"

He grabs his water bottle to unscrew it. "Nope. Just your normal crazy self."

"I can live with that. Crazy intimidates people."

"Not a certain person though, am I right?"

We both know who he's talking about, and immediately this feeling of slight manic energy spreads through my entire body at the thought of Gemma. It does come with a side of dark worries concerning her safety and well-being and wanting to kill everyone who looks at her wrong, but so far, I've been able to keep that side under control.

He copies my movements, pulling one leg up to his chest. "You know, I've never seen you like this with a woman. It's been interesting."

I'm quiet for a moment, processing his statement and thinking about the women in my past. Nothing but casual arrangements. I was focusing on my work and didn't want more than a hookup, or maybe I never met anyone who interested me enough.

"What are you going to do about her?" Ash's voice interrupts my thoughts.

I don't have to think for long about his question because there's only one answer. "I'm going to call off the engagement to her cousin, and then I'm going to beg her to marry me."

CHAPTER 18

GEMMA

"Both of our dads flew out to Las Vegas for some business stuff and took Frederico and a few others with them. Don't ask me how Niko knows all of this since I have no clue either, but he was highly amused about what happened at the restaurant and that Frederico is on a tight leash because of how he acted." Ally sighs into the phone.

"Ally, he reacted like I should have reacted, but I was just too shocked. My dad really must have kept it a secret from everyone." Getting a phone call from my cousin this morning has been such a pleasant surprise.

"All the damn secrets everywhere. It's driving me insane, especially something like marrying you off to an old creep who will take you to the fucking other side of the world. What on earth are they thinking? No way will you marry Emilio. We'll figure out how to fix this. For now, I've talked Niko out of taking out our whole family for what feels like a hundred times in the last few days, so there's that. Good thing is, it sounded like they'll be gone for a few days, or maybe even a week, so that gives us some time. And I'll be back next week, I think, so I'll try to help too. Maybe I can talk some sense into your dad, or mine for that matter."

I walk up to the window and stare outside at the beautiful city skyline. "I'm afraid my dad's a lost cause at this point. He might have always been, and I just didn't see it."

"I'm sorry, girl. I really am."

The corner of my mouth quirks up. "You know, there's a way you can make it up to me."

She laughs. "Oh yeah? What's that?"

"You could tell me all about Niko and you, for starters."

She chuckles and blows out a breath. "About thaaaaaat, phew, that's a long story. It's also something I don't really want to talk about while I'm here. I don't want ears listening in. Niko keeps reminding me that most people think I'm being held here against my will and to be careful until we've got this whole mess sorted out. He knows this could end in a blood bath if it all came to light."

Worry pools in my stomach for her safety, but she keeps assuring me she's one-hundred-percent safe and that she wants to be with Niko—she's given me that much—so I'm trying to trust her on this. At least as much as I can.

Voices float through the apartment, and a quick look at the clock confirms that this certain someone is here to see me. "I'm so sorry, but I've got to go. Zeno, or Mr. Grumpy Butt as I like to call him, is here to see me. And somehow, he doesn't strike me as the kind of guy who'd appreciate me being late. He's probably already annoyed enough that he has to do this with me at all."

"And here I thought my life had gotten interesting. Sounds like you've got me beat by a mile."

"I'm not so sure about that, but a lot has definitely changed."

"It has, but I think that's good. It's time to live our lives, Gem, especially you. We'll catch up soon, okay? Love you."

I smile like a lunatic, although I know she can't see me. "Love you too. Be careful."

"Always. Bye."

I end the call, just as a text message from Luna pops up.

LUNA

Sorry I've been so quiet. I've been out of town for work with my dad, and it's been taking longer than we expected it to take. But hopefully, we'll be back soon, so we can catch up! How have you been? Do you need anything?

There's a knock on the door, so I throw my phone on the bed, planning on replying back to Luna later. But it's nice to hear from her.

I take a couple of deep breaths and walk to the door to pull it open.

As expected, Zeno greets me with the biggest frown known to mankind, barely moving a muscle when I give him a small smile. "Hey, Z."

Fake it 'til you make it and all that.

His inky-black hair is as disheveled as always, and his ice-blue eyes look extra cold today.

He turns around without greeting me and walks a few steps before calling over his shoulder, "Let's get this over with."

I know he isn't thrilled about this arrangement, about helping with my training, but I am. Well, partially. I'm also a little scared because he could probably snap me like a twig with his bare hands, but I'm mostly excited. Matteo said Zeno is one of the best, and I trust his judgment.

Matteo joins us at the gym a moment later, and I can't decide if that helps my nerves or if it only makes it worse knowing he'll be watching.

He winks at me and waves me over so he can wrap my hands and tie my gloves. Matteo seems satisfied and leans in. He doesn't kiss me, but he whispers, "Try to get in and hit him on the right side, he's got an old injury there."

"I heard that," Zeno grumbles, his tone making it clear he'd rather be anywhere but here.

Matteo presses his lips together, his eyes full of mischief. "Ignore him. He's just a barking dog that never bites."

At this, Zeno growls, and I try to give Matteo a reassuring smile. I know Zeno is anything but that, but I also know he's Matteo's friend and he must be a good guy, or we wouldn't be here.

Zeno steps onto the mats—that Matteo has reassured me, with much amusement, have been deep cleaned—and slams his pads together in a thundering sound. "Come on, princess. I don't have all day."

Matteo whispers in my ear, "You've got this. Remember, his right side." Then he pats me on my butt and gives me a little push that almost has me stumbling forward.

Zeno and I stand only a few feet apart from each other while he goes over the basics of boxing again, like Matteo did the other day. I nod after everything he says, trying to remember every single word. Although I'm nervous because Zeno is a beast and Matteo is watching, I actually want to do well.

I enjoyed my sparring session with Matteo way more than I thought. It was different than anything I'd ever done before, and it was . . . empowering. For the first time in a very long time, I'm doing something for me, something that has my adrenaline pumping in the best way possible.

Zeno slaps his pads together once more, but this time, I give him a little glare that he ignores. I go into a fighting stance with my feet shoulder-width apart, and one foot slightly in front of the other. My knees are bent, and the heel of my back foot is lifted a bit, then I raise both hands in guard position, with my knuckles facing the ceiling, just above chin height.

I get a raised eyebrow from Zeno as he watches me, but this time, I slam my gloves together to tell him I'm ready.

And crap, does he mean business.

He's a brutal teacher and has whacked me more times than I can count—mostly on my arms and sides—but I'm loving it.

His pad connects with the side of my rib cage once more.

"Tuck your elbows in by your sides. You need to protect yourself." He lowers and raises his arms several times to show me exactly what he means.

I do better the next time, and he grunts his approval. At least that's what I'm telling myself he does.

A few minutes later, he straightens to his full height and removes his pads. "Take a quick break and we'll continue with some other stuff."

Other stuff turns out to be basic self-defense moves. He walks me through a series of kicks and hits, explaining how to do them before we practice a few times. It looked a lot easier when he showed them to me compared to me actually doing them myself, but a few rounds later, I slowly get the hang of them.

The front kick to the groin is definitely my favorite and Zeno's least favorite to practice.

"I think we'll move on to something else," he mutters, after he was almost too late to block me, Matteo chuckling from the sidelines.

Repeat, repeat, repeat. Hammer fist punch, palm heel strike, and a few others I already forgot the names of, but we keep going. My absolute favorite is where he tackles me from behind, and I bend down to grab his leg and try to pull it out from underneath him. This move will take a lot more work until I'm able to get him on the mat, especially since he's expecting it, but I can't wait for the day it'll happen.

We do this every day for the next week. Those few hours have quickly turned into my favorite time of the day, other than the time I get to spend with Matteo while he either fucks me senseless or we spend time together sharing a meal or doing other mundane things like two people who live together would do. Like a couple, a *real* couple. At least those are the silly ideas my heart keeps feeding my brain.

That same brain is distracted today because Matteo made me come so hard right before Zeno came over that I can still feel his tongue between my legs. That thing he did today . . .

Zeno sighs dramatically, and I snap back to reality.

Heat creeps up my neck, and I grimace. "Sorry. I'll be good now."

He gives me a glare that doesn't hide his disbelief one bit. "Weak spots."

I stand straight and rattle off, "Eyes, nose, throat, solar plexus, groin, knee."

Zeno nods. He likes it when I'm a good student, as much as he allows himself to like it, I suppose. The glares have definitely dimmed the tiniest bit this week, and sometimes, I could swear I almost see a little twitch at the corner of his mouth. Almost.

"Hands out," he says the command as I knew he would, but I still groan.

As usual, he ignores my protests and uses a zip tie to bind my hands together in front of me. We go through the motions we practiced several times, until I break free from it.

He gives me a minute to rub my wrists before he holds out another one. "Again. Make sure the lock is between your wrists and that you swing your hands down as hard as you can. And pull the elbows away from your body or you'll hit too low and the angle will be wrong."

"Got it." I'm in the zone now, going through all the steps several times in my head and with my hands and arms too. Then, it's time to try it, but, as before, I can't get through it right away. But the third time's a charm, which is the fastest I've been able to do it yet.

I bounce on my toes, beaming up at Zeno and lifting my hand. "I did it. High five."

To my utter surprise, he actually lifts his hand and lets me hit it.

Matteo had to deal with some business stuff, but he walks in at that exact time to catch my triumphant moment and stops dead in his tracks, his eyes wide.

"Ugh." Zeno turns away from both of us and grabs his bag in the corner. "See you tomorrow."

Matteo glances after his friend before turning to me. "Did he just high-five you?"

I grin widely. "Not completely voluntarily, but yes."

Matteo throws his head back and laughs. "You have no idea how much I wish I could have been there for that. What was it for?"

Instead of answering, I lift my arms and show him my wrists.

His gaze flicks up to mine. "How many tries?"

"Three."

He takes both hands and presses soft kisses to the red marks on my wrists. "Look at my little bird setting herself free so she can fly."

His words hit me like a truck, making it temporarily hard to breathe. He might only be talking about my training sessions and learning some important skills, but those words . . . they crawl under my skin and feed my soul. I want to be that bird who frees itself so it can fly, and I'm going to be. I am.

My hand goes to my collarbone, only to find it bare. No bird cage. I hate that I can't wear it during my practice sessions, but I'd hate it more to see it break. No one wants a broken bird.

Matteo takes my hand and tugs me out the door. "Come on, I got us some lunch ready. Afterward, I want to show you a new skill."

"Another one?"

He hums. "You were the one who wanted to learn how to fight."

"Well, I did. I just didn't expect it to be like this. It's like I'm doing survival boot camp or something."

He stops mid-step and spins around. "I don't do things halfway. Either I'm all in or all out."

"Okay." The word comes out softly.

Matteo studies me. "Is it too much?"

I shake my head. "No, no, no. I've just been surprised by it all, that's it."

"You sure?"

"Yup. I love it, and it keeps me busy. Which is a good thing since I have no idea what I'd do otherwise."

We get to the kitchen, and he pulls me to the island, where a bunch of food containers are laid out.

I crane my neck, trying to figure out what it is, but there's no logo or anything on the boxes. "What is it?"

"The steak and spinach mashed potatoes you liked so much. I had some more delivered for us."

"You did?" I smile because Matteo has been spoiling me with the most delicious food I've ever eaten. The fact that my dad didn't allow me to eat most of it makes it all the more delicious.

"I did." He leans in and gives me a kiss. It's quick but still drives the butterflies in my stomach wild. "I made sure to get some of your favorite ice cream too."

"Oh, thank you. Let's eat."

Matteo's eyes flare. "I don't know if I ever told you, but I love it when you get all excited about food."

I dart out my tongue and lick my lips. "You do?"

He nods. "Actually, I just love watching you get excited. Period."

I glance down and take one of the food containers so I

have something to do. I get all fidgety whenever he says stuff like this and don't know how to act like a normal person. "It looks delicious."

For the next few minutes, I stuff my mouth with some of the most delicious food I've ever had. We've always had someone to cook for us at home, but since my dad put a strict diet in place for me, it was restrictive in what I could eat. Which is another reason why I love working out so much too, since it allows me to eat even more.

We don't sit, just stand by the kitchen island, and it's one of the most comfortable meals I've had in a long time.

Once Matteo is done, he puts his fork and plate down, steps in front of me, and grabs me by the waist to lift me onto the counter. The cold granite makes contact with my exposed skin, and I yelp.

"You said earlier you wouldn't know what to do otherwise. Tell me what you meant by that." Matteo leans against the counter opposite me, watching me now that we're at eye level.

I shrug and take another bite of my steak. When I'm done chewing, I say, "You know my dad's always wanted me to be someone's wife. That's supposed to be my job for the rest of my life and why he didn't want me to go to college. He said it was a waste of time and money. And, God forbid, I'd do any kind of job in the family business or even worse, outside the family. The horror."

He's quiet for a moment. "But you kept busy at the cabin. You seemed . . . happy."

I nod. "I was happy. I can't even describe how amazing it felt, how amazing it still feels, to not be constantly monitored and watched, or told what to do and what not to do. And, of course, I love reading or watching a good show or movie. It's fun for a while, but I couldn't do it forever. My dad said it would only be a year or two before I had my first child to take care of, and until then, I'd have to keep my husband happy. He always told me it's an easy job, an easy sacrifice to make for the family." I snort. "That not everyone is that so 'lucky.' As if I should be grateful he's marrying me off for his own gain like a piece of meat. It's a joke. But I made a promise, and I thought I'd be okay with it."

Matteo steps between my legs. With his hands on either side of my hips, he leans in. "I'm going to officially cancel the engagement."

My breath catches in my throat. "You are?"

"Yes."

"And then . . ."

He stays quiet as if he's debating how to continue.

I lick my dry lips. "Then what, Matteo?"

"Then I want to marry you."

This time, the oxygen in my lungs disappears completely. "That's very sweet of you, but you don't ha—"

"Don't you dare finish that sentence. I've told you before, and I'll say it again, I don't do things I don't want to do." He comes closer, his eyes more black than brown.

"But then why?"

"I want to marry you because you're mine, passerotta. The thought of another man ever touching you drives me to a level of insanity I've never experienced before. Your father could try to sell you off to a million other men, and I'd kill them all before you ever walked down a single aisle."

The drumming in my chest gets so loud, it's almost deafening.

Our breaths mingle as he leans his forehead against mine. This is insanity. Pure insanity. And I want it.

I close my eyes and focus on my breathing, trying to tune in to myself like I've tried to do more lately. To find that feeling in my gut that's trying to help. But there's no churning in my gut, no nausea or immobilizing pressure on my chest. None of the things I felt for so many years every time I thought about marrying someone, even worse when my father told me he'd found someone for me. I always wrote it off as nerves. People get anxious about marriage and have their doubts, it's normal.

But what has never been there before is this warmth that's spreading through my body right now. It started at my chest and keeps expanding outward, filling my whole body with a fervor that I've never experienced before.

Not once.

Until now.

Until this beautiful man entered my life unexpectedly on one of the most depressing days of my life to lure me into his web. I was his from the second I felt the touch of this forbidden stranger, no matter how wrong or twisted it was.

"Say yes, passerotta."

"You're asking me?"

"I am."

He's giving you a choice because he doesn't want to put you in another cage.

All he's ever wanted was to keep me safe, inadvertently enabling me to break out of my cage. And somehow, deep down inside, I know that if I said no, he'd somehow find a way to help me stay out of my father's grasp.

But the thing is, I don't want to say no.

"Yes." The word is barely audible as it leaves my mouth, but I know Matteo heard it.

It's undeniable in the way he captures my lips, the way his hands bite into my hips as his tongue delves into my mouth, as if he's trying to possess every single inch of me.

He said I'm his, but he's mine too.

His fingers glide under my shirt to pull it off along with my sports bra. My leggings and underwear go next. We're both panting, and my clit buzzes with such an intensity, I'm afraid my heart won't be able to handle my next orgasm.

Matteo sheds his clothes too before he walks over to the freezer to get a round container of my favorite new treat, *Karamel Sutra* ice cream. I lean forward in anticipation, watching him as he grabs a spoon from the drawer and stops next to me.

I lick my lips when he opens it, and I see the chocolate and vanilla ice cream with the caramel in the middle. He gets some on the spoon and offers it to me.

The spoon disappears in my mouth, and I hum my approval. "God, I love this stuff."

He chuckles. "It's good."

We go back and forth a few times, and it's my turn again.

Matteo says, "Open up wide," and I part my lips eagerly.

This time, he shakes his head though, and before I know what's happening, he touches the spoon to my chest and lets it slowly descend across my stomach. But he doesn't stop there.

"I said, open up wide, passerotta."

JASMIN MILLER

The spoon reaches the top of my mound, and I finally understand his command. A shiver runs through me, and I spread my legs. Matteo steps between them, the spoon never leaving my body. Not exactly knowing what he's about to do has me trembling. I jump as the spoon descends farther and reaches my clit, but Matteo anticipates it and holds me down with his other hand on my stomach.

The spoon glides over and around my clit several times before he trails it even lower over my lips. The coolness mixed with the melting ice cream and caramel has me squirming against his restraining hand.

"Matteo."

"Lie down."

I lean back on my elbows first before I lie down completely, hissing when my back meets the counter.

His tongue hits my clit, and I feel like I've been electrocuted, unable to control how my body reacts. My inner temperature rises, and tingles rush through me like I'm on drugs. At least, that's how I always thought it would feel: a sense of euphoria and an out-of-body experience I can't fully escape. Not that I want to since this feels too damn good.

Since Matteo is still holding me down, I arch my back, unable to stay still while he licks me clean, long after there should be any ice cream left. The sparks grow, my clit tingling to the point that it's bordering on pain, but Matteo doesn't let up. The spoon clatters on the counter, or wherever he put it, but I couldn't care less. The whole place could be on fire for all I know because all I can focus on is his tongue and mouth on me.

Now that he has both hands free, he really goes to work,

pushing several fingers deep inside me while continuing to attack my clit like there's no tomorrow.

The pressure on my abdomen eases up, and I immediately use that chance to lift my pelvis off the counter so I can grind against his face.

"Oh my God." I whimper, several times, the pleasure this new angle gives me almost more than I can handle.

Matteo growls his approval, pulling his fingers out and gripping both of my ass cheeks from underneath so he can haul me against his mouth even more fervently.

My inner muscles constrict, and my insides explode into a million pieces, my orgasm hitting me so hard, I scream, something I've never done before. My breath comes out in quick pants as waves of endorphins rush through my body. Matteo is the only reason I haven't given myself a concussion by smacking back down on the hard surface.

He hasn't let go, kissing and nuzzling the skin around my clit, careful not to touch it.

"Holy shit." The words fly out of my mouth, and I throw an arm over my eyes.

My heart beats so fast, I'm afraid it might stop altogether from being so overworked.

Matteo chuckles against my skin and gently puts me down on the counter, right in front of him.

Then he lines himself up at my entrance, enters me, and then fucks me.

To my utter disbelief, he makes me come once more before roaring his own release.

We clean up in the shower, something that seems to have become our thing.

He comes over to give my ass a slap while I'm still getting dressed.

"Come to the gym when you're done, okay?"

I look at him with wide eyes. "Another workout?"

As much as I love it, I can only take so much.

He grins at me and shakes his head. "No, baby, we're going to play with knives. Afterward, we're going to pick an engagement ring."

CHAPTER 19

GEMMA

"**S**top trying to stab me, baby. Slashing, remember?" Matteo takes a few steps back.

I do the same, lift my hands, and groan. "I know, I know, sorry. I don't know why it's such a reflex. It's not like I've done it before."

"Don't overthink it. Just remember to slash. Forearm, biceps, triceps, and upper thigh."

Knife training is my favorite new thing, although it's annoying the crap out of me when I can't get it right. We've been training for two days now, with Matteo showing me different grips and ways to hold the knife as well as use it. Today, he thought we should try something different where he pretend-attacks me, so I can try to defend myself. Lucky for him, he gave me a rubber knife to practice with.

I take a deep breath and wait. He knows I'm ready and doesn't hesitate to jump me again. My limbs tingle with anticipation. I shouldn't find this exciting, but for some reason, I do. The fact I get to do this, and Matteo's the one doing it with me, is exhilarating.

He didn't just listen to what I wanted, but he went above and beyond to deliver. To other people, this might mean nothing, since it's their norm, but to me, it's everything. For so long, I've longed to be heard and not just seen. Now that it's happened, it feels overwhelming, but in the best possible way.

Matteo easily tackles me to the floor, and I giggle. He's got his arms wrapped around me and caught our fall by flipping us over and taking the brunt of it.

I put my hands on his chest and look down at him, at his beautiful face. His brown eyes watch me as warmth rushes through my chest.

"Thank you. For everything."

The space between his eyebrows tenses before it relaxes again. "There's nothing to thank me for, passerotta. The world is yours, all you have to do is ask for it."

My life has changed so much because of this man. In a way, he's truly saved it. Maybe I should mourn my old life, or rather the picture of the life I assumed I'd have. The romanticized version my mom convinced me wouldn't be so bad. But all I can focus on is this new joy for freedom, a taste of the life I'd written off so long ago. And butterflies, so many butterflies.

"I feel like I don't need the world as long as I have you." I stop breathing, unable to believe I just said that out loud.

Matteo grips the back of my neck and pulls me down for a torturing kiss. My heart has no choice but to speed up, while I'm trying to keep up with him. I didn't know it could be like this, that a simple kiss could make everything around me vanish like it never existed in the first place.

I don't know how long we kiss, but Matteo suddenly

groans. It's the realization that it's not a good groan that has me moving back.

My eyes widen when I hear my phone alarm.

Matteo tilts his head in the direction of my phone that's still blaring. "Is it time for you to get ready?"

I gulp and nod.

"Cold feet?"

This time, I shake my head and whisper, "No."

His hand cups my chin, his thumb brushing over my cheek. "Good. Get ready then, so I can officially make you mine."

I lick my lips, steal another quick kiss, and get up. Thankfully, the alarm on my phone snoozed itself.

The shower is exactly what I need after yet another strenuous morning, but I'm not complaining about the workouts. They might not be easy but they fuel my energy and my self-confidence like nothing else ever has. It's empowering.

The heat of the water soothes my aching muscles as I wash up. I set the timer early enough so I wouldn't need to hurry, which allows me to stay under the spray a little longer.

With one towel wrapped around my body and one around my head, I stand in front of the mirror and apply my makeup. Simple, yet classic with a winged eyeliner that I'll complete with my red lipstick once I'm done. My hair is next, and I style it into soft waves that are held back from my face by a small French side braid.

Then it's time for my dress. Matteo handed me a credit card a while ago and told me to get whatever I wanted. Since I have everything I need—mostly thanks to Luna—I haven't particularly felt comfortable spending his money. But I made an exception for today, since I wanted to wear something special, and I'm in love with the dress I found.

It's a sleeveless maxi dress with several lace layers, a high slit in the front, and a plunging neckline. I feel more beautiful than I felt in the couture wedding gown my father had custom-made for me. It covered almost every inch of my body like he was trying to hide me, the same way he had me hide my true personality. But I don't want to hide from Matteo or feel confined in any way.

And even though I know it's only going to be a quick courthouse wedding, I still want to look beautiful for Matteo. He's doing me a huge favor by marrying me, ultimately putting himself between me and my father. His decision doesn't come without risk, but I'm hopeful that there won't be any repercussions, and my dad will accept that I'll be out from under his thumb. Maybe there's some kind of deal we can make with him. There has to be *something*.

Matteo walks in just as I put on my birdcage necklace. He steps up behind me to help with the clasp. Then his mouth drops to my shoulder, kissing the soft skin there. I close my eyes, shivers running through my entire body at the gentle touch.

"Are you ready?" His hand glides down my exposed arm before it slides into mine.

"Yes."

I turn around, but Matteo lifts our joined hands and keeps turning me so I do one full spin in front of him.

"I cannot wait to call you my wife."

Heat creeps up my neck and cheeks because I've been thinking about the same thing, and how I cannot wait to be married to him and call him my husband. It's the first time in my life that thought excites me.

Ideally, I'd have preferred waiting until his engagement to Ally was officially canceled, and some dust had settled over the drama that will undoubtedly come from it, but now that my dad has a wedding planned for me this week, there's no time to waste. Matteo had to pull some strings, or rather, pay off some people, so we can get married this quickly.

Matteo puts one hand in his pocket and gets out a rectangular black box. "Early wedding present."

I lift my hand on autopilot, the box heavy as Matteo places it in my palm.

Swallowing, I peer up at him. "You didn't have to get me anything. But thank you."

One side of his mouth ticks up. "Trust me, you're going to love this."

I huff a nervous laugh and open the lid, my gaze immediately flying up to his.

He's already biting his lip—knowing exactly how much I love it when he does it—and then his lips grow into a beautiful, full smile. I see it so rarely, I'm stunned and simply stare at him like an idiot.

"Do you like it, passerotta? Take it out." His voice is closer than it was before.

I blink, and he's right there, in my personal bubble, brushing his knuckles across my cheek, which snaps me out of my trance.

I throw my arms around his neck and hug him tightly. His distinctive smell distracts me as I bury my face in his neck, trying not to get any of my makeup on his suit. "Thank you. I love it."

"I wanted you to have your own, and I don't ever want you to leave the house without it." His hands wrap around my middle, and he squeezes, securing me there until I move back.

The package is still in my hand, so I lift the lid once more and stare at the contents, taking a closer look this time. The smooth material of the knife is a matte black, similar to the ones he showed me while we practiced different holds. But this one is special, with an engraved bird on the handle. I run my thumb over it, smoothing it back and forth over the slightly uneven surface.

"It's beautiful." I take it out of the cushioning and flick it open and closed before putting it into my purse.

Matteo watches me with a content expression, patiently waiting for me to stow it as he offers me his hand.

I take it, letting the warmth from his much larger hand spread to mine.

The drive to city hall is short, and a familiar voice calls from the left as we step out of the car.

Ash's waiting for us with none other than Zeno.

I turn to Matteo, who only shrugs and whispers, "We need witnesses."

My mouth drops open because yes, we do need witnesses, but I thought we'd use the ones they provide, which thankfully is common practice when the bride and groom don't have any themselves. The fact that Matteo actually arranged for his friends to be here for our wedding was the last thing I expected. My eyes water, and I blink several times to push the overwhelming feeling away.

Ash gives me a half hug before Matteo can interfere.

Zeno lifts his chin and says, "Hey."

Even his signature frown is absent today.

Ash claps his hands together and rubs them. "Let's do this."

Everyone agrees, so we make our way up the steps of the beautiful and iconic city hall building. Inside, we take care of the paperwork and wait for our number to be called. It doesn't take long, and we follow the clerk from the small antechamber into a ceremony room, where he takes his place behind the podium and Matteo and I face each other in front of it, holding each other's hands.

He gives us a warm smile that drops a little the instant he sees our witnesses on the side, which I'm guessing is due to Zeno and the frown that is back in place. But the clerk composes himself and focuses back on us, spreading his arms wide.

"We have gathered here today—"

Matteo clears his throat. "Can we just skip to the important part?"

I squeeze his hands but only get a shrug from him. This man.

The clerk gives a nervous laugh and nods. "Of course, of course."

Then he begins again, glancing at the paper on his podium before looking at me. "Do you, Gemma Fiore, take this man to be your lawfully wedded husband, to have and to hold, from this day forward, for better, for worse, for richer, for poorer, in sickness and in health, to love and to cherish, until death do you part?"

My complete attention is on Matteo as the clerk reads the vows, and I'm trying hard to commit this moment to memory. Not only the way my heart is beating like a drum in my chest, but also how the tingling nerve endings in my body and the breathlessness add to this overall elation over my wedding to this man.

The clerk is done, waiting for my answer, so I smile at Matteo and say, "I do."

His eyes close for the quickest of moments, but I swear, I saw relief in them.

The clerk repeats the same vows for Matteo, and warmth fills every corner of my chest cavity when he doesn't interrupt the vows, so the promise can be like a living, breathing thing between us.

"I do." The two words come out of his mouth with ease, and without an ounce of hesitation, at least none that I can hear.

Matteo is the first to pick up my ring, and I marvel at how much I love it as it sparkles in the light. It was love at first sight, and I immediately knew I only wanted one ring. No extra band or anything else. Just this beautiful piece with a slim band and an oval cluster of different-sized diamonds at the top.

He slides it onto my finger and says, "I'm yours."

Two simple words that mean the world to me. To not just belong to someone, but to have that person belong to me too. We didn't talk about the wedding ceremony much before, and I thought we'd just repeat whatever the clerk told us to say, like it happened at my wedding to Luigi, but this . . . this small declaration is everything.

With shaky hands, I pick up the black tungsten wedding band and slide it onto his ring finger. To go along with his promise, I repeat the same words, "I'm yours."

Matteo yanks me against his chest and fuses his lips to

mine as I vaguely hear the clerk announcing us husband and wife. I'm not sure if he ever tells Matteo he can kiss the bride, or if he decided to throw in the towel. Either way, Matteo takes that part of the wedding ceremony seriously, thoroughly showing me how well we fit together.

Ash claps and hollers loudly when we pull apart and glance around, and Zeno tips his head in our direction.

"Congratulations." The clerk gains our attention once more and has all of us sign the marriage certificate. He explains the mailing procedure of the official document and leads us out of the room where we part ways to leave the building.

Outside, the sun shines down on us, and we make our way to the waiting car by the side of the building.

It's in the moment I'm almost pressed against the car door with all three men surrounding me like a shield that it hits me. We're out in public, with a crazy guy out there who seems to think I'm his. Is that why Zeno and Ash are here? For extra protection?

Matteo has kept me so busy that it feels like forever ago when he received those pictures of us. And all the training and wedding talk and preparation had me distracted that it slipped my mind, right until this minute.

Now, my heart races at the possibility that someone could be here to harm, not just me, but also Matteo. They sent *him* the pictures. He was the one they threatened.

I tug on his hand. "Can we go, please?"

His gaze finds mine immediately, his brows furrowing as he gets a good look at my probably panic-stricken face. He doesn't ask any questions, only nods his head. "Sure."

Turning back to Ash and Zeno—who now wear the same worried expression as Matteo—he says, "I'll call you later."

They nod and try to give me a reassuring smile, at least Ash does, but even he fails miserably.

Matteo opens the car door, and we both slide inside the cool space.

Now that we aren't out in the open anymore, I let out a sigh of relief.

The car moves, and Matteo squeezes my hand that he still hasn't let go of. "It shouldn't take long to get home, passerotta."

This is his way of telling me that he wants to know exactly what's going on once we're safely back at the apartment.

Home.

His home.

My home.

Our home.

What if something had happened to him while we were out there? A second husband dead on my wedding day?

My eyes burn, and my chest physically hurts at the thought, since it would hit differently this time.

The cityscape passes by without me noticing much of what's going on. Matteo's phone rings, and his hand stiffens in mine as he listens to whatever is being said on the line, only grunting a few times and ending the phone call with a "Yes," the moment we drive into the parking garage of his building.

Matteo pulls me out of the car and into the elevator, and in less than two minutes, we're inside the apartment and he's engaging the security system behind us.

He spins me around, his large body pressing me against the wall, and cups my face with both of his large palms. "Talk to me."

Three words. It only takes those three words for moisture to build in my eyes.

I inhale deeply and shake my head. "It's nothing, I promise."

"I want your nothings just as much as everything else."

"It's silly." Lifting my lids to meet his gaze, I chew on the inside of my cheek. "I kind of forgot about the threat out there, and the second I remembered it, I got worried something might happen to you."

The change in his expression is almost instantaneous. The frown disappears, and though he's not smiling, he doesn't seem concerned anymore either.

His thumbs rub over my cheeks. "I don't want you to worry about me, passerotta."

"But I do, okay?" The words shoot out of my mouth.

Matteo leans in and presses his lips to mine. This kiss is different from any other kiss we've shared before. He doesn't try to dive into my mouth with his tongue, or anything else. It's as if he wanted to say thank you, and this is the language he chooses to express it.

His phone beeps, but he ignores it and draws back.

I touch the side of his leg and hold on to his pants. "Check it, it might be important."

He exhales with a grumble but lets go of my face to get his phone out.

His fingers swipe over the screen a few times before he puts it away again. His gaze is pensive as it locks with my eyes. "Your dad will be back tomorrow evening."

The air whooshes out of my lungs. "Why didn't I realize I was in this amazing bubble this whole time, thinking everything would just solve itself if I pretended it didn't exist?"

The corners of his mouth tip up, but it looks like one of the saddest smiles I've ever seen.

"Trust me, if I could, I'd keep you in that bubble for the rest of eternity because I like seeing you happy and carefree."

I shake my head. "No, that wouldn't be fair to you either."

We're both quiet, and my thoughts are buzzing so fast in my head, I can barely make sense of them. "Will you do something for me?"

"Depends."

I wasn't expecting him to give me carte blanche, so I barrel on, "Will you get me up to speed and tell me what's going on with Nikolai and Ally, with my dad, everything?"

"Right now?"

I raise a shoulder. "Why not?"

He grabs my hand and touches my ring finger. "Maybe since we just got married, and I hoped we could consummate our marriage for the rest of the day?"

I take a step closer and put my hand on his shoulder. "What if I tell you, you can fuck me six ways to Sunday after our conversation."

Matteo leans in, brushing his nose along my jaw all the way to my ear, and whispers, "I'd say you have a deal, passerotta."

A shiver runs through my entire body at his raspy tone and those light, little touches. They drive me insane, and he knows it too. As if to prove my point, he kisses his way down my throat, gently sucking on my skin. My head falls back to give him more access, and he chuckles.

Then his lips are gone, and he's tugging on my hand so abruptly, I stumble for a step.

"Come on, passerotta, let's *talk*."

I huff and follow him to the large sectional on the side of the open living room area. I kick off my shoes and curl my feet under me while Matteo walks to the kitchen. My dress isn't necessarily meant for this position, but I don't care at the moment. I'm too lazy, and too eager to talk to Matteo, to change my clothes.

Plus, I did imagine him peeling my wedding dress off me, and I definitely don't want to miss out on that.

"Champagne or something else?" Matteo glances over his shoulder, standing next to the open fridge door.

"Champagne, please." All things considered, we do have things to celebrate, despite the shitstorm that's probably going to be unloaded on me in the next few minutes.

By some miracle, he manages to carry a bottle of scotch, a bottle of champagne, a water bottle, two flutes, and a glass back without dropping anything. He puts it all on the table, and I jump in my seat when he pops the champagne cork.

My pounding heart slowly calms down, and I take the filled glass from him. "Thank you."

Matteo sits next to me and turns my way. "Happy wedding day, passerotta. To you." He raises his glass. "Mrs. Santarossa."

I swallow. I'm Mrs. Santarossa now. It's not just a strange concept, or a wish anymore; it's my reality. For once, something I wanted became true, so I clink my glass to his. "Happy wedding day, Mr. Santarossa."

The champagne flows easily down my throat, the bubbles

and sweetness adding to the warmth in my stomach after it hits my taste buds.

Matteo finishes his glass and sets it down on the table to switch to his drink. Did he just have some champagne with me so we could toast on our marriage?

He picks up the bottle of scotch and says, "So, what do you want to know?"

I exhale harshly, staring at the ceiling in an effort to clear my mind enough to see through all the fog in my brain that's been created by denial and ignorance.

"Well, let's start with us. What's going to happen with us now? Are we going to tell my dad since he's coming back?"

Matteo takes his tumbler and sits back, situating himself sideways, so he can face me. "Yes."

I give him my best come-on-you-can-do-better-than-this look I've been perfecting since I met him, and he chuckles into his drink.

"Yes, they are flying back tomorrow evening, so I'll meet with your dad and uncle a day later to clear things up."

I almost choke on my drink. "What do you mean *you* will meet with my dad and uncle? I'm coming too."

Matteo sighs. "I think it might be better if you weren't around."

"I don't care. I want to be there. They're my family. Plus, we don't need anyone getting shot."

"Fair enough."

"That means Ally will come back too, right?"

He nods. "Nikolai will let her go after I talk to your uncle and cancel the engagement, yes. I'll meet with him tomorrow, and will make sure he upholds his side of the bargain too."

This time, I do choke on my drink and spill some of it in

the process. Matteo puts my flute on the table and reaches for a napkin to help me clean up the mess. By some luck, nothing got on my dress.

"You're going to meet with him tomorrow?"

He nods.

"When were you going to tell me?" I throw my hands in the air.

He's quiet for a moment. Too quiet.

"Matteo. Were you going to tell me at all?"

"To be honest, I hadn't really thought much about it. I'm not used to having to share my plans with anyone, unless I'm working with my team, so this is all new to me. My dad knows I'm doing my job and that I come to him if I need him for something. It's been like this my entire life."

My chest expands with my next inhale, a weight settling on my chest. "Okay, this is new to both of us and something we both need to get used to. Obviously, it's the opposite for me, and I'm the one who's usually kept in the dark, and I've always hated it. It makes me feel . . . I don't know, like I'm not important enough to share anything with, I guess."

He reaches out and puts a hand on my knee. "I don't want you to feel like that anymore. You know you're important to me. You're my life now."

Hope pushes some of the heaviness off my chest, and I whisper, "You're mine too."

"Come here." He grabs me underneath my legs and behind my back and slides me onto his lap. He presses a lingering kiss on my forehead before leaning his against mine. "I'll try to remember to tell you what's going on, okay? I just don't want to drag you into things that you don't want to be dragged into either. Or shouldn't be for that matter. I don't want to taint your light with the dark parts of my life."

"What if I welcome the darkness? What if that's what will allow my light to shine even brighter?"

"Then I promise I'll try my hardest."

"Thank you." This position isn't the best for having a serious conversation, but I enjoy the closeness and snuggle against his chest. Nothing has gone according to plan since the day he first came into my life, the day my whole life changed.

Even if he had no direct hand in what happened to Luigi, or even with Ally and Nikolai, he was still some form of catalyst for me, and I'll never forget that. I'll always be full of gratitude toward him for that. Maybe even more than that. No, I know it's more than that. He drives me crazy, but in the best possible way, I enjoy his company, and I can't stop thinking about him. Have I . . . have I developed feelings for my husband?

"Do you remember when I told you that this whole thing with Nikolai was about business?"

My mind comes to a screeching halt as I try to focus back on our conversation and his question. It takes me a minute to sift through what we were just talking about to remember our past conversations. "Mmm, some business beef, right? That's why you set up the whole engagement to Ally, to lure Nikolai out, or something like that."

"Well, it was never really about business. Not in the traditional sense. One of his guys killed one of my cousins, and I wanted Nikolai to hand him over. The second I found out about him and Ally, I knew I could use that info to my advantage. I didn't expect him to storm the bar, guns blazing, or that anyone would get hurt in the process, but in the end, it all worked out."

I try to pull back as much as I can to look up at him. "So he handed over the guy who killed your cousin?"

"Well . . . not exactly."

"I'm confused."

Matteo sighs. "Nikolai is convinced that his guy, Vladimir, didn't kill my cousin."

"He didn't?"

"He called me earlier to tell me he got the evidence to prove it."

I nod, trying to wrap my head around this whole story. It's definitely not the kind of thing that usually happens in my life, mainly because my dad always kept me in the dark about pretty much everything. "So now you're meeting with Nikolai tomorrow so he can show you the evidence?"

"Yes."

"And you're going by yourself?"

"No. Zeno and a few of the other guys from the team are coming with me."

"Okay." That makes me feel so much better, especially knowing Zeno will be there with him. "Do you think Nikolai's telling the truth?"

Matteo's forehead wrinkles. "Honestly, I'm not sure. Tommaso, my cousin, he got into drugs pretty badly. When we found him, we immediately assumed he'd overdosed, but then we saw the bags with the drugs next to his body, and it had *Italian bastard* written on it in Russian. We knew he got his drugs from the Russians, but at least their products are good quality. Tommaso met with Vladimir that night, so we put two and two together, especially once Vladimir disappeared."

"Shit, I'm sorry. I can't even imagine finding someone like that."

Matteo shrugs. "We knew it was going to happen eventually, but we can't just let someone kill him and not pay."

I stay quiet, not sure how to respond, my mind still going over all of this information until something stops me mid-thought. "What are you going to do if Nikolai is telling the truth and it wasn't one of his guys who killed Tommaso?"

His gaze locks with mine, his hand rubbing soothing circles on my back. "Then I'll reevaluate. If it really wasn't Vladimir, I hope that whatever proof Nikolai has might be able to tell us who actually did it."

"That makes sense."

I get lost in my thoughts once more, a swirling mess of Nikolai and Ally, my dad and Emilio, the arranged marriage to him and my actual marriage to Matteo, now my *husband*, and the chaos all of this will unfurl. Because there's no way my dad will just let me walk away like this. I'm his prized possession, and there will be consequences to pay. One way or another.

CHAPTER 20

MATTEO

"Again." I pump my fingers in and out of Gemma's soaking wet pussy and latch on to her clit once more.

"I can't. It's too much."

"Just one more, baby. Then you can ride my cock." Pleasuring Gemma has quickly become one of my favorite things to do. After our conversation yesterday, we had a nice dinner before we consummated this marriage. Over and over, all evening, in the middle of the night, an hour ago while it was still dark, and now again as the sun is rising beyond the city.

Gemma whimpers when I suck on her clit exactly the way she likes it. Her inner walls tighten around my fingers as the orgasm rocks through her and she cries out her release. Her cum runs down my fingers, and I leave my position between her legs to sit up on my knees and rub my wet hand all over my cock, stroking it a few times. Fuck, that feels good.

"Mmmm." Gemma's propped up on her elbows, watching me with excitement in her eyes.

I love she's so into sex and is as eager to learn as she is to please.

"You want some of this, baby?" My grip on my cock tightens, and I slowly lose control. That's what she does to me. My *wife*.

She nods and licks her lips, her gaze fixed on my dick.

I get off the bed and pat the end of it. "Come here and lie on your back with your head hanging off the edge."

The little minx makes her way over to me on all fours, her tits swaying, and her eyes never leaving mine.

Fuck. I'm not going to last long.

She gets into position and blinks up at me, waiting to be told what to do next.

My cock twitches.

"Such a good girl." I brush my hand over her cheek.

She turns into my touch.

So fucking perfect.

"Slide off the bed a little more and open your mouth, baby."

She does as I ask, her mouth right in front of my cock. I push in, and she groans around my length. Once she's used to this new position, she touches me wherever she can reach. My gaze is glued to her, to every little thing she does, and I follow the path she draws with one of her hands as she slides it down her chest and squeezes her tits, before she moves between her legs to rub her fingers over her clit in desperate circles.

Fuck. She's going to be the end of me.

Impatient, I pull out of her mouth and all but jump on the bed to lean against the headboard. "On my cock, passerotta. Right now."

She's unable to keep her grin at bay, smiling like the cat that got the cream. And cream she will get, so much of it pumped into her that it'll drip out of her for days.

With one leg on each side of me, she lines herself up, but I don't give her time to ease down. I thrust up, filling her in one go. We both gasp at the sensation, and Gemma falls forward, catching herself with her hands on my chest.

She closes her eyes and hums, the noise getting louder when I reach up and grab both of her breasts. I pinch her nipples, and she moans low in her throat, rocking back and forth on my cock. Her hips move so seductively, rolling forward and around to the back, I'm starting to see stars.

"Fuck." I grip her hips, holding on to her flesh, and pump into her like a mad man, chasing this over-the-top euphoria that only she can give me.

Her moans get louder in time with my thrusts, and the instant she tightens around me, I'm done for. I come so hard, my vision turns dark for a split-second, my grip on her the only thing that keeps me grounded.

Motherfucker.

Cum drips onto my balls as Gemma shifts forward to lie on my chest.

Snuggling as close as possible, she presses her face into the crook of my neck.

A perfect fit in every way.

She yawns, and her lips move over my throat. "Some days I feel like you're trying to kill me with orgasms."

A chuckle rumbles through my chest. "That's the last thing I want to do."

She snorts. "Yeah, life without me must have been pretty boring."

I smack her ass, immediately regretting it when she wiggles around and more cum runs out of her. Then my brain snaps back to her words. While life wasn't necessarily boring before, she's definitely added something to it that I didn't know was missing. Something I was chasing, without ever realizing what it was.

It was her. Her energy, her smart mouth, her dark side, her insatiable taste for sex, her sweetness, her curiosity. Everything about her has brought richness to my life. A new layer of living.

"It's certainly a lot better with you."

At my words, she lifts her head to look at me, and I take that opportunity to kiss her. I tug her lower lip into my mouth and gently brush my tongue along it. Her upper lip is next, and then I devour her mouth. We kiss until my phone alarm rings and I pull back with an annoyed sigh, swatting blindly for it on the nightstand.

Gemma pouts, her lower lip pushed out. "You already have to go?"

I nod. "Nikolai isn't known for his patience."

She presses herself up on my chest and bobs her head reluctantly. "Fine. I got this new book I wanted to read anyway. Or maybe I'll work out."

"I'll be back as soon as I can."

"I know." She gives me one more kiss before she gets off me and walks to the bathroom.

Satisfaction thunders in my chest at the sight of my cum running down her inner thigh.

My phone's alarm rings again, and I swing my legs over the edge of the bed. I turn the alarm off and make my way to the bathroom. Gemma's already in the shower, letting the water rain on her, cascading down her gorgeous curves.

Not right now. There's more time for that later.

I step into the large shower and go straight for the second showerhead. But not before slapping my hand on her fine ass. She chuckles and shakes her head at me, and we both wash up. She's still busy with her hair when I get out.

Once I'm dressed, I grab what I need and go back into the bathroom to draw a naked Gemma against my chest.

"I have to go, passerotta."

She heaves a heavy sigh, and I hate that she's worried. But there's no way I'm taking her to meet Nikolai. Even if we meet in neutral territory, the risk of something happening to her isn't worth it.

I brush my thumb over her frown, smoothing out her forehead. "I'll be back soon, and we can continue what we started earlier."

That makes her laugh. "I'm pretty sure we both finished."

I bite the corner of my lip and lean down. "There's more where that came from, baby. Always for you."

She groans and shoves at my chest. "Go. I can't take it."

I capture her chin and devour her mouth one more time to the point where she clings to my suit jacket like it's a life vest. A little taste to tide me over until I'm back in her arms and between her legs.

Eventually, I draw back, and she wraps her arms around her middle. "Come back soon?"

I nod. "Promise."

One last look at her, in all her naked glory, with her wet, dark hair framing her beautiful face. With that image imprinted in my brain, I turn around and walk out the door of the bedroom to make my way to the elevator.

In the parking garage, Zeno waits for me next to one of our blacked-out SUVs. He's not alone since Marcello and Leandro will be joining us today. Four of us and four of them, like Nikolai and I agreed on.

Leandro lifts his chin my way and says, "Hey, boss."

Marcello does the same before they slide into the back seat.

Zeno waits for me with his huge arms crossed over his chest and a frown marring his forehead.

I smirk at him. "You know, I left Gemma standing in the exact same position and wearing the exact same expression as you."

"Mmm." He grunts at me but doesn't bother changing anything. This man doesn't give in to pressure, which is one of his best qualities. Nothing can penetrate his focus or will, at least not that I've seen it happen.

"Let's go." I take my hands out of my pockets and get in the passenger seat while Zeno finally gets his ass moving and into the driver's seat.

I know he's not the biggest fan of meeting with Nikolai, but tough shit.

The drive is silent, something I'm used to after years of working with these guys. Marcello and Leandro aren't always on my team like Zeno, but I've worked with both plenty of times to know they're good at their job.

What's different this time is how distracted and restless I am. Thoughts about Gemma circle around in my head, and this nervous energy I haven't felt in forever buzzes through my veins. I don't like it.

We get to the agreed-upon warehouse in neutral territory, and Zeno drives into the open garage, stopping several car lengths away from another blacked-out SUV. I hate trusting people like this, but with how messy things are with Nikolai and Alessandra, and the fact that I married her cousin and best friend, I have to hope it'll be enough to keep things civilized today.

Marcello and Leandro get out of the back and approach the two guys standing next to the other vehicle. They talk for a minute and nod before coming back to us.

Leandro opens the back door. "Boss, they said it's only Nikolai and Vladimir in the car."

I snap my head around and stare at Zeno. "He brought Vladimir?"

Zeno's frown is even deeper than before. "Maybe he changed his mind and wants to hand him over after all?"

Marcello clears his throat. "Actually, Nikolai said to remind you to honor your promise."

I groan and hit my head against the headrest. "Fuck. Fine."

"What promise?" This comes from Zeno.

I don't look at him. "To hear him out before acting."

A grunt is all I get from Zeno, which is just as well.

I grab the door handle and say, "Let's see what he's got and get this over with."

Zeno moves at lightning speed, jumping out of the car and walking around it to be next to my door as I get out. Despite his size, this man is fast.

Nikolai exits his car as well, a cowering Vladimir following him. Nikolai gives him an exasperated glance before gesturing to the simple table and chairs that are several feet inside the warehouse. We all make our way there and take a seat on opposite sides.

Nikolai steeples his hands together in front of him on the table. "Thanks for meeting me. I . . . I appreciate it."

It sounds like the last few words are hard to get out, and I bask in his obvious discomfort, biting my cheek to keep from grinning.

"Like I said on the phone, I have proof Vladimir did not kill Tommaso." Nikolai lets his Russian accent come out, and at his words, my whole side of the table tenses.

He clicks on the tablet he placed on the table. It must be a photo or video since we're surrounded by signal jammers in the warehouse to keep people from listening in on us. It sucks to be cut off from outside communication for the time being, but it's safer for both sides.

Turning the tablet around, he offers it to me. There's a paused video on the screen, so I push the play button and watch as Vladimir meets with Tommaso, who seems jumpy as fuck. The neighborhood is dilapidated and dark, but I immediately recognize the clothes Tommaso's wearing, and the dirty store behind them. It's where we found him the next morning. They exchange cash for a bag of drugs, and Vladimir leaves. Tommaso shoves the bag into his jacket and turns to go as well, walking out of the frame with a cigarette in his mouth, and that's where the video ends.

I propel the tablet to Nikolai and glare at him. "That proves nothing. He could have come back and killed him later."

Nikolai elbows Vladimir in the side. "Tell them where you went after, durak."

I'm unable to hide my expression, flinching slightly at the

fact that Nikolai just called him an idiot in front of us. Not that that's a terrible insult, but Nikolai isn't known for handling his people like this in front of others.

Vladimir doesn't immediately react, so Nikolai smacks him on the back of the head. "Now."

At that, Vladimir sits up a little straighter. "I met with Tommaso and then I went to Maria and fucked her the rest of the night."

Out of the corner of my eye, I see Zeno's leg bouncing. Only once, but that tells me he's just as done with this as I am.

Nikolai tilts his head back and peers up, as if the answers to his prayers are waiting there for him. He spits out something in Russian that's too low and too fast for me to completely understand, but I'm pretty sure I heard "fucking moron" and "too stupid to live" somewhere in there.

Vladimir looks at the table and doesn't move.

Nikolai inhales deeply before glancing at me. "Maria is his sister-in-law. He was fucking his brother's wife, which is why he was hiding this whole time because his brother got wind of it and is out for his head."

Behind me, Leandro snorts, but that's the only reaction from any of us.

Nikolai drags a hand over his face before pushing around on the tablet again. "Fortunately—or unfortunately, depending on the situation—there is a video of that too. It's on the tablet as well, in case you're interested."

I'm just about to answer when Nikolai lifts a finger and continues, "But to make all of this as short and as pain-free as possible, watch this first."

Reluctantly, I grab the tablet once more, really not in the

mood to watch this Russian idiota with his sister-in-law, but I play anyway. I'm surprised to see it's not the expected sex tape, but the same location as in the previous video. It's lighter than before as Tommaso walks into the frame, the huge-ass grin on his face confirming he's high as a kite.

Annoyance floods through my blood, and I'm about to pause the video just as another person enters the frame. He's dressed in all black, and it's impossible to make out any features since his hoodie is drawn way down his face. There's no audio for the video, but it's clear that they get into an argument. Tommaso shoves the other guy, who's on him in a flash, forcing Tommaso to the ground like he weighs nothing.

With a knee on Tommaso's chest, he gets something out of his pocket and fiddles with it for a moment, like he needs to take it apart or something. The second he hits Tommaso's neck with it, it's clear what it is. A needle, probably full of cocaine, since that's what Tommaso officially overdosed on.

Zeno mumbles, "Figlio di puttana," and I couldn't agree more.

Son of a bitch, indeed.

Tommaso stops moving almost immediately, and the other guy goes through his pockets. When he comes across the bag in the inside pocket of his jacket, the guy takes it, produces something from his own pocket, and seems to be writing on the drug bag.

Fuck.

This is the guy who killed my cousin. It's clearly not Vladimir, since this guy not only has several inches on Vladimir but also a good fifty pounds.

The hooded guy jumps up and walks out of the frame,

not once looking in the direction of the camera, and the video ends.

Damn it.

I gaze up at Nikolai who's already watching me. "Any idea who this guy is?"

Nikolai shakes his head. "Not really, but I had my guys go through it with a fine-tooth comb, and they found something."

"What is it?"

"I will show you once you uphold your side of the bargain."

Since I expected him to pull something like this, I came prepared. I hope it'll be enough.

I place both of my hands on the table and say, "Trust me when I tell you there's no way I'll marry Alessandra."

His gaze zooms in on my wedding band before snapping up to my eyes. "Someone I know? A certain jewel . . . perhaps?"

The fact that he's not outright saying Gemma's name makes me feel a little more charitable toward him, so I nod at his questioning gaze.

In response, he does the last thing I expect. He throws his head back and laughs and laughs. Everyone except Zeno and me stare at him like he's just lost his marbles, and I can't blame them. They don't understand that I married the most perfect woman and that there's no way in hell I'd ever consider marrying someone else.

Seeing that Nikolai kidnapped Alessandra because he thought she was engaged to someone else proves he does understand what the right woman can do to a man.

Nikolai pushes his chair back, still chuckling to himself.

"Well, I guess congratulations are in order. I'm sure Alessandra will be thrilled about the news."

I was expecting he'd tell her, but this is too important to miss otherwise. I'll just have to ask Gemma for forgiveness if she's mad about her cousin finding out this way.

Nikolai takes the tablet from the table and puts his other hand in his pocket. "As soon as we're away from the blockers, I'll send you the still photo of the video that we think might help find the guy who did this."

I dip my chin. "Thank you."

With a nod, and still grinning, he heads in the direction of his vehicle, and so do we.

The other two guys who came with Nikolai and Vladimir walk ahead of us, chuckling about something. I don't hear everything they say, but I catch the end of it.

My blood freezes inside my veins. "What did you just say?"

Everyone stops dead in their tracks.

"You," I point at the right guy in front of us, "what the fuck did you just say?"

"Uh."

Nikolai hisses something at him.

The guy gulps. "I was wondering if you were the lucky one to take the Fiore princess for a ride since Luigi Rizzo never had a chance to before he was killed. No offense or anything."

I pull my gun out of the back of my pants and shoot him in the leg.

Nikolai yells something at the other guy before he even thinks about getting his gun.

The guy's on the ground, blood soaking his pants.

I close the distance between us in a few steps, holding my gun to his head. "Don't you ever talk about my wife again. Capiche?"

His eyes widen, and his mouth opens and closes several times. "I didn't . . . I had no—"

Nikolai clicks his tongue. "I'm sure that'll teach you to speak more respectfully about women, Ivan, won't it?"

Ivan nods, still clutching his leg.

"Perfect." Nikolai claps his hands. "Let's go."

Ivan scrambles up, mumbling an apology, before climbing into the SUV.

We do the same, watching them as they back out of the warehouse first. I'm drumming my fingers on my leg, still annoyed with Ivan, and also impatient for us to get out and far enough away from the signal jammers.

The moment we're in the clear, all of our phones chime with notifications, and Zeno stops on the side of the road.

I ignore all other messages, missed phone calls, and notifications, zooming in on the one that just came through from Nikolai.

The picture takes way too long to load, and when it finally does pop open on my screen, confusion spreads across my chest, followed by a sudden feeling of dread that snakes throughout my whole body.

Zeno leans in and scans my screen. "Isn't that the same tattoo as—"

"No, no, no." My brain is spinning a mile a minute as I dial Gemma's number. The call goes straight to her voice message. "Fuck. Why's it going to her voicemail?"

Zeno goes into action mode, getting back on the road while I check my security system and go through the different frames until I find Gemma taking a phone call right at the time we met with Nikolai. She looks panicked, with wide eyes and shaky hands, even on the video footage. I watch her running around the apartment, putting clothes on over her workout clothes, and doing who knows what, before she heads to the elevator and leaves.

"Where the fuck did she go?" I roar before pulling up the security footage from the building.

Gemma in the elevator, Gemma walking out of the building, and Gemma rushing to a black town car that's waiting by the curb. The passenger door opens from the inside, a hand reaching for her to help her in. It's clearly a guy, but he doesn't lean over enough for me to see anything above his chest. Like he knows exactly where the cameras are.

But what's easily visible, like a big, fat neon sign, is the tattoo on his hand. The same exact tattoo as the guy had who killed Tommaso.

"Motherfucker. I'll kill him, I will fucking kill him. If he hurts one fucking hair on her head, he'll be begging for a quick death."

CHAPTER 21
GEMMA

As soon as I wake up, I know something is wrong. My mouth and throat are dry like I haven't had a drop of water in weeks, and my head is screaming at me, pounding behind my skull. My brain is useless too, my memory and thoughts fuzzy, unable to help me figure out what's going on.

A fresh bout of pain shoots through my head, and I groan until the sound gets stuck in my throat as a soft creak comes from only a few feet away. My heart skips a beat, but my body is too out of it to truly react.

"You're awake."

I hear the voice and freeze, my sluggish brain trying to understand what's going on, but it's too hard to focus. My entire perception is distorted, and nothing makes sense. Even the voice in my head sounds odd.

Hair covers my face, and I lift my hand to push it away, but I can't.

I try to lift it, but cold metal immediately bites into my wrist, giving me little to no room to move.

To my surprise, my other hand isn't restrained, so I use it to brush my hair off my face. Then I peel my eyelids open and immediately regret it. The room is bright, and fresh pain explodes behind my forehead with every single movement. Unable to endure it, I shut my eyes again and take deep breaths through my nose to fight the rolling nausea.

"What's going on?" My words come out slowly and a little slurred, my voice weak and quiet. None of this makes sense.

I need to see where I'm at.

The light suddenly turns off, and I'm greeted with darkness the next time I pry my eye open. Since it doesn't feel like my head will explode any more than before, I open my other eye too. Too bad I can't really see much now in the darkness.

My heart is racing, and it's hard to breathe past the tightness in my throat.

"Water." I smack my dry lips together, no clue if that one word came out right or not.

Some movement around me creates noise, and I flinch when a wave of excruciating pain pierces my brain.

This time, my groan sounds like that of a dying person, or at least that's what it sounds like to me.

"I brought water for you. Open." The person—a man, guessing by the deep voice—puts a hand under my head to hold me in a half-upright position and presses something cool against my lips.

I eagerly open my mouth.

I drink and drink until the bottle is empty. Only then does my brain register the taste, and the fact that it doesn't taste like water. There's definitely something mixed in it.

"What?" It's all I can get out, my brain still fuzzy.

"It's just painkillers, I swear." He lowers me to the bed again—I think it's a bed—and smooths some hair away from my forehead.

I cringe at the touch, but my body is too weak to move away.

"Get some more sleep, bellissima."

His voice—and the way he says those words—triggers something in my brain, but the notion is gone before I can catch it, and the buzzing in my head gets too loud to think at all, pulling me back under.

The next time I'm conscious, my brain and body feel different. I'm still not a hundred percent, but I don't feel nearly as weak or disoriented as last time. I open one eye carefully, and when nothing but a low thumping comes from my head, I open the other one as well.

I have no idea what time, or even day, it is, but there's soft light coming from two high, narrow windows on one side of the room. A bedroom. It's bare, except for the bed I'm lying in, a small table next to it, and an armchair a few feet away.

It's facing my way, and the hairs at the back of my neck rise at the idea that someone might have been sitting there watching me while I slept.

While my brain feels much clearer, my thoughts sharper, my memories are still fuzzy. I remember a man talking to me, giving me some water to drink with painkillers, but that's about it. I have no memory of how I got here or what happened before I woke up.

Or how I got shackled to the bed. I glance at my wrist and gasp since the handcuff is gone. My bladder uses that moment to scream at me, and after scanning the room again, I'm hopeful that one of the closed doors leads to a bathroom.

I swing my legs over the edge of the bed, relieved when I see I'm wearing my own clothes and nothing looks out of place. My hoodie jacket is over my workout shirt and my sweatpants are over my workout shorts. Why am I wearing all of these layers? My brain continues to try and put the puzzle pieces together while I make my way to what I think is the bathroom on only slightly wobbly legs.

The bathroom is tiny and almost completely empty besides the toilet, a sink, and a bathtub. I ignore the surroundings and take care of business. The walk back to the bed is steadier than before, so I continue walking to the windows, hoping to see anything familiar that could help me figure out where I am.

But before I can make it, noise is coming from outside the door, and I slip back into bed, lying down with my eyes closed.

The door creaks open, and my body instantly reacts. My chest feels tight like my lungs aren't working properly, and my heart beats so wildly behind my ribs, I'm a little worried I might go into cardiac arrest.

Footsteps approach, stopping close to me from the sound of it.

"I know you're awake, piccolina."

The voice, my childhood nickname. My eyes fly open, and I stare straight into my cousin's face. Frederico smiles at me, and I bolt upright.

Despite feeling much better, I get a little dizzy from the quick movement and steady my position with my hand on the mattress. "What the hell is going on?"

He sits in the chair—my brain in total overdrive—as another thought pops into my head.

"You're back. That means my dad is back too."

Frederico opens his mouth, but I'm faster as something clicks in place in my brain. "Oh, my goodness. Porca puttana." Holy shit indeed. "I can't believe it. Did my papà set this up? Did he tell you to bring me here?" I rush to my feet, and once the dizziness subsides, I shuffle back and forth between the bed and the bathroom. I'm still a little sluggish and unbalanced but manage to stay upright.

My cousin watches me, but he stays quiet while I do all the talking.

I throw my arms in the air. "He totally did, didn't he? He couldn't take it that I was out of his grasp, and he knew I really didn't want to marry Emilio, so he sent you to do what, exactly? Keep me hostage until the wedding?"

That gets a reaction out of Frederico. He jolts in his seat, his whole body turning rigid. "You're not going to marry Emilio."

His jaw is so tense, I'm surprised he's able to unlock it enough to talk.

I nod in response. "Damn straight I'm not marrying Emilio. Never in a—wait, what?"

My brain finally catches up with what he said, and I stop dead in my tracks. "Did you just say I'm not going to marry Emilio?"

"I did."

"Why am I here then?" I point around the room. "Where are we anyway?"

"You're safe and with me, and that's all that matters. The second you stared at me at the restaurant with pure terror in your eyes, I knew I couldn't take it anymore. That memory has haunted me nonstop in my dreams."

305

"I'm sorry, I didn't mean to worry you. I was just so shocked, although I shouldn't have been. It's my dad, after all." I walk back to the bed and sit on the edge of it. "And I appreciate the help, I really do. But I'm okay now, I truly am. My dad is not going to marry me off anymore, I made sure of it."

He tilts his head to the side and studies me, and I wonder what he sees. Does he notice a difference? Do I look any different on the outside, since so much has changed on the inside?

Something cold and dreadful shifts inside my stomach while I watch Frederico's face change from his normal, calm facade to something else entirely. Something much, much darker. His nostrils flare, and he cracks his neck from side to side, the vein in his throat throbbing and straining against the skin.

He leans forward in his chair and places his elbows on his knees. His cold eyes penetrate mine, and he speaks in a voice I've never heard before. It's menacing and quite frightening. "Bellissima, did you fuck Santarossa?"

I swallow, willing my rolling stomach and the accompanying nausea to calm down. In one of my lessons with Zeno, he reminded me to never underestimate an opponent and to listen to my gut. Always.

But Frederico isn't my enemy. He's my cousin. He's *family*. The guy I constantly played with when I was younger. The boy who called me piccolina because I was the little one following him around everywhere.

So why is he acting this way?

And why am I feeling this sense of dread?

Do the men in my family overreact about old traditions

and upholding them? Yeah, maybe. But it's not the end of the . . .

An ear-splitting noise echoes through the room, and I immediately make myself as small as possible with my head tucked to my chest and my arms over my head.

Once it's quiet again, I glance up, my mouth falling open at the sight in front of me. The table that just stood a few feet away from me is now scattered around the room in dozens of pieces.

Frederico stands right next to the demolition spot, still clutching one of the table legs in his hands. He's breathing heavily, his chest rising and falling rapidly.

He takes a step in my direction, never letting go of the piece of wood. "Gemma, did you let Santarossa fuck you?"

He enunciates every word, every syllable, slowly, like he wants to make sure I don't miss a single one of them.

His expression tightens with every passing moment I don't answer.

"Gemma," he roars my name.

A shiver runs through me. "Why . . . why are you asking me this?"

He stops a few feet in front of me and bends down to be at eye level. "Because I want you to tell me if you opened your legs for that bastardo like a little whore."

A slap to the face couldn't have shocked me more than his words do. I rear back, my eyes going even wider as I stare at this man in front of me, who seems almost unrecognizable right now. It's like he put on a mask and turned into a different person altogether, a person I've never met before.

Or maybe it's the other way around, and I've never known him in the first place.

I open my mouth and close it again.

Suddenly he's right in front of me, grabbing my hair and yanking my head back so hard, the sharp pain shooting through my skull has me seeing stars.

"I will ask you one last time, piccolina. Did you let Santarossa fuck you, yes or no?"

"Yes." I barely get the word through my teeth, trying not to move, while also still trying to figure out what the hell is going on. My mind is in total overdrive, trying to find the missing puzzle pieces in this whole fucked-up situation, since I'm clearly missing something big.

He lets go of me, and I sigh in relief, massaging my scalp where I'm sure a few strands of hair are missing now.

Frederico paces the room, staring at the ceiling with his hands crossed behind his neck. "Why would you do this? I should have known this would happen . . . No . . . After everything I've done for you . . . for us . . . so we could be together. He forced you, didn't he? That's the only thing that makes sense . . . because you wouldn't do this to me, would you?"

My brain comes to a screeching halt.

The nausea from earlier comes back twofold, and I press one hand against my stomach, hoping to keep its contents in.

"Frederico, what are you talking about?" My voice sounds way calmer than the tornado of dread that's circling inside my stomach. "What did you do?"

The laugh that escapes him lacks any trace of humor. "I kept you safe, that's what I did. And trust me, it wasn't always easy. And sometimes I had to wait a while, watching you be in pain, just as much as I was, while we were kept apart once more. The way it's been our whole lives. There was always someone keeping us apart. I was just waiting for the right time, for your dad to see me the way he was supposed to see me, but then he ruined it all by selling you off to Emilio. I knew I couldn't just take him out like Luigi, especially once he got you out of the country, so I had to take you away and—"

"*You* killed Luigi?"

He stops his pacing and gives me a small smile, resembling the man I thought I knew once more. "Of course I did. And although you had to grieve in public, it was easy to tell how happy you were that he was gone." His expression flips again, the angry mask firmly back in place. "Then Santarossa came along and had to ruin it all. I knew I could talk your dad into letting us get married after Luigi's death, I was working on it. He was about to finally acknowledge we belonged together, that we were a perfect match, and suddenly you were gone."

There's no way I can currently process all of this, even if my brain was working a hundred percent. Maybe I'll wake up soon and this will all have been a dream. My head spins back to the time I first woke up here, handcuffed to the damn bed.

I don't think, I just talk. "Did you drug me?"

He lifts a shoulder and drops it again. "You were frantic when you realized Ally wasn't here, so I had to calm you down."

Ally?

The memory pops into my head at the mention of my best friend's name. Frederico texted me that Ally was dropped off somewhere by the Russians and needed our help. I called her phone, but it went straight to voicemail, so I didn't even think twice and quickly put on clothes to meet Frederico. Then we drove here, and then . . .

My hand flies up to my neck, touching the tender spot on the side. "You put a needle in my neck."

He shrugs again. "It's the fastest way."

He's crazy, absolutely crazy.

And I have no clue how to get out of this.

Frederico laughs. "You know, you might have actually done me a favor by fucking Santarossa. Like you said, your dad might not sell you anymore. And I can swoop in and offer to take on the tainted principessa that no one else wants. I'll just have to fuck Santarossa out of you until you're pure again, so I can put a baby in you."

This time, I can't keep the bile down. I turn to the side and heave, emptying whatever I had in my stomach on the floor. This is too much, all of this. Dealing with my crazy dad was one thing, but at least I knew what I was working against. This thing with Frederico came so out of left field, I can't wrap my head around it. I'm still not a hundred percent sure I know what *it* is.

"Amore mio, Frederico is an adult now and working with your papà, so he can't come over to play anymore. He said not to bother him, capiche?"

I still remember that day and how my mom distracted me with ice cream and pizza, all in secret, of course, so my dad wouldn't know.

What if . . .?

My gaze snaps up to Frederico's, and I wipe my mouth with the back of my hand. "Did you ever tell my mom I should leave you alone? After you started working for my dad?"

At my question, he stalks over to me and gets in my face. "Is that what she told you?"

I nod, unsure how to react anymore. Anything I do or say can set him off, but I have no way of knowing what it could be.

"Figures that's what she told you. I shouldn't be surprised." He lets his head drop and stares at the floor before he goes back to pacing the room. "She caught me a few times staring at you and said it was inappropriate. But I couldn't help myself, so she kept me away from you. Should have killed that bitch sooner."

My whole body freezes, a coldness creeping into every single one of my pores in a way that's both suffocating and excruciatingly painful. The pressure of it pushes on my chest, and my breaths come out shallow.

No, no, no, no. That can't be right. I must have heard wrong.

"You—" I press my lips together, and my eyes burn like they're on fire. "You killed my mom?"

He looks at me with wide eyes, like I'm the crazy one, and says, "Of course I did. She wouldn't let me see you."

"You broke into our house."

"Did you hear me? She. Wouldn't. Let. Me. See. You." His voice is so flat, he sounds like a robot.

My brain goes back to that horrible scene from five years ago when I lost the most important person in my life, the only one who was ever truly on my side and tried to protect me the best she could.

I heave again at the gruesome memory, thankful that nothing comes up this time. "My bunny."

311

Frederico shrugs. "You loved that bunny. I thought maybe if you were in pain, I could be the one to console you."

My body convulses over and over, and the sour smell permeating the room from my stomach contents on the floor only worsens it. But in the bigger scheme of things, it's a small problem compared to the reality that my cousin is actually a delusional psychopath.

His words trigger something, and my thoughts jump to when I found the dead bunny on the porch at Matteo's cabin. "Oh my gosh, that was you upstate with the bunny? And the . . . and the pictures."

It seems like that was the wrong thing to say because Frederico stops walking and comes for me once more. But this time, he doesn't stop in front of me; instead, he goes straight for my throat, squeezing so hard I gasp for air, but none comes.

"At first, I wanted to kill you for that, but then I remembered that you had no choice. You only did it since you were scared and didn't want your dad to sell you again."

The pressure on my neck lessens. It's still hard to breathe, but not impossible anymore. But with how things have been going, that might change any second, and this will indeed be the last thing I'll ever see in my life.

Just when I was finally happy, when I had a husband I actually loved. Crap. I *love* Matteo, I really do. I've fallen for him somewhere along the way but never allowed myself to feel it, not truly, let alone tell him.

My eyes fill with tears, and they overflow one by one as I glance up at my cousin, the same person I laughed with a million times in my life. The person who killed my mother. I cry and I cry and I cry, the dam in my brain broken down completely.

"Shh, bellissima, it's okay. I forgive you." He lets go of my throat and wipes at my tears before picking me up and lying down with me, cradling me in his arms.

I'm not sure how long we stay like this, only that it feels like hours, but I don't dare move. This might be my only chance to think and attempt to regain more of my strength and wits.

However, at some point, my bladder complains, and I have to shift around to alleviate the feeling.

"What is it, piccolina?" His breath hits my neck.

I bite the inside of my cheek to contain the shudder that wants to rush through my body at having this monster so close to me. "I need to use the bathroom."

"Go ahead." He opens his arms, letting me out of his cocoon. "I'll wait."

"Okay," I whisper the word as quietly as possible, trying to sound and appear as friendly and as weak as possible.

I have no way of knowing if he'll turn into a monster again, so I need to be smart about this. My steps are light and quiet as I walk to the bathroom, carefully avoiding the vomit on the floor. Once I'm inside the small room, I close the door and pee.

Everything in my brain is flitting around manically, trying so hard to come up with a way to get out of this situation.

Bedroom windows? Too high and too small.

Bathroom window? No window.

Anything that can be used as a weapon? Not unless I get my hands on one of the broken table pieces.

That's how far I get until he calls out, "Everything okay?"

His voice still sounds calm and nice, but my heartbeat picks up a notch.

"Yes, I'm almost done." Keeping my voice steady, when all I want to do is cry or scream, isn't easy, but since he only says, "Okay," I'm guessing it was good enough.

I pull up my workout shorts and brush along their sides to slide up my sweatpants just as I feel something hard. My hands shake while I brush over it again. I close my eyes and press my lips together, hoping it'll help me keep my emotions at bay since they're trying to overflow in all directions.

My knife is in the side pocket of my workout shorts. I put it in there, so I could practice some more with it, while Matteo was meeting up with Nikolai. When I left the apartment in a panic, I only threw on my sweatpants, not even thinking about the knife.

Now it's burning a hole in my pants. I take it out and stuff it into the deep pocket of my hoodie. I'm yanking up my sweatpants just as the door flies open.

My chest is so tight, it feels like my rib cage might burst soon.

You can do this.

I have no clue how to get out of here though. I'm not even sure where here is. And despite having my knife, I'm not sure I can take on Frederico. He's not a small guy, not to mention he's a total psycho and completely unpredictable.

Since I don't have my phone, or keys, or anything else on me anymore, I'm assuming he searched me and took everything I could use as a weapon. It's a miracle he didn't find the knife, and I might only have one chance to get away, so I need to plan it wisely. I'm also incredibly relieved I took off my jewelry like I do before every workout. Somehow, I don't think it would have gone over well if Frederico had seen my wedding ring.

I take a step forward, just as my stomach growls.

His eyes briefly narrow to slits, then he holds out his hand. "Come on, let's get you something to eat."

I don't bother reminding him that food is probably the last thing my stomach wants after I just threw up. My skin crawls as I place my hand in his, but staying in this room won't help me escape. And hopefully it's a good sign that he wants to take me somewhere else.

We walk through an old, dingy hallway, and step into the open kitchen and living room area. A sense of unease instantaneously washes over me, and I can't help but feel like something's wrong.

Frederico drags me in the direction of the fridge, and I look around. Big mistake. There are two elderly people sitting next to each other on one of the couches, both of them with identical gunshot wounds to the forehead.

I cover my mouth and recoil from it all. This room, the dead people only a few feet away, the smell of their decomposing bodies slowly penetrating my nose, my psychopath cousin, everything.

Frederico turns around and stares at me when I yank my hand out of his.

He tilts his head to the side and pouts. "What's wrong, piccolina?"

My eyes betray me, and they flick over to the dead bodies.

He sighs like this is just another bad day at work. "Yeah, I know. Sorry about that. They wouldn't cooperate, but I needed to make sure we'd be safe here. I did this for you, bellissima. Only for you."

He opens his arms and gestures for me to come to him.

I can't.

I just can't.

I told myself maybe I could play along for a bit, make him trust me, so I could escape easier, but I can't. He killed two innocent, old people in their own home, just because he didn't get his way.

There's so much blood on his hands that I know of, and probably so much more I don't. Who's to say he's not going to snap and kill me too?

So despite trembling from top to bottom, I shake my head.

He exhales loudly. "Always so sensitive."

I don't reply.

Suddenly, he moves, coming straight for me.

I shriek and run. Where, I'm not sure. I didn't even have time to peek around the room after I saw the dead people. There's a door on the far right. Not sure where it leads, but out the window, I can see some sky in the distance.

I almost make it there as a shove from behind sends me flying to the floor. I catch myself on my hands and knees, pain ricocheting through my entire body on impact.

Frederico spins me around and climbs on top of me, boxing me in with his legs.

Then he slaps me so hard across the face, my vision turns blurry, and I taste copper in my mouth.

Fuck.

"Don't worry, bellissima, you'll learn." Then his hands are on my breasts, squeezing them through my sports bra, and his erection is digging into my stomach. He slides up my shirt far enough to expose my stomach and to trace my scar with his fingers. The scar *he* gave me and is now admiring.

Shit, I didn't even think about that earlier.

Disgust fights with panic in my body, my brain not knowing what to do. The only thing I know is I will not let him rape me. No way in hell. I will fight tooth and nail before that happens.

He moves his hips back and forth and groans while I try to remain as still as possible.

In most situations, you'll only get one chance. Use it wisely.

Zeno's words echo in my head on a loop, and I try to remember what else he said.

Ear, nose, throat, solar plexus, groin, knee.

I take a moment and think. Frederico just got turned on when I fought him. Sick bastard. But maybe I can use that to my advantage. It might completely backfire, but I have to try. I need to get him off me so I can get to my knife.

After a deep breath, I wiggle under him like I'm trying to get away. "Please don't, Frederico."

The grin on his face turns into a full-blown smile. It's sickening to watch, and for that alone, he deserves to die. He palms himself through his pants, watching me while he's trying to make up his mind. Then he goes up to his knees to unbuckle his belt and to open his pants. He pushes them down far enough to get his dick out, and I focus on what I'm about to do.

I move around once more, whimpering, "No, no. Please, don't do this."

He wraps his hand around his dick and pumps into his

palm a few times, groaning loudly, his gaze never leaving my face. "Touch me, piccolina."

I make a choking noise in my throat but slowly reach out with my left hand. My entire body shudders when I wrap my hand around him, at the same time as I slide my right hand into my pocket to tightly grip my knife before I pull it back out.

Once I'm sure I've made the best fist around the knife, I take my hand off his dick and slap both of my hands on his ears before drawing my right hand back and hitting him in the nose as hard as I can. Then I buck my hips up, which makes him fall my way. Thankfully, I practiced this exact same thing with Zeno countless times, so I try to focus and do the hand and leg motions he taught me in order to flip Frederico over, so I'm on top of him.

He howls in pain, blindly grabbing for me while I scramble backward. I'm able to get far enough away to stand, but so does he.

"You fucking bitch. You're going to pay for this."

I stumble, quickly realizing I'm backing myself into a corner since the door is behind him.

Fuck.

He must have come to the same conclusion because he grins at me. His smile is what nightmares are made of, his teeth completely covered in red, with more blood steadily dripping down from his nose.

If he gets his hands on me now, I might not get another chance. With my thumb, I push at the blade in my hand, and with an upward flick, it opens and clicks in.

Matteo tried to teach me this one over and over, but I

never got it right. Too bad that the time I finally master it, I'm possibly about to be raped and murdered.

Frederico stops and regards my knife. He's probably as surprised to see it as I was when I discovered it.

But then he advances again, and both Zeno and Matteo yell at me in my head.

You have one chance. One chance, Gemma.

I have to injure him badly enough so I can escape, nothing more. One opening so I can run.

Frederico makes the first move and jumps toward me, and I swing my arm toward his forearm. Slash. No idea if I got to the bone like I was supposed to, but Frederico hisses and withdraws. His biceps and triceps are next. Slash. One more, the front of his thigh right above his knee. Slash. Not sure how much damage I did through his pants, but he collapses to his knees before toppling over and rolling onto his back, with his good hand holding on to his injured arm.

There's so much blood everywhere, but he deserves it.

Now run, Gemma. Run.

But somehow, I can't.

My feet finally unfreeze, but they don't carry me to the door. Instead, they bring me closer to Frederico, who tries to kick me as soon as I'm within reach, right before I manage to cut his other leg above the knee too.

"That was for my mamma, you sick bastard."

Then I give him matching wounds on his uninjured arm.

"And that was for giving me a fucking scar."

At this point, he barely moves anymore, so I slash at his throat. His head lolls to the side, his hands falling to the floor.

"And that one was for killing not one, but two bunnies, you motherfucking psychopath."

After that, things get a little blurry. I slash all the other spots I remember from my lessons again and again, not caring if they cover me in blood too. Then I sit on the floor at a safe distance to make sure he's not going to get up again.

I'm still in that exact same position when a door opens somewhere and footsteps approach.

CHAPTER 22
MATTEO

" Downstairs. I found her."

It's Zeno's voice in my earpiece, and Ash and I rush toward the door that should lead us downstairs.

Finally. Fucking finally. It took us almost two days to find her, and I haven't slept or eaten much in that time.

Please be okay, please be okay.

Zeno hisses. "Holy shit. Gemma, look at me. Fuuuuck. Gem. Hey, over here. It's me, Zeno."

Ash meets my gaze with wide eyes. I don't think either one of us has ever heard Zeno talk like that—to anyone. My feet move even faster than before, and I almost trip down the stairs in the process.

I jump off the last few steps and turn the corner to the open room, but nothing, absolutely nothing could have prepared me for this.

"Motherfucker." Ash comes to a halt beside me before we both jump into action, running to Gemma, cautious not to slip in the blood that seems to be everywhere around her. On the floor, the ceiling, the walls. And on her.

Zeno spins our way and shakes his head. "She's not responding. She just keeps staring at him."

That's when I notice Frederico for the first time. He was hidden by the kitchen island as we came in, but fucking hell, he resembles something out of a slasher movie.

And *she* did this.

My fiery queen who looks like she was born from blood.

"Passerotta." My voice sounds as pained as the darkness and sorrow I feel inside my body right now.

Gemma's eyes widen, and her head snaps in my direction. Then she's scrambling to her feet, needing several tries to get up without slipping. She runs to me, and I open my arms as wide as I can, catching her as she collides with my body and sobs.

"It's okay, baby, I've got you." I brush over her hair that's crusted with blood. How long has she been sitting here like that?

Ash walks around us, his concerned gaze scanning over what he can see of her. "Gem, are you hurt? Is any of the blood yours?"

She takes several deep breaths and slowly untangles herself from me. I don't ever want to let her go again, but Ash is right, we need to make sure she's okay.

"I'm . . ." She clears her throat.

Ash produces a water bottle from his backpack that he unscrews and hands to her.

She takes it and hisses but still lifts it to her mouth, draining the whole thing.

"Did you hurt your hand?" Ash gingerly takes her hand

to examine it. It's covered in cuts, but he doesn't appear too concerned about those.

Gemma flinches a few times but doesn't say anything.

Ash grimaces. "Sorry, Gem. We need to get some X-rays done to double-check, but I'm pretty sure you fractured your hand."

Gemma nods. "It hurt like a bitch when I punched him, but then I didn't feel the pain as much as I was . . . you know . . ." She glances around and rolls her lips.

I put my arm around her, touching her wherever I can without being in the way of Ash. "It's okay. It's over now."

Zeno calls Ash over, and Gemma stays quiet, lost in thought.

The next time she stares at me, her eyes are still slightly glazed over. "I . . . I slashed like you told me to."

Fuck me, this woman.

My beautiful wife slayed her dragon and bathed in his blood.

I cup her face and caress her cheek. "Good girl."

Then I press my lips against hers.

We found her, and she's safe.

Everything else can wait.

Gemma looks up at me, and then her eyes roll back. I catch her right before she goes limp in my arms.

"Shit." Ash is back, immediately checking her breathing and pulse. "She seems okay. Hopefully it was just from the exhaustion. Let's get her home so we can take care of her properly."

After checking with Zeno to make sure he'll take care of the cleanup, Ash helps me to get Gemma in the back of the

SUV with me before he hops in the driver's seat, and we get out of this shitty neighborhood.

Gemma stirs and blinks open her eyes, peeking up at me from beneath her long lashes.

I brush my thumb over her frown. "Hey, passerotta."

"What happened?"

"You fainted. How are you feeling?"

She inhales deeply before she answers, "Okay, I guess. Just really tired and a bit dizzy."

"We'll be home soon."

She nods and snuggles closer, her injured hand carefully tucked against her chest and her feet elevated on Ash's bag. I watch her chest rise and fall and the vein in her throat pulse for the rest of the drive.

Ash helps me get out of the car with Gemma still in my arms.

She lifts her head. "You can let me down. I should be good to walk."

"Not happening." My voice comes out low and gravelly, but I soften it for my next words: "Just let me do this for you."

She whispers, "Okay," and we head to the apartment.

Ash tells me to get her cleaned up while he gets everything set up.

We don't talk while I take Gemma into the bathroom, where I take off her clothes.

We don't talk as I step into the shower with her and wash all the blood and grime off her body.

We don't talk while I dry her off, get clean clothes for her, and help her put them on.

All I need right now is to be with her, to be able to see her and touch her, to know she's alive and all right.

Everything else can come later.

I put my arm gently around her shoulder as we walk to the spare bedroom Ash has set up as his medical room.

I watch both of them while he does a thorough checkup and takes X-rays of her hand with the portable machine.

He regards the digital X-ray and points at the screen. "Yup. Boxer's fracture, right here."

Gemma groans. "Seriously?"

Ash turns back to her. "Good news is I don't think we need to correct anything. A splint for a few weeks, and you'll be as good as new."

She exhales loudly. "Great."

Ash rolls the machine away and gets up. "Sorry, Gem, but you did good. I don't have a splint here, so I'll go and get one."

"Thank you."

"Of course." He nods to me and walks away from the bed.

Gemma closes her eyes, and the moment Ash closes the door behind him, a tear runs down her face. Another one joins, and another. She presses her lips together so hard they turn white, and my chest hurts like someone sliced it open.

I climb onto the bed next to her and gently pull her against me. "Shh, it's okay. You're safe now."

She sniffles. "I didn't know if I was going to make it out alive, or if I'd see you again. I never even got to . . ."

Her mouth turns downward, and more tears flow over her cheeks.

"Never got to what, passerotta?" I prompt her, needing to hear whatever she has to say.

She opens her amber eyes that glitter with moisture. "To tell you I love you."

I lean my forehead against hers as I struggle with the onslaught of emotions this whole situation and her words have brought along. "Fuck, baby. Don't you ever do anything like this to me again, you hear me? I won't survive it a second time. It felt like I was dying without you, like you took my heart with you. And you know what? I don't want it back, capiche? It's yours, amore mio. Ti amo tanto."

I love her so very much.

"Matteo." Gemma sobs, tremors rolling through her entire body while I hold her.

Eventually, her sobs slow down, and her breathing evens out, but I never let go of her. This is how Ash finds us when he pokes his head into the room. He grimaces and tips his head toward the hallway. I get out of bed as carefully as possible, relieved to see I didn't wake her.

I join Ash in front of the room, instantly on alert because of his dark expression. "What happened?"

He brushes a hand over his face, just as the elevator doors open on the other side of the long hallway and Zeno steps out, his glum expression mirroring Ash's.

His eyes narrow as he walks toward us. "Did you tell him?"

Ash shakes his head.

I lift my hand and point in the direction of the living room, no words necessary for them to understand what I want from them.

Once there, I turn to them, my friends, my partners in crime and some of the only people I'd trust with my life, and now Gemma's too. "Someone tell me what the fuck is going on."

Ash sighs. "Someone snitched about Frederico, and the news has spread like wildfire among the families."

I rub the back of my neck. I hate snitches and the chaos they create. It's exhausting, and I'm tired. All I want to do is stay in bed with my *wife* and hold her. Instead, I'm going to have to deal with this shit.

I sigh. "Do they know who killed him?"

Zeno shakes his head. "Nope. Only that he was practically massacred and that we were at the scene."

My jaw is hurting from all the clenching I've done the last few days. "Lorenzo?"

Zeno's mouth is set in a straight line. "On his way."

"Great."

And because the timing couldn't be any worse, my phone rings.

I pull it out of my pocket and frown at the caller ID. I don't want to deal with this shit, but I swipe the screen anyway and lift the phone to my ear. "Ciao, Stefano."

"Ciao, Signor Santarossa. Sorry for the interruption, but Signori Fiore are here with two of their men." The words come out in a rush, and I can just picture the old man's eyes flitting around nervously due to his company.

"It's okay, Stefano. Send them up. I'll unlock the elevator on my side once they're here."

"Will do, signore. Grazie."

I hang up and put my phone back in my pocket, walking to the elevator and staring a hole into it. I don't need to check behind me to know that Ash and Zeno are right there, always having my back.

The monitor for the security system comes to life as I press it, and we watch via the live feed how Lorenzo, his brother, Toni—Ally's dad—as well as two of their men, enter the elevator and ride up. The monitor makes a beeping noise when the elevator arrives at the penthouse. Only people with the code can open it from the other side, so I unlock it by pressing my thumb on the screen, and the doors quietly open.

The four men walk in, and Lorenzo's eyes immediately zoom in on me. He points at me. "You."

The only reaction he gets from me is a raised eyebrow. Not only does he show up uninvited, but he also barges into my home, just to point fingers and yell at me. Not happening. If I wasn't this damn tired, I'd have a gun aimed at his head by now.

I pick an imaginary piece of lint off my shirt before I give him a bored stare. "Say what you came here to say and leave. You're not welcome here."

His nostrils flare as he stares me down like I'm nothing, or I assume that's what he's trying to do. Toni stays quiet, but his fingers curl by his sides. The two men with them scowl at me but show no other reaction so far. That might change in the next few minutes if Lorenzo doesn't get his shit together.

Lorenzo takes a step toward me. "Is it true that Frederico's dead?"

"Yes."

Color rises up his neck and into his face. He looks like he might explode soon. "And he was murdered?"

I'm about to answer when a quiet, "Yes," comes from somewhere behind me.

All heads snap to where Gemma's standing in the hallway, appearing small in her oversized hoodie and sweatpants, her arm cradled to her chest. I feel terrible that she still hasn't had the medical treatment she needs. I'm also irritated as hell that she's up at all and not still asleep like she should be. Fucking Lorenzo.

She walks over to us, and I feel marginally better the moment she stands next to me, surrounded by Ash and Zeno.

Lorenzo tsks at her, disapproval written in the tight lines of his face. "Gemma, let's go."

The "*Fuck, no,*" is sitting on the tip of my tongue just as Gemma says, "No."

One word. Two letters. Zero room for arguing.

His lips form a tight line in disgust. "Gemma, I said let's go. Stop being a brat, we're going home."

No matter how much I want to glance at Gemma, I don't dare take my eyes off Lorenzo. But out of the corner of my eye, I can see she stiffens at his words.

Then she shifts and raises her chin. "I said no."

Lorenzo's breathing gets louder, like he's an angry bull getting ready to charge. Even the vein in his neck is pulsing aggressively. His behavior seems to trigger the man standing next to him because his fingers twitch, slowly moving up his leg.

Lorenzo blatantly ignores his daughter and turns to me. "What the fuck is this, Matteo? I thought we had a deal. Alessandra is back home, and Emilio will be here in a few days for the wedding. Everything can go back to the way it was planned."

"I'm not marrying Emilio." Gemma's tone is firm.

Lorenzo's eyes narrow to slits as he glares at her. "I didn't ask what you wanted. You're going to marry Emilio."

She shakes her head. "I can't. I'm already married."

He rolls his eyes at that. "Don't be stupid. Luigi is dead."

"I wasn't talking about Luigi, Papà." She pauses for a beat. "Matteo and I got married."

That bomb has everyone reacting. Lorenzo and Toni both shout at the same time, and the two other guys have their hands carefully inching closer to the inside of their jackets.

Movement to my right has everyone freezing.

I finally look over, and what a sight.

Gemma's holding one of my guns with her uninjured hand, raised high enough to aim at her father's head. "Don't test me, Papà. I'm not your little puppet anymore. You heard what happened to Frederico."

"Figlio di puttana." He continues to cuss under his breath, a bead of sweat forming on his forehead. "What the fuck is wrong with you? *You* killed your cousin?"

Gemma swallows. "He was a psychopath."

Lorenzo throws up his hands. "So what?"

Gemma engages the grip safety, and the men opposite her notice it.

"He drugged me, handcuffed me to a bed, said we'd get married and was about to rape me. I'm sorry if that level of psychopath isn't concerning to you, *Father*, because it should be. You should be the one protecting me from monsters like him. He killed Mamma."

The last words come out in a whisper, and my brain is reeling from all the info. We still haven't had a chance to catch up yet, but shit, that sounds even more fucked up than I thought.

Lorenzo's eyes widen in surprise, but he stays quiet.

Gemma laughs humorlessly and shakes her head at him. "Papà, did you hear what I said? Frederico killed Mamma."

This time, she yells, and while I couldn't care less if she shot Lorenzo, I know she would. She's not a cold-blooded killer.

"Passerotta." I put my hand over hers and take the gun from her, keeping a tight grip on it before addressing the men. "Well, this was very unpleasant, so it's time for you to leave. As you heard, there will be no wedding for Alessandra or Gemma, and I never want to see your faces here again."

I wave the gun in the direction of the elevator, and the four men reluctantly walk toward it, Lorenzo at the back of the group.

He suddenly stops and turns around, a disgusted glare aimed at his daughter. "You're a disgrace to our family. Your mamma would turn over in her grave if she could see you."

One second he looks like he's about to spit on the floor, the next he's howling in pain when one of my small throwing knives hits him in the upper thigh.

"Don't you ever talk about Mamma again." Gemma hisses in pain, cradling her right hand to her chest.

"You bitch." Lorenzo crosses the distance, charging straight for her, malicious intention written all over his face.

I step in front of Gemma before he can reach her, raising the gun and pressing it straight to his forehead. His eyes bulge as I step closer.

"Listen very carefully to me, Lorenzo, because I will not repeat myself. You're going to walk away right now and stay completely out of our lives and affairs. Consider all ties with the Santarossa family cut, including Gemma since she's my family now. You're not going to contact her or even look at her. Forget she exists since you never deserved her in the first place."

Without taking my gun off him, I walk him to the elevator, only relaxing once the doors close and I activate the keypad.

Then I'm by her side where Ash and Zeno are already tending to her.

Ash is tsking. "Seriously, Gem. You could have let someone else have some fun too, you know?"

"Sorry." That's all she gets out before she grimaces.

Ash sighs. "Come on, you wild cat. Let's see if you managed to damage your hand even more."

By some miracle, the injury is still the same on the X-ray, and Ash finally puts the splint on her, saying, "No more funny business, okay? I doubt you'll be this lucky next time."

She nods with a small smile. "I'll try."

Both Ash and Zeno leave with the promise to catch up the next day, after we all get some much-needed sleep.

Gemma doesn't protest when I take her to our bed, where I carefully strip her down and climb under the warm covers with her. She snuggles up to me, and I cradle her as much as her injury lets me, both of us needing this close contact.

Her breathing slows down, and she mumbles, "I love you, Matteo."

I press my lips to her forehead. "I love you, passerotta."

EPILOGUE
GEMMA

"Yes, sweetie, just like that. Hit him again. Show him who's boss." I pause on the side of the mat, watching Grace with Zeno as he first corrects her stance and talks her through the combination again, then holds up his pads to let her try it.

She lands her next combo correctly, and the exuberant smile on her face is why I'm doing this. These kids and women deserve a chance to be able to stand up for themselves, especially if they aren't always given a choice.

Six months ago, after another intense training session with Zeno, I had a moment where I felt this overwhelming gratitude toward him and thought about how there are so many other women out there who could benefit from the fighting/defensive skills Zeno, Ash, and Matteo have been teaching me. The prospect kept nagging at me, so, later that night, I searched online to see if there are places that offer the kind of help I've received. Plenty popped up, but most were expensive gyms, which a lot of women in difficult situations wouldn't be able to afford.

When I mentioned it to Matteo, he said I could always open a self-defense place for women and children in need, and that we could set it up as a non-profit business. Together, with the help of Matteo's men and Luna and Ally, we were able to open the place two months ago, and I've been loving every single minute of it. Seeing that empowering spark enter the students' eyes as their confidence grows is one of my favorite things to witness. We work closely with the local women's shelters, and I'm planning on expanding the studio and adding more places over the next few years so we can help more people. Matteo hired some security, just in case, and Zeno offered to help with the classes alongside the other trainers.

Grace smacks Zeno's pad before giving it a swift kick too, the combination hard enough for him to crack the tiniest of smiles and for Grace to throw herself at him for a hug. Despite his intimidating stature and his massive frown, the kids have been drawn to him. It's been interesting to watch. The moms and other women are more cautious than the kids, which I don't blame them for; he's definitely a bit scary at first.

Zeno pats Grace on the back awkwardly until her mom calls her from the other side of the room. My stomach churns every time I see the mom's bruised arms. That's my least favorite part of my work, seeing and knowing what some of these women go through. While I was a prisoner in my own home, I was at least never physically abused. But that's what we're here for, to help as much as we can, so these women have a better chance of taking care of themselves since that might be their only way out.

The bell above the studio door chimes, and the instantaneous chatter that follows makes it easy to know who it is. Luna and Ally take off their shoes at the entrance and make their way across the large room.

After another, "Good job," at Grace, I make my way to the two most important women in my life.

Luna shakes her head at me. "What on earth do you think you're still doing here?"

Ally wrinkles her nose and points at me. "Are you sweaty?"

I press my lips together at their antics. "Hello to you too. And yes, I worked out, so I'm sweaty. Is there something wrong with—"

Luna holds up her finger. "I swear to you, if you say anything about this being just another normal day, I'm going to lose it."

Ally nods because that's what these two like to do, gang up on me until I have no choice but to go along with their crazy plans. Like today, even though I'm not mad about it at all.

Heavy footsteps come from behind as Zeno walks up to us, a deep scowl firmly in place. "You guys are scaring the kids." He turns to me. "I'll lock up, leave."

Luna bursts into laughter and pats him on the arm. "*We're* scaring the kids? Oh, Zeno, you should have become a comedian."

He narrows his eyes at her, and for a moment, I think he's going to ignore her and walk away, but then he says, "Why don't you worry about your own problems? Like maybe figuring out who's stealing our fucking money?"

Ouch. He knows how to land a punch.

Luna knows it too, the corners of her eyes tightening as

she pokes him in the chest. "I hope you'll enjoy all the dildos and anal plugs I'm going to have delivered to your place."

At that, his eyebrows rise, but this time, he stays quiet. As scary as he is, Luna is the way bigger pain in the ass with her mad computer skills.

Zeno stares at the ceiling, as if he can find some strength up there to deal with Luna before he turns his back to her, so I'm the only one in front of him. "Please get them out. I'll see you soon."

"Thanks, Z. I appreciate it." I raise my fist, and with an eye roll, he bumps his knuckles against mine. This man is too easy to rile up.

He walks away, and I focus back on my friends, who are both staring at me.

Ally wrinkles her nose. "I hate to say it, but Zeno is right. We have to get out of here. From the looks of it, it'll take a while to get you ready for your big day."

I sigh because we've talked about this before. "Ally, it's not my—"

Luna grabs my hand and pulls. "Nope, not listening to this again. You owe us a beautiful wedding day, and trust me, you'll love every single second of it. Especially all the gorgeous pictures, since you basically have none from your actual wedding."

I know she's right. It's something I've regretted a few times since our wedding last year. Even though Matteo and I have other pictures of us, I'd have loved to have more traditional wedding pictures too. The ones you show everyone, the ones you hang on the wall and show your . . . kids, and your grandkids.

Kids.

Our kids.

What will life be like once it's not just the two of us?

Ally jabs her elbow into my side.

I sigh. "Fine, let's go."

It doesn't take us long to get to the wedding venue, where Luna and Ally usher me into the suite to take a shower. The moment I'm out, the makeup artist, as well as the hairstylist, are ready to perform their magic.

I try to relax as much as I can, peeking out of one eye when something pokes the back of my head.

A glance in the mirror shows the hairstylist attaching a bunch of lace to my soft waves and Ally and Luna watching with huge smiles.

Last year, I wasn't thinking too much about if others might feel left out if we got married without them. I had too much on my plate with Ally gone, having been half-kidnapped by Matteo—even though I wasn't really resisting—plus Frederico sending threatening mail, and my father trying to get me back so he could sell me to the next wealthy guy.

After Matteo and I got married, and all threats were taken care of, I started to feel like maybe we should have at least attempted to set up something for people to join us. Which is why I agreed to this, even if Matteo couldn't have cared less. He left it up to me and told me if I didn't want to do it, he has enough info to blackmail not only my best friend, but also his sister.

My only stipulation was to keep the wedding small, with only the people I actually know and want to share this meaningful occasion with. Luna and Ally had a blast planning most of it, with the help of a wedding planner, and I'm grateful to have this memory with the people I care about most.

Luna and Ally help me into my dress, this time something a little more lavish, a sleeveless princess gown with a plunging V-neck, a beaded-lace bodice, and a ruffled tulle skirt. It's fun and flirty and absolutely gorgeous.

Ally steps back first, glancing at me with shiny eyes.

I shake my head. "Hey, didn't you hear the makeup artist? No crying allowed."

"I'm pretty sure she was talking about you and not me." She chuckles and wipes at her face. "You look beautiful, Gem."

"Thank you." I reach out and squeeze her hand.

Luna goes to the door and peeks outside before closing it again. "My dad's here."

I let out a long breath and press my hands to my stomach. The butterflies are wild and uninhibited, knowing this is special. Taking into account that Matteo's dad, Giulio, is the one walking me down the aisle today isn't helping either. He's quickly become yet another Santarossa family member in my life who I value dearly. It still hurts to know what my family life, my relationship with my father could have been yet wasn't, but I've been trying to focus on the future and the fact I do have all these amazing people in my life now.

Luna and Ally squeeze me one more time each before they leave the room. Giulio waits in the doorframe, an older version of his handsome son—all tan skin, dark eyes, and dark hair. Even though his is peppered with gray streaks. He's a lot like Matteo, reserved around most people but the ones he's close with.

"Sei assolutamente bellissima. My son is a lucky man."
He smiles widely and offers me his arm.

I close the distance between us to loop my hand around
his elbow. "Thank you, I'm just as much of a lucky woman."

"That's why I like you so much. I've always wanted partners for my children who can acknowledge them for who
they really are. My wife took great pride in raising our kids
with a big heart and a smart mind. In the case of Luna, with a
smart mouth too."

I laugh at his comment, knowing how much Luna drives
everyone nuts at times. But there's never been a single doubt
over how much Giulio loves his two children, or how much
he adored his wife before she passed.

That's what the ultimate goal of love and life is, to leave
an imprint on your loved ones and to be cherished and
adored long past your time.

Together, we walk onto the manicured rooftop garden
where our friends—and most importantly, my handsome
husband—wait for us. My heart soars as we celebrate our love
surrounded by amazing views of Manhattan and the beautiful loft space inside.

SEVERAL HOURS LATER, Matteo's hand wraps around my
throat, and he presses me against our bedroom wall. "I asked,
have you been a good girl today?"

The air vibrates in my windpipe when I push out, "Yes."

His other hand goes under my short dress. As much as I
loved my wedding gown, I wanted something less restrictive
for the reception. I also wanted something that wasn't white.

The second I saw this short red number, I knew I had to have it.

Matteo's hand slides up the inside of my leg. "You're such a fucking tease. Dancing in front of me in this dress all night. I wanted to bend you over the table and show you how hard you made me."

I moan at the picture he's painting.

"Open my zipper, passerotta. See what you do to me."

My hands are steady while I open his pants and shove them down, as much as I can in my position, and do the same to his boxers. His long erection twitches as I wrap my hand around it and squeeze.

"Harder." Matteo pumps into my hand and crushes his mouth on mine.

The kiss is rough, and he devours me like this is our first time and he can never get enough of me. His lips are soft and demanding, his tongue slick and hot, and I love the sparks that rush through my body at this contact. I will never tire of this feeling or this man.

He bites my lower lip and pulls back, his pupils dilated. "Do you think you deserve a reward for being a good girl?"

I nod, my breasts straining against my dress.

I don't know if he notices it too, but his hand leaves my throat and palms my breast through the material. He does this at the same time as his other hand reaches my panties, and as usual, he doesn't waste any time, thrusting them aside in one swift move so he can sink a finger deep inside me.

"Baby, you're soaked."

I writhe against his hand. "I've been thinking about your cock inside me all day."

He groans against my neck, biting my skin before

soothing the spot with his tongue. "On your knees for your reward."

He withdraws his hand, and I sink to the floor, not wasting a single moment before I lick up his shaft and take him deep into my mouth, reveling in the taste of his salty precum.

"Fuuuuuuuck." Matteo growls and slaps a hand against the wall.

I make quick work of his pants and boxers, dragging them off completely so I have unrestricted access to him. His skin is warm against my fingertips, and I glide them up his legs. I give his muscular butt a squeeze and drag him more firmly against me before wrapping one hand around his shaft to pump up and down in sync with my mouth.

He gathers my hair in one fist, using the leverage it gives him to take control. His pumps become wilder, his cock hitting the back of my throat viciously, and I love every single second of it.

Some people might enjoy sex because they know it leads to an orgasm; to some, it might be an act of duty, something that's expected of them. To me, sex is an expression, my love note to adventure and a different side of myself. It's the power and control, playfulness and pushing limits, combined with this man and the trust between us that makes it as enticing and addictive as it is.

Matteo slows down, but I won't have it. I tug him to me and move my mouth faster, until he snaps and roars his release. He pumps one more time, then stills with his hard dick in my mouth, his salty cum shooting down my throat and tears running down my cheeks.

When he pulls out, I lick my lips and stare up at him with a grin.

His eyes turn to slits, and he hauls me over his shoulder and yanks up my dress.

Cold air hits my butt, right before his hand meets one butt cheek.

Slap.

One more on the other side.

Slap.

Then I'm flung on the bed, belly down, and pressed into the mattress by Matteo's weight.

"You wanna play dirty today, passerotta?"

His cock is lined up against my ass, rubbing over the fabric of my panties. It creates friction along my pussy, and I whimper.

His weight lifts off me, and a moment later, my panties are gone and Matteo presses my legs forward so I'm on my knees with my butt in the air. I fist my hands into the blanket, my hard nipples still confined in my dress, not giving me any kind of relief.

Shifting my head to the side, I peek over my shoulder at Matteo. But he isn't glancing at me, his gaze is solely fixed on my exposed body.

"Such a pretty pussy. And it's all mine."

His hand comes down on my butt.

"All of this is mine."

Slap.

"You're mine." He growls the words and his gaze snaps to mine. Right before his palm connects for another slap, but this time, right on my pussy.

My eyes widen, and I gasp. Then I close my eyes and

revel in the sparks that shoot outward from my groin. A moan leaves my mouth, but it doesn't even sound like it belongs to me.

"Your pleasure is mine too. Look at me." He slaps my pussy again before dragging his fingers through my folds. "Fuck, you're soaked."

I wiggle against his touch and rub my fingers over my lips before pushing one into my mouth.

"So greedy, passerotta." He rubs my clit in firm circles. "But I'm greedy too."

He latches on to my clit with his mouth, and I moan loudly. I'm so turned on, so close already that it doesn't take long and I scream my release. Matteo lets go of my clit once the spasms subside, but he's far from done. He licks over my lips in slow strokes, making sure to mark every inch of skin all the way from the front to the back.

Just when I think I can't take it any longer, his thick head nudges at my entrance, and we both groan as he thrusts in. He stretches me, the pleasure so intense, I bite my finger. Matteo pulls out, just to ram back in again to the hilt, repeating the motion over and over until we're both slick with sweat and panting.

"Say it, baby." His grip on my hips tightens, and his movements speed up. "Say you're mine."

I'm holding on to the blanket for dear life, unsure of how to survive the next orgasm that already seems so much more intense than the last one.

"I'm yours," I moan. "We're both yours."

Fireworks explode in my body, and I come so hard, I tremble from head to toe.

It feels like it'll never stop, propelling Matteo over the

edge too. He pulses inside me, muttering a string of curse words and other unintelligible things I can't make out.

Then he lies down next to me and immediately drags me toward him.

Cradling my face in his hands, he stares into my eyes, his gaze flicking from one eye to the next. "Did you just say you're both mine?"

I lick my lips and nod.

"You're pregnant?"

I nod again, tears forming in my eyes.

We weren't exactly planning for this, but we didn't try hard to keep it from happening either, following my implant removal two months ago. Ash said most pregnancies happen within six months to a year after the removal. For us it happened much sooner than that, but there's nothing I'm more excited about than having a little bambino or bambina with this man.

His lips close over mine in a tender kiss, showing me exactly how much he loves me. How much this means to him. And that he's mine.

Forever.

Because family *is* everything. Sometimes it just takes a while to find it.

Author Note

Thank you so much for reading my words. It means the absolute world to me.

If you enjoyed *Forbidden Freedom*, I'd appreciate it a ton if you could leave a review. Word of mouth and reviews always go such a long way.

For more books and bonus scenes (including one for Gemma and Matteo), please visit my website www.jasminmiller.com

ACKNOWLEDGMENTS

Wow. Where to start with this book? It's the first one I've published in almost a year and a half after going through a major burnout that threw me into a dark and scary place I hope to never visit again. Thankfully, I was able to slowly find my way back to life, to smile again, to enjoy music again (and slowly books as well) and to fill me with a happiness not much else can compare with. And there's a reason for that, or rather, seven. Thank you to Kim Namjoon, Kim Seokjin, Min Yoongi, Jung Hoseok, Park Jimin, Kim Taehyung, and Jeon Jungkook. Thank you for bringing me back to the light. The best is yet to come.

Now to the "real" people in my life. LOL

My husband was a tremendous help while I was trying to find my footing again, and there aren't enough words to show my gratitude and love for this man. Thank you! I love you more!

Alicia, thank you for being there for me every step of the way, as always. I'd be a mess without you. Borahae. Forever and ever.

A big shout-out to my wonderful editors and proofreader Rebecca, Emmy, and Karen. This book definitely wouldn't be the same without you and all your hard work. Thank you!

Thank you to Sara and Lissanne for the feedback (you're amazing), and to Lynn, Courtney, and Felicia for all the teaser help and your excitement for the story. You know how to make a girl feel special, and your love and support means so much.

To all the ARC readers, I can't tell you how grateful I am that you're (still) excited about my work. Thank you, thank you, thank you! You're the best!

And then there's Najla, my cover queen. Thank you for this beauty!

Last but not least, the biggest thank you and hug to every single person who reads this book. I mean it from the bottom of my heart when I say thank you for reading. Out of the millions and millions of books you picked mine, and that means the absolute world to me. ♥♥♥

ABOUT THE AUTHOR

Jasmin Miller is a professional lover of books and cake (preferably together) as well as a fangirl extraordinaire. She loves to read and write about anything romantic and never misses a chance to swoon over characters. Originally from Germany, she now lives in the western US with her husband and three little humans that keep her busy day and night.

If you liked *Forbidden Freedom* and would like to know more about Jasmin and her books, please sign up for her newsletter on her website. She'd love to connect with you.

www.jasminmiller.com
jasminmillerbooks@gmail.com
Facebook.com/jasminmillerwrites
Instagram.com/jasminmiller
Twitter.com/JasminMiller_
Facebook.com/groups/jasminmillerpeeps
tiktok.com/@jasminmillerbooks

Printed in Great Britain
by Amazon

24018213R00209